"Did I say I wanted your money?" Brett asked suavely.

"You did earlier. For rent, food, and gas, remember? Three things that sex wouldn't pay for."

"With the others, no. With you I'm not so certain." Brett's desire flared as quick as Honey's temper. He sat beside her, gathering her quivering body close. He held her head still, taking her mouth to drown out any further impertinence.

He didn't know what to believe. Her words contradicted her appearance. She sounded like a pathological liar and looked like an angel, and was much too delectable to kiss to worry about analyzing her personality quirks.

His mouth molded tenderly to hers, warm and certain. Her lips were shaped as perfectly as her body, both waiting to be seduced....

ABOUT THE AUTHOR

Popular romance novelist Alice Morgan claims
she writes sensual stories as a "tribute to the
loving reality of an exceptional husband."
Over the years she has raised champion
quarter horses, served as a policewoman, and
marketed fancy citrus fruit. Married for thirty-
three years, Alice now resides in California.

Books by Alice Morgan

HARLEQUIN AMERICAN ROMANCES
35-BRANDED HEART
68-DECEPTION FOR DESIRE

These books may be available at your local bookseller.

For a list of all titles currently available, send your
name and address to:

Harlequin Reader Service
P.O. Box 52040, Phoenix, AZ 85072-2040
Canadian address: P.O. Box 2800, Postal Station A,
5170 Yonge St., Willowdale, Ont. M2N 5T5

Deception for Desire

ALICE MORGAN

Harlequin Books

TORONTO • NEW YORK • LONDON
AMSTERDAM • PARIS • SYDNEY • HAMBURG
STOCKHOLM • ATHENS • TOKYO • MILAN

Published August 1984

ISBN 0-373-16068-2

Chapter One

"I want a sexy looking man by Sunday. He must be openly affectionate and crazy in love with me from two to ten o'clock in the evening."

"Is she for real, Aunt Gladys?" Brett asked in astonishment, as he watched the videocassette tape reproduce a young woman's unique beauty with vivid clarity on the screen before him.

His pulses leaped wildly as he observed her abundant auburn hair tumble in deep waves around slender shoulders. The texture of her skin looked like rich satin and he gripped his hands to tamp the impossible urge to touch it. He could feel his heart skip a beat when her soft gray eyes looked straight toward him beneath their frame of heavy black lashes. When she raised her passion-shaped mouth in an enticing smile his own lips thinned in a vain attempt to deny his thoughts.

He had a compelling urge to hold her tight to his body, to feel the flutter of her lips beneath his mouth, and to taste the silky textured sweetness of her skin. Entranced, he watched a tiny dimple wink in one cheek, appearing enticingly often while she talked.

"What's her problem?" Brett asked with forced gruffness. "Doesn't she know you run a marriage bureau and not an escort service?"

Staring at the rounded contours of the girl's figure, emphasized by the thin material of her blouse and bias-cut skirt, he ached to get his hands on her narrow waist and caress the curve of her hips.

When her tender breasts rose and fell as she moved, his

throat felt dry and keen eyes darkened beneath their shadow of lashes. He was stunned by the sudden feeling of unbidden desire in his loins. Not comfortable with his intensity of interest in an unsophisticated woman, he tried to ignore the innocent face that seemed to pierce into his mind like an arrow from one of his aunt's many hearts and cupids adorning the office of Happy Hearts Marriage Bureau.

"Shush, Nephew, and listen further," his aged relative scolded.

"You see," the feminine voice continued, "I'm committed to a wedding party at Wayfarer's Chapel, then a reception, and I've told a lie that backfired on me."

"Typical female," Brett scoffed. He was furious with himself for his excessive reaction to her femininity.

"My mother wants me to marry her wealthy friend despite the fact she knows I hate the man. To end her constant nagging I told her—and a few girl friends too—that I've just become engaged to a man I met since I moved to Long Beach four weeks ago."

"Stupid fool," Brett complained. "This sounds like the plot of a B-grade movie. Why would she need to hire an escort anyway? No man in his right mind would kick her out of his bed."

"Watch your tongue, Bretterson Robert Weston!" Aunt Gladys scolded, raising both plump hands in chagrin. "For the life of me I don't know how you've managed to build up a prosperous business and run around like you do too."

"Years of practice, the mind of a computer, and outlook of a cynic," Brett answered back, annoyed when his relative shut off the tape and the alluring image left the screen.

"Every month you appear with a different woman in our local scandal sheet," she admonished firmly. "Yet you won't let me, your only living relative and without peer as an entrepreneur of selective and harmonious introductions, find you a nice girl."

Refusing to be sidetracked, Brett shrugged aside her criticism, insisting, "Tell me more about this ridiculous female who came to you for a man."

The old woman glared at her nephew's lack of compassion, continuing sympathetically, "Shame on you! The little thing is committed to being maid of honor at a wedding this detestable man is attending. Since she can't back out of the bridal party she came to me, hoping to hire the services of an escort willing to pretend to be her fiancé for one afternoon."

"My God!" Brett exclaimed, one hand rubbing the nape of his neck as he spun around. "This story gets more corny all the time. Next thing you'll tell me she has an aged grandmother and crippled brother to support too."

"Well, she did mention she was really on a tight budget," Aunt Gladys mentioned with concern. "Her clothes weren't the quality your women wear either."

Brett ignored that, sat on the couch, and crossed his long legs. His eyes never left the shiny tips of his handmade shoes as he spoke. "I'm certain she could easily pay for a man's time without spending a penny. Her body's definitely built for bartering."

Stopped by the snort of censure from his aunt, who was quick to catch the meaning of his comment, Brett looked at her. His eyes held her glance arrogantly, not the least embarrassed by his words.

"Come off it, Aunt Gladys. You're well aware it's the 1980s. This is the age of the liberated female, remember? Nowadays it's hard to find a female that doesn't beat the man to the bedroom door, and frankly, I like it. It saves a lot of unnecessary double-talk."

Brett raised one dark eyebrow in an arch of disdain, adding wryly, "I haven't had a single female say no since I started college."

"Maybe that's your problem, Bretterson," his aunt scolded, reverting to his full name again. "If you ever find one to refuse you, you might give her more than a month or two of your time."

"My dear prudish aunt, today's liberated way of life is far better for both men and women," he contradicted with conviction.

"You're wrong, Brett. Your own dear mother and

father—God rest their souls—couldn't have been more happily married." Tears came to her eyes at the thought of her brother's and sister-in-law's deaths twelve years earlier.

"True, but they were the exception not the rule." He certainly didn't have many friends who enjoyed connubial bliss. Quite the opposite in fact.

"Despite a letdown in conventions, over two and a half million couples get married each year in the United States. What do you think of that, Nephew?" She waited for his answer, her bright blue eyes flashing excitedly above heavily rouged cheeks.

A high-necked, pink-flowered dress tightly covered the stiff corseted figure beneath. All her life she'd worn the same style, with three strands of pearls resting on her plump bosom and spotless white thick-soled shoes on her stubby little feet. She was seventy-five, a spinster, and devoted to bringing romance to others.

"Not much," Brett laughed.

He paced the cluttered room, staring at the photographs of couples his aunt had introduced. Many had yellowed with age and were far older than his own thirty-four years. It was like being in another era surrounded by her antiques and old-fashioned office furnishings.

He suddenly turned back, a devilish smile tugging his lips. He knew she enjoyed their arguments as he did. "It seems a waste of time to bother with a legal ceremony at all. After the short bliss of a honeymoon, a man is faced with the cold reality of a marriage. That's not for me, I guarantee you."

With added emphasis he bluntly informed her, "My single life, aunty dear, is one long honeymoon!"

"I'll thank you to remember you're not in some barroom bragging about your sexual behavior, Nephew. Watch your tongue."

Unperturbed, Brett laughed, changing the subject abruptly. "You didn't answer my previous question. Why can't the girl pick up some guy off the street? There must be plenty of young men willing to go along with her scheme just for the free eats at the reception."

"Unfortunately she gave her mother a complete description of her imaginary fiancé." Aunt Gladys eased her well-padded hips against the heart-shaped back of a red velvet chair that clashed horribly with her frizzy orange hair, inviting, "Now, where on earth could the child hope to find in one day a man like she described?"

Brett leaned one wide shoulder against his aunt's filing cabinet. "What's this paragon of a fiancé supposed to look like...this figment of her overactive imagination?"

Aunt Gladys chuckled, moving her hands about. "Tall, powerfully built, tan, and fit."

"A low mentality muscle-bound beach bum, no doubt. The sands are crowded with her type in June."

"Let me finish! She also told her mother and friends he was intelligent, successful, had dark hair, and striking green eyes. To add emphasis to her lie, she said he was shopping for her engagement ring."

"With a mind that muddled she shouldn't be allowed to run loose on the streets."

"You're forgetting, Brett, that it was her only defense against her mother's persistent demands. That loathsome creature's unwanted attentions since she graduated from college have forced her to move from her hometown of San Diego." A glimmer of tears shone as Gladys continued. "She acted so proud of her degree and seems quite hopeful of finding employment soon in her chosen field."

"There's not much demand these days for college-trained liars. She'd be better off marrying the lovesick idiot that wants her before he changes his mind," Brett retorted glibly as he checked the thin gold watch strapped to his left wrist.

"I've got to get back to work, love." Brett smiled, kissing his relative's soft lavender-scented cheek. "My workload's getting heavier all the time and you know how I like the challenge of besting my competitors."

He gently assisted the old woman from her chair before they walked to the entrance of her outer office.

"You work too hard, Bretterson," his aunt scolded softly. Her eyes were filled with pride and love for the young man beside her. Her heart had gone out to him from birth and they shared a special bond of love.

He hugged her good-bye. "Lately I find work more enjoyable than making love. Do you think I've reached a midlife crisis already?"

"No," she called out. "Only boredom with a chase that always ends in the same catch."

Opening the driver's door of his gleaming Ferrari, Brett laughed back. "You know I've always had a decided preference for tall, well-endowed blondes."

He waved and pulled from the curb, contemplating the pleasure of running his fingers through a heavy mane of vibrant red-brown hair.

"Darn! Darn! Darn!" Honey exclaimed in frustration after circling the wide block for the third time. Frantically searching for an empty parking place, she spotted a car pulling from the curb.

"Hurry! Please hurry!" she pleaded, giving a sigh of relief when she drove forward, before backing into the narrow space.

Surprised that she had successfully maneuvered into the tight spot on one try, she switched off the engine, reached for her purse and file folder, then rushed from the car. A hasty peek showed several minutes left on the parking meter, but another glance at her watch proved she was late for her job interview—a job she needed desperately.

With her gray plaid skirt hem flying, she ran forward, uncaring of the curious glances her quickened stride caused. The black blazer separated, revealing the rapid rise and fall of full breasts covered by her only silk blouse.

Unable to spare the time to check her reflection in the wide glass doors of the luxurious building, she rushed through. Vainly trying to catch her breath, she took the waiting elevator to the third floor. Her stomach was tied in knots as she gave her name to the smiling secretary. She couldn't remember when she had felt more nervous. So much depended on her making a good impression.

Ushered into the plush office, Honey forced aside the feeling of dejection that threatened to overwhelm her.

"Hello, Miss Bowman. I'm Mr. Jordan. Preferred Pension Counselors' personnel director."

She handed her résumé to the kind-looking older man and sat down. It was her third interview in as many weeks, and she had an intuitive feeling she would be turned down again. The B.Sc. degree resting in her dresser drawer was apparently less important than her low grade-point average in the final year of college.

Her attention never left Mr. Jordan's somber expressions as he scanned the damning form. His brows drew together sympathetically as he read her G.P.A. and lack of job experience. With hands clasped tightly in her lap, shoulders held straight and chin tilted at a proud angle she braced herself for the usual "Sorry."

Mr. Jordan cleared his throat and prepared the best way to explain his employer's adamant demands on hiring only the top graduates in their field. "Miss Bowman." His voice lowered, husky with compassion as he leaned forward. "Our company has prided itself on the number of actuarial assistants we've trained in all phases of pension planning, but you must realize your grades are far below that which a company of this caliber would require."

Honey nodded, overcome with weariness.

"Would you care to explain? Your high school grades and first year at college were the highest possible." He glanced at the résumé before him. "I notice you waited two years before entering college and then took a one-year leave of absence during."

A rush of sadness filled Honey's heart, remembering each traumatic stroke her father suffered. Without remorse she took time off from her studies to nurse her bedridden parent tenderly until his death. Her mother's refusal to care for him during his long, unsuccessful recuperation caused a permanent breach in the slender threads of their relationship. Aware of Wendell Foster's wealth and paranoid attraction to her, her mother had withdrawn all financial assistance in an attempt to force a marriage she thought would benefit herself. The only possible way to continue her education, despite a college scholarship, had been through part-time jobs.

A deliberate cough brought Honey's attention back to the kindly personnel manager. "I have no excuse, Mr. Jordan." She certainly didn't intend boring him with her reasons. It wasn't his fault she couldn't keep up her college grades and work several jobs too.

Honey tilted her chin, looked Mr. Jordan in the eye and promised, "I'll do my best if given a chance."

Claude Jordan smiled at Honey. Faith in her ability surged through him. Her haunting eyes were filled with a sad vulnerability and he wanted to help.

"Despite your damaging résumé, Miss Bowman, I feel you would be an asset to our company." Reluctant to build her hopes up too high, he was forced to add, "Unfortunately I don't have the final say on hiring new employees unless they meet our stringent requirements. I have an appointment with the president at five. I'll plead your case and let you know one way or the other by six o'clock tonight."

"Will you phone me at work?" Honey asked quickly. She wrote down the café's number, handed Mr. Jordan the slip of paper, thanked him, and left.

Honey rushed from the building. It would be a miracle if she arrived at the Savory Seafood beachfront diner on time. She pleaded with her old car not to give her any trouble, pushing the accelerator to the floorboard as it sputtered its way along the street.

A frown crossed her face as she entered her single-room apartment and started removing her best clothes. It was small, gloomy, and barely adequate but the only one she could find on short notice with a severely limited income.

Hanging her clothes neatly on racks, she placed them on one of the large nails stuck around the walls in lieu of a closet. Dressed in a snug-fitting black body suit, red-and-black plaid mini skirt, and black net hose, she grimaced at her reflection in the small wall mirror. She hated the blatant sexuality of her uniform. Her legs were purposely exposed, drawing unwanted attention as she waited tables at the diner five nights a week from five-thirty until two in the morning.

Honey secured her hair into a chignon, giving up when several curls refused to be confined. Fresh lipstick, a brief spray of perfume, purse and jacket over her arm, and she was ready to return to her car.

It was an even fifteen minutes since her arrival. Another ten minute drive would get her to the diner with five minutes to spare. Despite the poor locale and bad reputation of its food, she was pleased to be working.

"Lillian," Brett commanded his secretary over the intercom, "call Jordan and tell him to get up here now!"

With barely a chance to swivel his executive chair around and see if he could catch a glimpse of Santa Catalina Island some twenty-five miles off the California coast from his tenth-floor office, he was interrupted.

"Mr. Jordan's here, Mr. Weston."

"Send him in," Brett replied, leaning back as the outer door was pushed open by his amiable employee. He knew Claude to be an astute judge of character and had always relied confidently on his decisions for keeping their busy company fully staffed with competent people.

"Sit down, Jordan," Brett motioned, smiling broadly. Without preamble he inquired, "Did you fill the two vacancies today?"

Claude leaned forward, placed two folders on the massive desk and watched intently as Brett surveyed their contents. He knew his employer would pay strict attention to his comments as he read the résumés.

"I'm going to hire Dan Hector," the personnel manager told Brett. "He graduated top of his class and wants to work for us because he knows we're the best. Now the other"—he cleared his throat—"I—"

Brett raised his face, his eyes narrowing with disapproval and surprise. "Why take up my time with this? You know we don't hire anyone in the lower third of her class. I pay the highest wages in the area and feel entitled to insist on employing the best."

Claude briefly refused to meet the probing eyes across from him, uncertain how to start his plea on behalf of Miss Bowman. "I feel you're too harsh in this case. I'm certain this woman will be an asset to our company."

"Why?" Brett demanded, leaning back in his chair.

"For one," the older man answered sincerely, "she graduated from your alma mater as a math major."

"So?"

"A degree from Harvey Mudd College should over-shadow her grades not being up to your normal demands since it's academically one of the toughest."

Brett raised his hand to stop Claude's speech. "I also have to rely on some basis for comparision. A grade-point average is normally extremely indicative of one's capabilities."

He pointed to the résumé before him. "She's twenty-six years old and hasn't worked a single day in her life."

"But she really needs the work, Brett," Claude pleaded.

"They all do. I can't risk the reputation of my company by hiring every unemployed applicant."

"Won't you reconsider if only to help out a fellow alumnus?" Mr. Jordan asked hopefully.

"I donate several thousand dollars a year to the alumni fund. I don't feel obligated to hire the entire graduating class as well."

His employer's granite expression pierced through him. It was obviously useless to plead Miss Bowman's case any further. "All right, Brett, you're the boss." Claude rose, took the folders, and turned to leave.

"Hire Dan Hector immediately. Phone the girl and tell her to get married. With her grades she'll probably find it impossible to find work anyway."

"You're hard, Brett," Claude told him bluntly.

"I know. I have over three hundred and fifty employees and a multimillion dollar company to keep solvent. It doesn't leave me time to wet-nurse a young woman." Brett turned his attention to the papers before him, in-stantly engrossed in the figures and unaware when his per-sonnel manager shut the door.

The image of a shapely young woman with lustrous reddish hair and a sweet innocent look suddenly crossed his mind. He raised his face and closed his eyes in a vain attempt to blot out her image. He could feel heat course through his veins just thinking of her soft, curvaceous figure and enticing mouth. Unaccustomed to any woman coming between him and his work, he didn't like it one bit.

Deliberately forcing her to the back of his mind he refused to acknowledge the ache in his loins was desire. Hot throbbing desire for an alluring face and seductive body.

"Damn you! Why the hell should I want you more than any woman I've ever known?" he growled irritably.

His dark brows furrowed in contemplation of his lifestyle. He acknowledged having had many women. He enjoyed pleasing them, whether it was with his company, the sophisticated places he escorted them to, his lovemaking that often ended their evening, or the expensive presents he gave them. It was adult fun and games until their brief interlude ended.

Lately, the science of mathematics was more of a challenge than any woman. They were all so easy to comprehend. So effortlessly placated. He leaned back, contemplating in silence, as the solemn gray eyes in the perfect oval face returned as if to bravely chide him for his past actions.

Annoyed, he read the letters again, slashed his bold signature across the bottom of the pages, and set them aside for his secretary to mail.

"Hey, Honey! Mr. Jordan wants to speak to you."

Honey rushed to the messy office, crossing her fingers that the news would be good.

"I'm sorry, Miss Bowman," Claude apologized. "I'm certain you'll find work soon with a less exacting boss."

"That's okay, Mr. Jordan," Honey assured him. She replaced the receiver, returned to the kitchen, and calmly picked up a waiting order of seafood. A dimpled smile crossed her face, highlighting its youthful beauty and the

determined angle of her upraised chin. She eased gracefully across the crowded dining room, counting the hours
until her shift was finished.

Events compounded, and by Sunday afternoon Honey
humorously decided to petition having Murphy's Law
changed to Bowman's Law. She walked into her best
friend's room amazed she wasn't late for the wedding.

"What happened?" Marcie asked. "You look worn
out."

"And you look like a bride-to-be." Honey smiled,
pleased her friend was so happy. Carefully laying the plastic carrier holding her long gown on the bed, she sighed.
"Steve's a lucky man."

"Thanks, Honey. Now tell me what caused the dark
circles beneath your eyes."

"I had to work until two this morning, I couldn't sleep
when I got home, and my darned car wouldn't start so I
had to take three different buses to get here."

"Did you get the job Friday?" Marcie asked in a hopeful voice as Honey helped her into her wedding dress.

"No. The big boss man himself decided I wasn't qualified to work for P.P.C. I honestly don't blame him but it's
still a blow to my ego."

Satisfied her wedding gown was perfect, Marcie watched
as Honey removed her slacks and blouse. "What did the
personnel manager say when he read all the places you
had worked?"

"I didn't include them in my résumé. Waiting tables,
baby-sitting, typing invoices, selling clothes, stuffing envelopes, and working a switchboard have nothing to do
with pension planning." Honey's voice was muffled as
she slipped her gown over her head.

"But without those jobs you haven't worked anywhere."

"I know it," Honey laughed. "But do you think any of
them would be of importance as an actuary?"

"No," Marcie answered truthfully, "but they'd show
you weren't idle. Gosh, Honey, you usually juggled two or
three jobs at once just to pay your tuition."

"I'm not complaining. Dad was so proud that his only

child was accepted at a top-rated college, it was all worth-while. It seems a betrayal to him to wait tables now."

Honey's eyes filled with sadness as she thought of her father. He had been so gentle with her. The exact type of man she hoped to marry.

Loud laughter interrupted their thoughts as the three bridesmaids burst into the room.

"Where's your fiancé, Honey?" Wanda asked as Kathy and Sharon looked on inquisitively. "He sounds perfect and we're dying to meet him."

Honey bent to pick an imaginary thread from the hem of her gown, flushing with remorse at the proportions her lie had taken. "Actually he can't make it to the wedding after all." She straightened up, folding her slacks and blouse and placing them in the garment bag with her shoes and purse.

Sharon broke in. "I never did understand what you didn't like about that Wendell Foster guy. Any socially prominent man with his kind of money and good looks can give me a call, day or night. Just what's wrong with the man anyway?"

Honey stared at the bridesmaids. She was physically tired, her mind fatigued from the hard night's work, and she felt older in years as well as outlook. Her friends seemed terribly young and immature.

"You wouldn't like him, Sharon. He's too sexually ag-gressive. He scared me the way he stared. Like he's biding his time to attack me." Filled with anger at the memory, she told them, "I dated him one time and had to fight him off. I still have nightmares at the memory of his hot mouth and groping hands. He was actually tearing my dress off when some people came along and intervened."

Honey's stomach clenched, recalling her mother's fury at spurning Wendell's attentions. She remembered the ac-cusations that her daughter was frigid and cold, could hear the complaints that Honey should be grateful he was willing to tutor her until she was experienced enough to satisfy his needs no matter what they were.

"You're from the dark ages, Honey. What's the use in saving it?" Wanda blurted out. She surveyed her friend, envious of her beauty in the long gown. It outlined the tilt of her full breasts and tiny waist and made her own slender figure seem shapeless in comparison.

"Lay off, Wanda," Marcie scolded. "Honey's too intense to enjoy a short-term relationship. Her quick engagement proves that."

"The limousine's here," Marcie's mother called out, entering the room to give her daughter's gown a final inspection.

Time passed in a blur as the wedding party was driven to the chapel situated on a hilltop of the Palos Verdes peninsula. Intent on avoiding Wendell, Honey stayed close to Marcie's side prior to the ceremony. While sounds of "The Wedding March" resounded through the glass-walled chapel, she slowly preceded her friend up the aisle.

A tremor ran down her back, causing her to shudder. She glanced quickly through lowered lashes to her right, instinctively knowing Wendell was staring at her with his hooded blue eyes. She clutched the dainty nosegay with shaking fingers. One fleeting glance had taken in the raging animosity held in tight check. It was obvious that her mother had told him about the supposed engagement.

Honey's mind reeled, wishing for a forceful man to act as a buffer between her and Wendell's inevitable confrontation. She stood proudly, nerves too taut to hear the words or take in the beauty of the ceremony.

Loss of sleep sent waves of tiredness through her body, intensified by the minister's monotone voice droning on and on. Thoughts of the lies she told her mother and friends weighed heavily on her mind.

Sighing with relief when Steve and Marcie were pronounced man and wife, Honey attempted to slip unseen to the side of the chapel. She felt a desperate need to be alone.

"Come on, Honey, we're going to the reception hall now," Marcie whispered, secure in Steve's possessive hold as they ducked to avoid the traditional shower of rice.

She was gently pushed into a comfortable backseat along with Sharon, Wanda, and Kathy. Content to remain silent, she listened to their noisy chatter. She gave them a bright smile when the driver stopped, and then followed the crowd into the plush atmosphere of the rented hall.

Separated from her friends, Honey was amused to spot them flirting outrageously at the bar. She knew it wouldn't be long until they enticed three of the male guests to escort them home.

All she wanted was to count the hours until she could politely slip away from the lavish buffet and dance arranged by Marcie's affluent parents.

Chapter Two

Successful at avoiding Wendell during the wedding and the trip to the reception hall, Honey searched for his tall figure. Her dusky eyes widened with dismay, noticing him pushing his way through the crowd. His long stride would carry him quickly across the width of the hall.

Chilled by his sullen features and the speed of his approach, she spun rapidly, awkwardly falling against the steely contours of a towering man who loomed close behind.

Her naked shoulders were clasped in his strong hands. Startled, she raised her face, concerned that a stranger should hold her so intimately. Smoke-gray eyes fringed by heavy lashes were held by the penetraing sea-green gaze fixed on her flushed face.

Mesmerized by the man's piercing look beneath furrowed brows, she swayed forward. Her heart beat in wild confusion at the shock of being securely held within the grip of an aristocratic-looking stranger. She watched hypnotically while he lowered his head, his image blurring when his sensuous mouth took her trembling lips. The contact was electrifying. She could feel the force of it spread throughout her body.

Sliding his long fingers from the satiny smoothness of Honey's bare shoulders to her neck, he held her oval face still, cupping her suddenly pale cheeks with tenderness. His fingers threaded through the unruly tendrils of auburn silk, his mouth prepared to quell the burning rage threatening to explode from the astonished woman in his arms.

Feeling a surge of temper rapidly building up inside her

enticing body, he raised his head a breath away from the
sweetness of her quivering lips.

"Cooperate, you little fool!" he prompted impatiently,
his voice filled with husky authority.

Coerced into temporary obedience, Honey froze, strangely quiescent. Disgusted with her abnormal submissive-
ness, she started to protest only to feel his mouth clamped
over hers, instantly smothering rebellion before it had a
chance to commence.

She fit into the stranger's arms as if formed especially to
mold to his contours. To those noticing their embrace it
appeared they were lovers reunited after a long absence.
Passionate sweethearts influenced by the romance and
gaiety of the wedding festivities.

The fire of his dynamic, sensual mouth was breathtaking. His practiced expertise burned through Honey, causing her to tremble against him in alarm. Her mind reeled
and she was feeling faint as she tried vainly to recover
from the violation of his intimate embrace.

She twisted her head to break contact with his persuasive mouth and the control of his hands.

"Stop..." she gasped, feeling hysteria rise in her
throat. Her frightened whisper fanned his mouth, widespread fingertips unsuccessfully trying to pry a space between them.

His hands lowered to her shoulders, drawing her tight
against the hard wall of his muscular chest.

"Please...stop!" Unable to avoid his lips relentlessly
caressing her face, she became more desperate by the second.

"Shut up, woman! I'm your fiancé from Happy Hearts."
He nipped her earlobe sharply, kissed the dimple in her
cheek and the corner of her passionately shaped mouth.
"Kiss me now and act like you mean it!"

Shocked by his declaration, Honey raised her mouth
obediently. Out of the corner of her eye she noticed Wendell attempting to get around a large group blocking his
way. He was scarcely yards from them. She could see his
eyes, alarmed by the disgust and hatred directed at her and
the man holding her the full length of his body. Anyone

seeing the loathing in his face now would never call him handsome, she thought.

Thrilled by the sudden turn of events, Honey placed both slender arms around the stranger's neck, letting her fingers trail lovingly through his shiny ebony hair. Her lips softened, parting eagerly in response to the seeking mouth caressing hers with the intensity of an adoring lover.

Staggered by the ability of the Happy Hearts's owner to find her a suitable escort, Honey let her body melt into his. *He's perfect,* she thought, even to having thick black hair and green eyes.

Honey completely forgot the subterfuge and pretense that were the reasons behind her escort's caress. She clung to him, raising on tiptoes to deepen the pressure of his stimulating mouth. Blood pounded erratically through her veins, the expertise of his kiss drawing the very breath from her body.

Uncaring of their surroundings, she made no objection when his hands slid from her shoulders to her back in an intimate caress. She could feel the heat of his palm through her dress, the pressure of his chest crushing her breasts. There was no pain from his strength, only pleasure, and she wanted it to go on forever.

He was the one to end their embrace, his chest rising and falling with each rapid breath. His eyes narrowed, staring at her dazed, slumberous expression. He watched her irises darken, the gray depths turning to shimmering charcoal with the heightened emotions aroused by his searching caress. The heady scent of her perfume filled his nostrils. It was too soon, yet he felt as if he had hungered for her his entire life. The touch of her body, the sweetness of her mouth, was beyond his expectations, surpassing anything he had experienced.

"Oh, honey, I needed that," he husked intimately. His face lifted with reluctance to observe the stunned expressions of three young women looking on fixedly.

Wendell, stopped by an encounter with a persistent friend, was watching in disbelief, his focus never leaving Honey. Wanda, Kathy, and Sharon walked forward, envious of the startlingly handsome man holding Honey. They watched him smile at her tenderly, then lower his face to brush her forehead with his lips in a loving caress.

Honey lay her head on his chest, whispering weakly, "How did you know my name?"

He trailed his mouth from her forehead to her ear, murmuring, "I don't. Since we're about to have company, tell me quick."

She clung to his wide shoulders, astonished by his unforeseen appearance, trying vainly to quell her attraction. "But...you called me Honey." The intoxicating smell of his after-shave and faint aroma of tobacco clinging to his jacket added to his intense masculinity, making it impossible to gather her senses.

He rained kisses around her dainty ear, murmuring gruffly, "That was an endearment. You wanted an ardent lover, didn't you?" He spun her around, keeping between her and the startled eyes of her approaching friends.

"Yes. Actually, my name is Honey. You surprised me."

She leaned into the strength of his body, her lips close to his throat. "What—what's your name?" she stuttered, her nerves shaken by the impact of his closeness and experienced kisses. They made any caress from her past fade into oblivion.

Aware of her turmoil, he ushered her into a private reading room behind them, slamming the door abruptly before turning the lock. Assured they wouldn't be interrupted by her advancing friends, he released her.

Without the strength of his muscular arms, Honey stood motionless in the middle of the paneled room. Her face was pale, dilated eyes filled with indecision. The overhead light picked up shimmering glints in her auburn hair, which framed her face with a fiery halo.

Breaking the silence, she blurted out, "I can't believe it. The old lady was emphatic about not supplying escorts." She raised her hands in a pleading gesture. "I don't even know your name, but I'm thrilled you're here. Desperately happy, in fact."

He noticed the pallor of her face, the weariness visible in her shadowed eyes. His heart beat irregularly, filled with sympathy for the woman before him. It had never happened before. He had always prided himself that he never lost control of his cool, precision-prone mind.

"My name's Brett Weston." He would do anything to ease the stress visible to his keen glance. "Don't worry, Honey. I'm here to see you avoid any complicated situations."

"Thank you, Brett." Already she was secure in his forceful presence.

"If it's an ardent fiancé you need, remember to cooperate. You pulled away when I first held you, which didn't give anyone the impression I was told you were trying to imply."

Brett stood before her, long legs slightly splayed, one hand cupping his chin, all the time nonchalantly scrutinizing her curvaceous figure. His bold eyes darkened, lingering momentarily on the rise and fall of her breasts, outlined by the gown. Their brazen message was nearly as intimate as his touch.

Honey flushed at his audacity. His gaze acted like a shot of adrenaline. She felt the beginning of a fine temper, more exhilarated than she remembered being in weeks.

"I certainly hope I don't have to pay for the rental of your formal suit in addition to your wages." She couldn't resist the urge to put him in his place. Her chin raised defiantly, unflinching glance attempting to intimidate.

"What?" Brett was amazed by her outburst and sudden rebellion, clearly visible in her sparkling eyes. His brows drew together, a grim expression hardening his features for a moment. Abruptly a mischievous smile lifted the corners of his mouth, deciding it was time to teach her a lesson in manners. His eyes danced with humor, turning to jade when he teased devilishly.

"We, er, professional escorts have to supply our own wardrobe suitable to meet any social occasion."

Amused by her naiveté, he thought of the exorbitant cost of his tailored wardrobe, handmade shoes, and custom silk shirts. It also occurred to him she might not be as easily constrained as he wished.

"How... how much do you normally receive for a job

like this?'' She feared it would be more than she could afford. He looked so elegant, his roguish features handsome, his manner assured and confident. It surprised her a man of his appearance should seek employment as a professional escort. His work was certainly questionable, leading to all kinds of curiosity about its legitimacy.

She looked him over boldly, trying to analyze his personality. He seemed too aggressive and acted much too intelligent. He would be in demand, she surmised. His good looks also showed strength of character. Each feature indicated pride and breeding. Quite unique, really.

My God, she thought, *I'm scrutinizing him like a prospective buyer looks over a racehorse before purchase.*

"Don't worry about my fees, Honey," he purred seductively, annoyed by her impudent sizing of his character. "Surely we can come to some kind of an agreement, suitable and...satisfying...to both of us later tonight. Don't you agree?'' His eyes darkened to forest-green, roaming slowly over her body with deliberate intent to taunt.

He waited for her reaction, amazed by his weakness in giving in to the compelling need for this woman. His pulses raced wildly and his loins ached as he remembered the feel of her curved body resting close. He swallowed to ease the tightness in his throat, the taste of her mouth lingering like an aphrodisiac on his lips. He wanted her and he intended to have her.

A sense of devilment made him decide to continue with his act of being an escort. He knew the occupation irritated her despite admitting she needed him. She brought him back to the present abruptly with her outspoken threat.

"If you mean what I think you mean, forget it. I pay my debts in cash only!'' Her eyes turned frosty, showing anger at his blatant suggestion. "And furthermore I will demand a receipt marked paid in full!''

Brett started toward her, ready to give her a lesson in the merits of quelling her impertinent tongue.

Honey stood her ground, slender chin uptilted defiantly, smoky eyes shining with indignation. Her fiery expression matched the glints visible in her silky hair. "I...I...''

Checked by a hard pounding on the library door, Brett paused. They could hear the loud giggling of her girlfriends demanding that Honey come out and bring her fiancé with her.

Fearful she could never get away with her deception, Honey's face paled, her eyes pleading with Brett to help her.

He took her into his arms, clamped his mouth over her parted lips, and proceeded to kiss her until she clung weakly to his shoulders. He released her mouth slowly, looking at her stormy face.

"That's better," he insisted arrogantly. "I think a fiancée should look thoroughly kissed and well-loved at all times." He reached up, smoothing a finger over her pulsating lips in a slow caress. "You certainly look that way now with your glossy lips soft and quivery, eyes dilated, dark with mysterious depths of inner excitement."

"It's agitation...not excitement!" she shot back.

"Little liar," he told her, bending to brush her mouth in a deliberate provoking gesture.

He placed an arm around her waist, opened the door, and, looking at her girlfriends, demanded casually, "Introduce me to your lovely friends, darling." He turned his head, bending toward Honey to place a solicitous kiss on her forehead. The long fingers pinching her waist was his reminder for her to behave. He appeared to be so much in love, he was unable to spend even a fraction of a minute without touching her intimately.

Bemused by the touch of Brett's unyielding body hovering protectively close, Honey felt spellbound. She was awed by his ability to take charge of the unreal situation caused by her lie. She glanced with apprehension at her friends, making the introductions quickly.

She watched as they fell under the hypnotic spell of his husky authoritative voice, striking looks, and lithe physique. His assured manner convinced them beyond doubt that Honey had every reason to act dazed with her overwhelming fiancé.

Brett's social poise matched his appearance. He conversed briefly, told them he wished to dance with his fiancée, and guided her with one large hand in the middle of her back toward the dance floor.

The reception hall was crowded with happy guests, either filling plates with hot and cold delicacies from a sumptuous buffet or dancing to the music of a local band playing on a raised dais in the corner of the room.

As they neared the bar Brett's hand tightened painfully on Honey's waist. Her body had tensed at the same moment he spotted Wendell Foster set a drink down and move toward them.

Honey glanced sideways at Brett for encouragement, her shock increasing on noticing his eyes narrow with dislike. Icy disdain hardened every feature of his handsome face. He acknowledged Wendell's presence with a cold taunt.

"Well, well, Foster. I haven't had the misfortune of seeing you during the last few years. Still treating the ladies to your tender touch?"

An ugly flush tinged Wendell's smooth cheeks. "I can't say I missed your company either, Weston," he shot back. "I witnessed your crude display of passion earlier and want to know what the hell you're doing holding on to Honey." In a voice edged with rage, he demanded, "Get your hands off her. She happens to be mine!"

"You're the bastard!" Brett exclaimed grimly. His astounded glance raked Honey's white face, seeking confirmation of Wendell's statement. She trembled within his clasp, giving him an imperceptible nod. His fingers tightened on her waist involuntarily when he realized she was being sought by a man he had hated for years.

Brett's powerful shoulders tensed, his hand leaving Honey's body to form a tight fist. She stood speechless, watching he and Wendell brace themselves like wild stags sizing each other up before they charged into battle with deadly intent.

"No bastards in my background, Weston," Wendell challenged recklessly.

"Hell, no, you're the first!" Brett pointed out sarcastically. "Speaking of crude displays of passion, you're a master of the art of brutal persuasion. Do you still special-

ize in unwilling innocents?'' His furious voice hissed with
loathing, remembering the animosity and involvement
during their college years.

Wendell ignored the inflammatory remark, his eyes
never leaving Honey to demand arrogantly, ''Why the
hell was Weston holding you?''

Dazed by the actions of both men, Honey spoke for the
first time. She was relieved they were in a secluded area,
concealed from the others by large potted palms.

''This is my...fiancé.'' She held her chin high, gaining
confidence from the knowledge Brett was at her side. His
undaunted attitude gave her enough courage to challenge
back. ''Didn't my mother tell you I was going to be married?''

With both fists clenched at the sides of his fashionably
attired hips, Wendell admitted begrudgingly, ''She ranted
on about you meeting someone since moving here. I
don't see a ring on your finger.''

''I...er...I...'' Honey's lashes lowered, shielding her
bewilderment. She should have bought a cheap ring at the
dime store. Anything that could have passed for an engagement ring from a distance would have added conviction for her deceptiveness.

Interested in the reason preventing Brett and Honey
from dancing, Wanda, Kathy, and Sharon wandered over,
arriving in time to hear Brett announce calmly, ''If
Honey's friends hadn't interrupted us in the library,
Honey would be wearing her ring now.''

He turned to Honey, took her hand, and raised it to his
lips. He kissed each finger with deliberate slowness. ''I
just got it back from the jeweler's today, darling. I hope it
fits better now.'' He glanced at the others. ''She has such
slender fingers, you know.''

Grateful for the impulse that caused him to bring his
mother's ring, Brett slipped it on Honey's finger. He
kissed the top of her hand, turned it over, and pressed his
lips to the trembling palm. Then he drew her into his
arms, her hands clasped between them.

He was filled with a rush of satisfaction knowing he had

helped his bemused fiancé daunt any plans made by her uncaring mother and his longtime enemy.

"There, my dearest, you have your ring at last. How does it feel this time?" His inquiry was made deliberately, the fury on Wendell's face the exact effect he hoped to create.

Filled with disbelief, Honey stared at the brilliant lights flashing from the huge solitaire diamond nestled between a cluster of perfect rubies gleaming with a deep rich burgundy fire of their own. The antique gold setting enhanced the beauty of the exquisite ring.

"It's perfect, Brett. The most gorgeous ring I've ever seen."

He gripped her shoulders, reminding her she should have seen it before.

"As...as I told you before...darling." Nervous tears shimmered in her shadowed eyes. Trying to suppress them, she was unaware how alluring she looked staring in wonderment at the ring. Her hand was pressed flat on Brett's chest, vivid against his black suit. Two moist tears trickled down each cheek, sparkling when she raised her face to Brett.

Brett leaned forward, kissing each salty drop away before placing a lingering kiss on her trembling mouth. Raising his head, he stared arrogantly at Wendell, his narrowed eyes challenging him to question his right to Honey's affection. Hoping he would try to interfere, Brett ached to bruise his knuckles on the taut chin of the man he loathed.

"Convinced now, Foster?" Brett looked at Honey's wide-eyed girlfriends, nodding politely. "Excuse us, please. I wish to dance now with my delightful fiancée."

He brushed aside Wendell, deliberately goading the man, his hand guiding Honey through the crowd at the bar. He took her smoothly into his arms at the edge of the dance floor. Holding her firmly against his body, he led her around the sleek floor to the melodic sounds from the band, his steps sleek and practiced.

Honey placed her arms around his neck, her breath

catching when she felt him place both hands possessively on her hips before sliding to the small of her back. She felt his lips move, softly raining tender kisses on her brow.

Held tight in her husband's arms, Marcie had Steve stop close to Brett and Honey, uncaring they were in the middle of the dance floor.

"Introduce me, Honey, and congratulations!" she exclaimed, catching a glimpse of Honey's ring. Her parents were extremely wealthy, but she knew her mother would be green with envy over the costly ring on her friend's finger. Obviously Honey's financial worries were coming to an abrupt end.

Brett took another introduction in his stride, congratulated Steve and Marcie on their marriage, apologizing sincerely for missing their wedding.

Marcie's eyes sparkled with love and the effect of numerous glasses of champagne. "I'm glad you arrived, Brett. Honey probably told you she had to take the bus to my house. Now you can take her back to her room. My parents will be pleased also. Dad's had too much to drink and mother shouldn't be allowed to drive, she's so nervous."

Embarrassed, Honey started to speak up when Brett hushed her with a quick meaningful kiss on her opened mouth, his eyes ardent.

"Seeing the way you're looking at each other now," Marcie said, giggling, "I know you'll want to be alone later. Frankly, if Steve had acted like Brett during our college days, I know neither one of us could have handled a four-year celibate engagement."

Honey laid her flushed cheek on Brett's sleeve, lashes shadowing her eyes to conceal the turmoil Marcie's outspoken comments caused. Marcie was right, she thought. No woman could hold a man at arm's length if he had the seductive charisma, ability to make love, and sensuous appearance of Brett.

Dismayed by her intrigue with Brett, Honey remembered he was paid to be attentive. The disgusting man had undoubtedly trained for years, acting the part of a lovesick suitor, she reflected contemptuously.

My gosh, she speculated in silence. *Brett's nothing but a gigolo!*

She attempted to pull away from his grasp, no longer wanting to be enfolded in his enticing arms. Without his touch she hoped to end the emotional havoc that had mesmerized her from the first. Peeking through her fluttering lashes, she saw his eyes narrow in inquiry.

"Steve, I know you're anxious to glide around the floor some more with your lovely bride and I feel a sudden urge to hold my darling Honey close in my arms again. What do you think about continuing our dance?" Brett's voice was silky smooth, warning Honey he had sensed her thoughts.

Without another glance at her friends he pulled Honey into his arms, his mouth close to her ear as the lights dimmed, giving them privacy.

"Give, Honey! Why that look of distaste while I talked to Marcie and Steve? I felt you pull away as if you couldn't bear for me to touch you."

"I...I...If you must know, I was thinking of all the women you must have made feel cherished, like you are doing to me. You are giving an Academy Award-winning performance, Mr. Weston. My friends will never doubt that you are actually in love with me and our engagement is real." Honey stuttered nervously, adding with unaccountable jealous resentment, "You're a—a—gigolo!"

Brett nuzzled her neck, giving her a fierce, angry kiss. Infuriated by her insults, he punished her further by a sharp bite on her tender earlobe before blasting her with verbal condemnation.

"Gigolo, be damned! You're lucky we're in a crowded room or I'd show you just what I am, you little witch." His words were barely above a whisper. Spoken into her ear they sounded like thunder and he wasn't finished chastising.

"Are you forgetting that *you* sought to buy my services? Did you forget it was *your* lies that got you into trouble? Did you fail to remember it was *your* bungling, indecisive inability to convince Foster you didn't want anything to do with him that brought about this problem in the first place?"

"But... but... you..." she tried to explain, straining away with hopes of breaking his tight hold.

"Shut up!" he commanded impatiently, drawing her back into intimate contact with his body. He circled among the dancing couples, never missing a step despite his annoyance. His penetrating gaze fixed on her face, her flush visible despite the dim illumination.

"Don't go criticizing me. It was *your* wayward, lying little tongue that placed you in this predicament! Now relax, Foster's watching, and I want to earn my money today by convincing that bastard once and for all that he's to get any ideas out of his creepy head that he'll ever possess you. I'd even marry you myself to prevent that scum from ever laying a slimy hand on your beautiful, provocative body!"

Aghast at Brett's impassioned speech, Honey lay her forehead on his chest, letting the music lull her into a false sense of peace. She refused to question the reason for her contentment or the cause of the stirring receptivity aroused by the touch of a man she had hired for one day. She let her body relax, following his lead as if in a dream.

Brett deliberately held Honey in a close embrace, refusing to release her in order to prevent Wendell from cutting in. He guided her smoothly through song after song. When her body started to tremble, he lowered his head, whispering against the side of her neck. His lips trailed to her ear, his nostrils inhaling the fragrant scent of her fine skin.

"What's the matter, Honey? Are you hungry?" he questioned, curious about her sudden lethargy.

His warm breath caused a resurgence of desire. Her senses responded unbidden to each movement of his body and the hypnotic tone of his deep-timbred voice. She raised her face, murmuring wearily.

"Frankly, I'm ready to collapse. I just want to relax with my eyes closed."

Brett stared at her pale face, the dark shadows beneath her eyes visible in the dim light. His heart surged with compassion. Annoyed by his inability to control his mounting interest, his words were brusque. "Why the hell are you tired? At your age you should be able to party all night!"

"I do!" Honey blazed back, her stormy eyes holding his boldly. "During the day I lie on the sand and admire well-muscled bronzed men wearing sexy bikini swimsuits play volleyball. At night I idle the hours away in a luxurious restaurant surrounded by hordes of ardent admirers until long after midnight. My debauchery doesn't leave me much time for sleep!"

"Burn the candle at both ends, do you?" Brett snorted in censure.

"Certainly! And furthermore I shall continue to do so until there's no wax in the middle!" Infuriated by his scorn, her back stiffened, causing her to step on his foot. *Arrogant beast,* she thought. *Making fun of my fatigue when he lives off the hard-earned money of lonely, defenseless women.*

Hoping she had scuffed his elegant shoe, Honey demanded, "Take me to the lounge now. I'm going to phone for a taxi and go home."

Brett pulled her tight to his solid chest, scolding angrily. "I'm taking you home tonight. It's all part of the services of a gigolo." Damn her! He had never in his life encountered a more recalcitrant, impudent, delectable female.

"No. Definitely not," she started to protest, her words interrupted by the look in his narrowed eyes. Her heart began to race as his head lowered. He was much too close to elude. It was impossible to avoid the contact of his mouth.

His lips took hers masterfully, only intending to stop any further rebellion. Instead they lingered, absorbing the heady sweetness of her response. Her body became pliant, the contact bringing him pleasure. Uncaring they could be observed, he kissed her thoroughly, the sheer physical bliss of her soft mouth more astounding with each touch.

"Agreed?" he prompted, his lips caressing her neck while he regained his breath. Pleased by his ability to kiss her into acquiescence, he observed her nod silently.

"That's better. As a professional...escort...I detest an independent, continually dissenting woman. You're paying me to make an impression. Everyone, including Foster, is now convinced that you're passionately loved. Frankly, I think I'm doing one hell of a job today," he bragged deliberately, taunting her for her assumption he was a gigolo.

Honey regarded Brett with disturbing awareness, ired by his look of confidence. It bordered on smugness and provoked her feminine independence.

"What talent you've gained was undoubtedly acquired through continuous practice and thought of the easy money you would earn. Personally, Mr. Weston, I think you're terribly conceited and overconscious of your limited talents!"

Unseen by the guests crowded on the dance floor, Brett slid one hand over Honey's hip. He pulled her to the length of his hard body in a punishing gesture, forcing her to remain intimately close. So near, he could tell from the flush on her cheeks she could feel his desire— desire to seek her full capitulation through the act of love.

Honey met his eyes squarely, knowing her derogatory comments about his character incensed him. She was embarrassed that despite his indignation the touch of her thighs on his body and her breasts crushed to his chest aroused him. Unlike Wendell's repugnant virility, Brett's need tempted her to press her hips forward. His palm spread hard across her spine kept her from drawing away when she attempted to ease a more conventional distance apart.

"If you don't remove your hand from my back, I'll put a hole in the top of your foot with my heel." Her eyes glimmered with temper, the dimple in her cheek appearing with each word.

"Furthermore, I intend to report you to Happy Hearts. I asked for a fiancé...not an opinionated disciplinarian!"

Brett's hand slid to her nape. What looked like a loving gesture was a firm reminder he was still in control. His head bent to her neck, his strong teeth nibbling along the side between his exasperated retort. "What you need is a keeper, you temperamental witch! My other dates have been older and therefore easier to handle." He laughed inwardly when he felt a sharp tug on his nape. He felt entirely capable of controlling her but not easily. He raised his face. Staring at her, his eyes warned of later punishment.

It occurred to Honey she would regret her retaliation. Every time she snapped out an impertinent retort Brett quelled it. She had noticed a cynical smile on his lips and didn't like being anyone's source of amusement, much less a man for hire by the hour. He was the antithesis of her father.

"How old are you?"

"Twenty and then some!" Her exact age was none of his business.

"That explains it. You're too damned young to learn to put a restraint on your vicious little tongue," he told her glibly, his glance cautioning her to keep quiet. "I should demand compensatory pay for today's assignment. The hazards and hassle of putting up with an undisciplined, enticing termagant like you should be worth triple my normal fee."

Honey inhaled sharply, Brett's insulting comments causing her to stutter furiously. "Why—you—"

Brett swept her into an isolated corner well hidden from the other guests. He smothered her exclamation with the fierce possession of her tightly clenched lips.

Honey found herself responding instantly. Her feeble attempt to crush the enjoyment of his sensual mouth moving persuasively on hers was short-lived. The contact changed, becoming warm and gentle. His lips soothed until hers parted willingly, then increased their pressure. Her hands left his shoulders to tighten on his nape. Instead of pushing him away she drew him to her, raising on tiptoe until her head spun with the sensuality of his embrace. She clung weakly, all desire to argue leaving in a surge of exhaustion.

Honey made no protest when Brett ushered her smoothly through the reception room in preparation to taking her home. A sudden outburst of excited squeals from the single women as Marcie raised her arm to throw her wedding bouquet stopped them.

Brett's towering frame easily pushed Honey through the shifting crowd. He held her slender figure in front of him, his arms enfolding her like a safeguard. When he realized Marcie's intentions, he whispered in Honey's ear, "Catch it, sweetheart. She's deliberately going to throw the bouquet to you."

Honey raised her hand, deftly grabbing the cluster of white orchids, their silver ribbons streaming behind. A tinge of rose colored her cheeks when the other women congratulated her before questioning Brett about the date of he and Honey's wedding.

Undaunted by their personal queries, Brett commented loudly, smiling at Wanda's, Kathy's, and Sharon's envious expressions. "Honey will become Mrs. Weston as soon as I can make arrangements to leave my work." He placed a kiss on her brow, his eyes never leaving her profile. "No more than two months at the most."

He shot one last look at Wendell's face, his eyes scathing, mouth thinned in distaste. Filled with satisfaction at his wrath, he ushered Honey through the crowd, his hand never leaving her waist until they were alone.

Wendell Foster stood silent, brooding in the doorway, an angry witness to Brett's taunting wedding plans.

Honey felt dazed. Since Brett's appearance she had lost control of the events happening around her. She gathered her purse and clothing from the ladies' lounge, making no protest when Brett drew her to his side, through the lobby, down the broad stairway, and across the paved driveway toward his waiting car.

It was already dark, a narrow sliver of a new moon barely visible in the black sky. It seemed as if a lifetime had passed instead of one afternoon.

Honey came out of her reverie when Brett stopped to open a car door. She gasped at the sleek black Ferrari gleaming beneath the parking lot lights. She raised her eyes in despair.

"Oh, no! Why did you go to so much expense? I only

intended to hire an economy escort. The no-frills type!"
She shook her head in dismay, wailing plaintively, "I'll
never be able to afford all these extras." Her mind reeled
with the estimated expense of one afternoon's services.

"I promise I'll never tell another lie as long as I live,"
she cried poignantly, looking at Brett's strong profile as he
bent to open the passenger door. "This car must have cost
at least thirty thousand dollars. One day's rental would be
more than my weekly income."

Brett assisted her into the low-slung bucket seat, scooped
her trailing gown up, placed the plastic bag in back, threw
her bouquet on the floor, and closed the door. He walked
to the driver's side, easing his long legs beneath the steering wheel. He watched her awed expression as her widened eyes took in the plush interior.

"Quit worrying. I borrowed it from an affluent friend of
mine. It won't cost you a penny extra despite the fact you
insulted it's one-hundred-thousand-dollar price tag. This,
my uninformed young woman, is a custom-made Ferrari.
I suppose you drive an old wreck?"

He leaned over to fasten her seat belt before hooking
his own. The instant he turned the ignition key the motor
purred to life, its controlled power delighting his sense of
male pride, adding to the satisfaction of owning a fine
piece of luxurious equipment.

Put out by his attitude that assumed she owned an old
car, she retorted, "The kind of automobile I drive is none
of your business." Her eyes were drawn to the masculine
grace of his well-shaped hand when he shifted gears, remembering how enjoyable that same hand felt touching
her face or clasping her waist. She had to quell her interest!

"Furthermore, see that you take me straight home. I
don't normally ride in cars with strange men, Mr. Weston," she warned him primly, clasping her purse in the
middle of her lap like a shield.

Brett's eyes darkened to forest green, narrowing with
irritation. "Call me Mr. Weston once more and you'll
never get home. I've held you in my arms, kissed you
innumerable times, felt you return each one when you

forgot to fight me, placed a ring on your finger, pretended to be your fiancé, and declared my intent to marry you, all in the space of a few hours. That should certainly take us beyond the stage of being called Miss Bowman and Mr. Weston.''

Thoughts whirled through Brett's head. He vaguely remembered seeing Ms Bowman neatly typed on the résumé Claude handed him the previous Friday. It couldn't be! Surely fate wouldn't play into his hands twice in one day. Impossible. He shrugged, easing his car from the club onto the busy coastal highway winding around the edge of the Palos Verdes Hills.

He glanced imperceptibly at Honey's profile, admiring the purity of its line. The small straight nose, exciting mouth... God, how sweet it was... firm, defiant little chin, and long slender throat. She had the kind of beauty that would be even more appealing as she matured. The knowledge she was passionately loved and loving in return would add mysterious depths to her bewitching dove-gray eyes. Unable to resist a sudden compulsion, he pulled abruptly into a lay-by, stopping the car smoothly along the edge of the viewing area.

Startled by Brett's sudden stop on the dark road, Honey tensed. She had been thinking of her last traumatic date with Wendell. Her body trembled, suddenly frightened thinking Brett might attempt to force her to submit to his brutal sexual demands too.

Stunned by her quick cry and the fright in her eyes visible in the faint light from the dashboard, Brett demanded, "What's the matter, Honey?" He instinctively reached for her shoulders to comfort her when she twisted frantically, trying to free herself from the seat belt.

"Take your hands off me! You can't expect me to pay for your time this... this... way?"

"What way?" he murmured huskily, bewildered by her withdrawal.

"By letting you make love to me," she whispered back, her lashes lowered to stop the flow of nervous tears threatening to spill.

His fingers tightened, a heavy silence between them,

until he released her trembling shoulders to relax in his own seat. His glance didn't leave her face until she looked up. Forcing her to listen, he admonished her firmly.

"My God, I can't believe the way your mind works. Do you actually think I could pay my rent, buy food, much less gas, on that kind of payment? If that was the type of compensation I received each time I took a woman out, I'd have been a physical wreck in my teens!"

Honey turned away, staring at the blackness outside her door window. Her voice was a faint murmur as she apologized. "I'm sorry. I panicked." Tears blurred her eyes, a shudder running the length of her spine. "The last time I went out my date stopped like you did and I was almost... unable to stop him from..."

She couldn't continue, remembering Wendell's rough groping hands, hot seeking lips, and the weight of his body crushing her below him. She turned to Brett. The deep concern and understanding in his eyes made her realize intuitively he would never have to resort to physical force to make a woman submit.

"Your date was Foster, no doubt?" he blurted out grimly. "He should be behind bars." His hands lifted to her bared shoulders, soothing her fears with circular caressing motions. "You're lucky you escaped intact. Now relax. Manhandling is not my style."

He released her seat belt, drawing her unresisting body into his arms. His only interest was to reassure her of his intentions. She needed comfort now. His deep voice lulled her despite the intimacy of her position and the privacy in the darkened car.

"If you were more experienced, I'd show you soon what I mean. When you're older..."

"I'm twenty-six!" Honey interrupted, strangely intent on him knowing she was of age to do anything she wished.

"Hush!" he whispered, his hand moving over her back to mold her closer to his chest. "When you feel within yourself the need to attain womanhood, some lucky man will rush to oblige. It would be an invitation from the gods to tutor you in the arts of love, but never with force. The correct approach would make it unnecessary. You've an extremely passionate nature, which will be an unending delight to your first lover."

"But why did you stop the car?" Honey questioned, embarrassed equally by her false assumptions and his blunt speech.

Brett raised his hands to her face, cupping her jaw, his fingers moving slowly over her ears in a seductive caress. "This is why, Honey."

Too bemused to speak, she remained still. He gently removed each hairpin from her upswept hairstyle, placing them with the tiny white blossoms on the carpeted floorboard.

Threading his fingers through her hair, he spread it in heavy silken waves around her shoulders. His hands were as gentle and soothing as a lover's caress.

"That's better. You have hair a man wants to bury his face in. I could inhale its sweet scent forever and will lay awake all night wondering how it would feel across my bare chest." His words echoed in the car, closing them in with the implicit intimacy.

He lowered her window, easing her tenderly into her seat. She turned her face toward Brett, watching mesmerized as he started the motor and pulled into the light evening traffic. The breeze blowing by the open window whipped her hair back from her face, its soft touch a cool welcoming caress.

"Don't wear your hair up anymore," Brett told her, his swift glance taking in the beauty of the lustrous auburn strands flowing freely around her lovely face.

She closed her eyes, heavy lashes casting crescent-shaped shadows on her cheeks when Brett drove beneath overhead streetlights. The luxury of being driven home and self-satisfaction at outwitting Wendell were a heady combination. Exhausted, she dozed, unaware when Brett slid to a smooth stop for the second time.

Cautiously easing her purse from her lap, he removed her wallet. A brief glance at her face assured him she was sound asleep. He smiled tenderly at the enticing disarray of her wind-tossed hair. Finding her billfold, he searched for her driver's license, thankful she had the Department of Motor Vehicles type her Long Beach address on the back.

A frown furrowed his brow at her location. He knew her street was in a less desirable section of town. Unashamedly looking through the bill holder, he noticed with chagrin the small amount of money neatly tucked inside.

God, he thought, she really does need a man to care for her. The independent little witch can't even afford the price of a decent purse. His sophisticated companions wouldn't be caught dead with a cheap plastic purse like Honey's. He returned her wallet, placing the purse back onto her lap before driving to the section of town where she lived.

Within minutes he was pulling to a stop along the broken curb of the poorly lit city street. He observed with distaste the unkempt old home sitting squarely in the middle of a small shabby unfenced yard. A rusted junk car filled the narrow driveway amidst scattered trash. A worn path led to the rear of the house, stopping in front of a private entrance.

Brett eased his length from the driver's seat. He walked around the car, quietly opened the passenger door, and reached for Honey's purse. He removed her keys, striding across the yard to the side door. His assumption was correct when the third key opened the lock. He returned and lifted her into his arms. The air was cool with the dampness of a foggy night ahead.

Honey fit into his arms easily, her head resting on his shoulder during the short walk to her room. Holding her firmly to his chest, he kicked the door open with his foot before stepping inside.

Aroused by the movement of Brett's body, Honey blinked, her eyes filled with disbelief to find she was in her room. She squirmed from his grasp as he set her on her feet.

"Where's the damn light switch in this box?" he inquired, annoyed the room was too dark for him to see his way about clearly.

Honey reached toward the middle of the room, pulling the string that turned on the single uncovered overhead bulb. Embarrassed by the expression of revulsion on Brett's face as his eyes scanned her tiny room, she tilted her chin, ready for battle.

"You don't need to look like that. It's only temporary until I have time to seek something better."

"Don't spend so much time on the beach or dining out, and you'll be able to get a decent place," he growled, misunderstanding her reason for living there.

"Cheap apartments for rent are hard to find."

"Apartments! This unfit hovel is nothing but a rabbit hutch. I wouldn't keep a dog in anything this small. Where do you sleep?" he demanded, not seeing a bedroom door. "Where do you cook? Does the damn thing even have a bathroom?" he questioned, appalled she lived in such terrible surroundings.

Honey spun around, hands braced on her waist. Dressed in the elegant long dress, she looked out of place in this drab room. Her vibrant hair shone beneath the bulb, the only bright thing visible.

"Number one, I sleep on the daybed next to your long legs. Number two, I cook on a hot plate beneath the shelf next to a small portable refrigerator, and number three, of course I have a bathroom. It's behind the curtain. It contains a metal shower, which I detest, a toilet, and a small sink that doubles as dishwasher and washing machine."

She was becoming more incensed by the moment and didn't care what he thought. "I suppose with your... job...you can afford an elegant penthouse suite and a country estate?" she taunted defiantly, detesting her room intensely but too proud to admit as much to him.

A loud shrill voice grated on their nerves, interrupting Brett's response. Honey turned with resignation to see her stern landlady braced before them, hands placed belligerently on her fat lumpy hips.

"Miss Bowman! I thought I had made it clear that I would not allow you to entertain men in your apartment at night. You either abide by my rules or get out. I have a long waiting list for this lovely room and won't have my reputation ruined by your loose morals!"

Brett's temper escalated at the nerve of the old woman

to suggest Honey was in the habit of amusing men. He stared with piercing eyes at the woman, his features hardened with the force of his anger.

"I'll tell you only once to keep a civil tongue in your head when speaking to my fiancée, who will be vacating this dingy cell within days. This is also a one-family residential area and I feel inclined to report you to the proper commission in the morning."

Honey's landlady gushed apologetically. She had taken a second glance at Brett and regretted her hasty words. His expensive cut of clothes and confident threat had her worried.

"Sorry, my dear. Spend as long with your gentleman friend as you like." Her attitude became subservient, face mottled with fear that her lucrative rental would be stopped. "It will be a shame to lose a lovely young tenant like you."

Brett kicked the thin door shut with his foot behind her fast retreating figure. He turned to look at Honey.

"How dare she insult you?"

Tears spilled from Honey's eyes, her hands outstretched in dismay. "How could you tell her I'm moving?" she cried out. "I'll never find another place I can afford within commuting distance of my work." She sat on the edge of the lumpy daybed, bowed head cupped in her hands, for once uncaring of its hideous-looking faded cover.

"I thought you idled your days away at the beach."

"I do!" she sobbed, remembering the single day since she had lived in Long Beach that she strolled the sands.

"And your nights are spent in restaurants with hordes of male admirers."

"So what?"

"So when the hell do you have time to work?"

"I manage," she told him, glaring at his towering figure. He dwarfed her room, and she knew his image would be hard to blot out of her mind when he left. "Don't worry, you'll get paid," she told him, misinterpreting her query about being employed.

"Did I say I wanted your money?" he asked suavely.

"You did earlier. For rent, food, and gas, remember? Three things that sex wouldn't pay for."

"With the others, no. With you I'm not so certain." Brett's desire flared as quickly as Honey's temper. He sat beside her, gathering her quivering body close. He held her head still, taking her mouth to drown out any further impertinence.

He didn't know what to believe. Her words contradicted her appearance. She sounded like a pathological liar and looked like an angel, and was much too delectable to kiss to worry about analyzing her personality quirks.

His mouth molded tenderly to hers, warm and certain. Her lips were shaped as perfectly as her body, both waiting to be seduced.

Honey raised her slender arms to Brett's nape, like a young child seeking comfort. She arched her throat when his lips left hers to trail across her face. She was dazed, whether with fatigue or his sensual expertise she didn't know and didn't care. His mouth caressed every inch of her face, working magic wherever it lingered, matching that of his hands stroking her back.

The sweetness of his massaging fingers changed as tension left her weary body. Deep in the pit of her stomach she began to learn the power of igniting passion. She rapidly found that the feel of his mouth lingering on her throat was astonishingly perfect.

She ached with indecision, uncertain whether to pull his face upward to her lips or to guide his head lower to seek pleasure from her breasts. No man had ever touched her intimately or seen her body unclothed, yet she hungered to cradle Brett's raven-black head on her naked breasts and feel his long length stretched over hers with nothing between them but desire.

Her sensuous body moved instinctively in ways to excite him, soft fingertips unconsciously stroking his nape in featherlight circles. Aware the instant Honey's needs overcame her wish to deny him, Brett drew away and stood above her.

Honey pulled herself upright, fighting back the shame of his rejection. "How much do I owe you, Mr. Weston?"

Angered by her stubborn defiance, his words were sarcastic. "Consider your fee paid in full."

Vibrant hair framed her pale face in tumbled disarray. "I pay my debts in cash." She glared rebelliously.

"You belligerent brat, if I don't want your cash, you'd better remember it. Now get to bed, you look ready to drop on your feet. I'll get the rest of your things from my car."

Brett left the shabby room, his back stiff with annoyance. He was too damned old to put up with such nonsense, regretting the sudden rush of conscience that kept him from seducing her earlier. Her writhing body and hot little hands pulling him closer proved her willingness beyond doubt.

He returned with her plastic carrier bag and bridal bouquet to find her standing in the center of the room, her crumpled dress evidence of her response to his lovemaking.

"Get to bed and make certain you lock this door behind me. This thin door and ineffective lock will stop an intruder long enough for that old battle-ax landlady to save you. Her dragon face would scare anyone off."

Honey grabbed her purse, rooted through it for her wallet, took out some bills, and thrust them at Brett defiantly.

Grabbing her slight body, he pulled her roughly into his arms. Her determination to defy him grated on his nerves, arousing his fury. Her arms were crushed between them helplessly. He took the money from her fingers with one hand, the other molding her to the hard muscles of his lean hips and braced legs. He forced her soft female form to feel the hardening of his masculinity.

She squirmed feebly, attempting to get away from the intimate contact. His hand raised to her nape, his mouth mercilessly clamping over her parted lips. His punishing kiss continued until her head spun. She was barely aware of his free hand boldly inserted into her low neckline. His fingers stroked the rounded curves, cupping the weight in his palm until she called out, her mouth pulling away.

"No! Stop...please." Her body's response was frightening. She had no idea the tips of her breasts were so sensitive. She had felt tremors of pleasure ripple throughout her body when his thumb rubbed the soft nipples until they hardened with erotic excitement.

"You're too slight and damned passionate to succeed in defying me," he pointed out in a velvety voice. Velvet over steel and as hard to alter.

He slammed out of her room, his reminder to lock the door echoing in the silence. The sound of his car pulling from the curb in a rapid burst of speed followed immediately.

Shocked by her response and eager submission to a paid escort, Honey looked at her face in the chipped bathroom mirror. Her eyes were alight, lips full and parted, hair a gleaming tumble of waves. All because of a stranger who made his living seducing any willing woman with enough money to hire his services. She had actually offered her body to a gigolo!

Coming out of her shock, she felt the rough touch of paper against her breasts. Oh, Lord, she thought. His intent had not been an overwhelming desire to fondle her body but retaliation for her insistence on paying him with cash.

She removed the crumpled bills. Without his forceful presence to dominate her, she deliberately disobeyed his wishes, found an envelope and a small slip of paper, and sat down.

Honey enclosed an estimated accounting of Brett's fees, giving him all but five dollars of her money. She licked a postage stamp, stuck it belligerently on the upper right hand corner, addressed it to Happy Hearts Marriage Bureau, then propped the envelope on top of the small dresser.

Smugly elated, she removed her long gown, smoothed it carefully, and placed it in its plastic cover. While rigorously scrubbing her teeth, she felt the weight of Brett's ring. So what? she thought. Serve him right if I kept it! She rinsed her mouth free of its minty taste, undressed, and walked into her living area. Rooting through her dresser, she pulled out a pink baby doll nighty, pulled it over her head, and turned to make up the narrow daybed.

Fatigued by the day's events, she slipped between the

faded college dorm sheets Marcie had given her after graduation. A smile touched her mouth when she thought of her life-style. She lay between cotton sheets printed with the cartoon figures of Snoopy and Peanuts while yearning for designer sheets by Diane Von Furstenberg of slinky satin.

She tossed restlessly, her thoughts lingering on the emotional upheaval of Brett's near seduction. Abruptly remembering she had neglected to secure the door, she rose, groped for it in the dark room, turned the lock, and returned to bed.

Immediately falling into a deep sleep, Honey refused to admit she had followed Brett's last command before he stormed from her room.

Chapter Three

"Lillian!" Brett shouted unnecessarily into the intercom.

"Yes, Mr. Weston," his secretary answered promptly, at the same time placing her purse in the bottom drawer of her desk. Her eyes glanced at the large stack of mail to be opened. A typical start of another routine work week.

"Get Jordan on the phone immediately." Brett tapped his gold pen restlessly on the leather-bound blotter protecting a small portion of his desktop. His mind was in a turmoil and he was impatient to receive the answer to his suspicions.

"Your call's ready, sir," his secretary buzzed from her adjoining office. "Line one, Mr. Weston."

Brett leaned forward, pushed the button, simultaneously picking up the receiver. Questioning his personnel manager without preamble, he barked with irritation, "Jordan, what's the full name of that girl whose résumé you showed me on Friday? The one with the low G.P.A. Get me her address also."

Resentful at the delay while his manager found the file, Brett swiveled around in his chair. He stared without interest at the heavy early morning traffic crossing the distant Queen's Way Bridge.

"Her full name is Honey Eileen Bowman," the personnel manager replied within moments.

Brett's breath caught in his throat on hearing the name. He listened intently, already aware the address was one he knew well.

My God, he thought. *I actually turned that enticing, lying minx down. My adamant denial prevented her the chance to*

*earn a decent living and to afford the rent on a livable apart-
ment.*

"Jordan," he interrupted intentionally, "get her on the
phone immediately and hire her. I want her working here
tomorrow morning. Give her a month's advance starting
from the first too. Arrange the offer. Now get to it and let
me know as soon as she agrees."

"But, Brett, what happened? You told me Friday you
weren't interested. You were absolutely emphatic about
not hiring her. Adamant, in fact. I'll look like a fool calling
her back now and begging her to work for our company."

Brett answered his manager in a firm, clipped voice.
"Jordan, need I remind you that the biggest advantage of
being the boss is that I don't have to give an explanation
to anyone for a single decision I make? Now get on it!
Spend your time getting in touch with Miss Bowman instead of questioning my motives."

Hanging up the phone, Brett swiveled back and forth, a
smug smile twitching his lips at the thought of Honey's
shock when she found her gigolo of the night before was
her new boss.

The reminder of her daring to defy him throughout
their afternoon together still rankled. She actually called
him a hired seducer of women. A gigolo! Belligerent little
brat, he reflected with amusement.

His eyes lit with hidden fire remembering her soft body
moving with his, the sweet feel of her surrendering to his
caresses, the wild pounding of his own pulses when he
cupped the voluptuous fullness of her naked breast. He
had hungered all night dreaming of the sweetness of her
taut nipples in his mouth, his tongue making rapid strokes
across the tip until she begged him to take her. The
thought made him break out in a cold sweat.

Displeased with his adolescent infatuation, he walked to
the well-stocked bar concealed in the paneled wall. A
touch of a button and a section of polished mahogany slid
aside, revealing a wet bar. He took a glass down, poured a
double shot of his best bourbon, and let the entire contents slide down his throat in one swallow.

The little witch even has me drinking at eight in the morn-

ing, he thought. He hadn't been able to get her image out of his mind since he had first seen her on the screen. Meeting her in person had only added to his agony.

"I walked the floor like some obnoxious sex-starved teenager," he mumbled bitterly, brooding over his sleepless nights. "She probably slept like a baby until dawn," he groaned, his head suddenly throbbing with the beginning pain of a tension headache.

"I must be losing my mind!" He went to his chair and leaned back with eyes closed. All he could see was the oval face and uptilted chin of a young woman no more wise to the ways of the world than a mere child.

He rose, crossed to the corner table, and poured a fresh-brewed cup of coffee from the automatic percolator, drinking it black. He took the heavy pottery cup back to his desk, thinking of another idea to ease his worries about Honey's welfare. Pushing the buttons on his outside line, he sipped the hot liquid while listening to the ringing of the phone.

"Weston Towers. Bryson speaking."

"Bryson, I want you to have one of the maids clear out all the personal belongings from my suite. Box them up and lock them in my office. I rarely use it anyway. I'm going to sublet it for a couple of months to a Ms Honey Bowman."

"Sure, boss. When's she moving in?" his apartment manager asked.

"As soon as you get my things out of the way. Another thing, I don't want her to know I own the building. She's my guest and I don't want her bothered about anything. If you need me, call me at P.P.C."

"You want the maids to clean it three times a week like usual?"

"Certainly. Also see that the refrigerator's well-stocked by tomorrow at the latest."

Brett leaned back, the phone held casually to his ear. He felt better just thinking of the many ways he could bring Honey pleasure. She'd be so pleased with her change of fortune, it would probably soften her sharp tongue. Toning her fiery temper down and taming her into a sweet, agreeable, and pliant companion would make the longer drive from his estate to work worthwhile.

"Anything else, boss?"

"Yes. Make certain there are fresh flowers in the rooms to give it a semblance of a woman's touch." He paused, contemplating if he had forgotten anything to bring Honey additional enjoyment.

"Yes, sir, Mr. Weston," Bryson replied, undaunted. He was used to seeing his employer's orders were taken care of without question.

Brett swallowed the last of the coffee and leaned back with complete self-satisfaction while waiting to hear from Jordan. He was confident in his power to manipulate and manage things to his liking at all times.

For all this, he thought smiling, *she'll be begging me to share her bed within the week.*

Awakened by a pounding on her door, Honey murmured sleepily, brushing the auburn strands of hair from her eyes as she stood up. Slipping an old red flannel robe over her skimpy nightie, she opened the door, peeking warily around the side to see who it was.

"Oh, hello, Mrs. Dodson. I'm afraid I was still asleep. Is anything the matter?" she asked with alarm, remembering Brett's brazen announcement that she would be moving soon.

"Heavens, no, Miss Bowman," her landlady cooed. "You're wanted on the phone, dearie. No need to dress. I'll make us a cup of coffee and we can have a nice chat. I've been meaning to ask you in since you've been living here," she lied. Anything to keep the girl's fiancé from reporting her.

Her hypocrisy caused Honey's mind to reel. The old witch had never invited her in even to collect the weekly rent.

She rushed after her retreating figure, floppy slippers hastily pulled on to keep her feet clean across the dirty yard.

Hovering in the background in order to hear each word, Mrs. Dodson busied herself at the sink as Honey lifted the receiver.

"Miss Bowman speaking," Honey answered, her voice husky with sleep.

"This is Claude Jordan from P.P.C. I have excellent news for you. My employer has had a change of heart and insisted I contact you immediately before you were offered employment elsewhere. Will you be able to start work with our company tomorrow morning at eight o'clock?"

Stunned by his words and the prospect of working for the highest-rated pension planning company in the western United States, Honey nevertheless hesitated before agreeing.

"I don't know, Mr. Jordan. I'm still not employed as an actuary, but frankly I don't like the indecisiveness of your employer."

Honey's ego had been hurt by the man's rejection and she had never feared letting anyone know what she thought. She considered it only fair that the head of P.P.C. find out from the start that she was no coying female.

"I can't understand how he could be so adamant about *not* hiring me last Friday. My qualifications haven't changed in the interim."

Honey was puzzled. He sounded like a crotchety old man with an unstable personality. Surely he couldn't be approaching senility?

"It seems odd," she continued, her narrowed brows furrowed in contemplation. "Strange, really, that he should ask you to wake me early Monday, then expect me to start work the following day." She could hear Mr. Jordan's shocked murmur at her hesitation.

"Miss Bowman, I assure you it's unwise to question his motives." Claude laughed inwardly at her youthful daring despite her desperation to find work, telling her sincerely, "The experience gained from our staff would be valuable even if you decide later that P.P.C. doesn't fulfill your expectations."

It was hard to keep from chuckling out loud at her

miffed attitude and strong pride. Their files were filled with applications of qualified people seeking employment.

Honey sighed. Mr. Jordan was correct. It was the first good job offer she had received and she'd better accept it before he changed his mind again.

"All right, Mr. Jordan," she replied in a lilting voice. "If you're short of help, I'll be happy to start tomorrow."

Aware of her short temper, Honey decided it best if she added a condition to her agreement. "I'd prefer not to meet my employer until I've proven to him and myself that I can handle the position."

"My dear, Miss Bowman, the owner rarely leaves his office to greet his employees. He's much too involved in public relations work to be on a first-name basis with three hundred and fifty people. You'll be a statistical trainee working on the fourth floor, and I personally guarantee you won't be bumping into your boss at the water fountain."

Claude pictured their ten floors of offices, number of staff, and the heavy case load their company handled. Miss Bowman couldn't get an appointment with Brett if she tried, he thought wryly. He couldn't remember if he had ever seen his employer taking time to scrutinize any of his employees on the lower floors.

"Where do I report in the morning?" she asked, elation filling her at the realization she had actually been hired.

"Come to the personnel office so my secretary or I can explain the numerous company benefits you'll receive. We have a lucrative profit sharing plan, hospitalization, dental care, normal vacation and holiday time off, and, of course, an excellent retirement plan."

Dazed by her change of luck, Honey said good-bye, hung up the phone, and turned to her landlady. "That was certainly good news. I've been offered a great new job."

Honey turned down the offer of sharing coffee with her landlady, hurried back to her room, and gave a shout of joy. Her mood was jubilant as she took a box of dry cereal from the meagerly stocked apple crate that served as her cupboard. She removed a quart of milk from the tiny refrigerator, frowning when she felt the barely cooled sides of the carton. It was on the blink again. "I haven't had an ice cold drink since I've lived here," she grumbled out loud.

Crunching on the chewy granola, Honey thought of all the things she would do that day in preparation for her change of occupation. First she had to get the battery in her car charged, see that her clothes were clean and mended, then resign from her job at the diner. She knew she would be rushed trying to finish by the time she had to work that night.

Finished with breakfast, she washed the cereal bowl and spoon in the small chipped bathroom sink, quickly dried them, and set them on the unfinished shelf below the hot-plate.

She folded her sheets and single blanket, placing them neatly beneath the daybed before showering in the detestable metal box with its depressing stiff gray and black striped plastic curtain.

Honey stepped quickly from the hard, erratic spray of tepid water, drying her glistening body on a thin towel provided by her landlady. She caught her reflection in the mirror, a sudden flush of color tinging her creamy toned skin. She placed a hand against her cheek, shuddering at the sudden memory of Brett's passionate lovemaking. Most shocking was her own uninhibited response. It had never happened with any other man and she wasn't certain if she was emotionally ready to delve into the reasons for her unaccustomed receptivity.

She reached for her carefully hoarded bottle of scent, looked at the scant amount left, and decided to save it for work. It would be at least a month before she received her first paycheck. Her budget would be stretched to the breaking point by then and perfume was definitely still a luxury item.

Just wait. When I'm in the chips I'll absolutely wallow in Chanel No. 5, she reflected joyously.

With the envelope containing Brett's payment in her purse, Honey gathered it up, noticing the ring. It shimmered with fire, the perfect stones vivid against her smooth hand. It fit perfectly and she luxuriated in the feel of the heavy gold setting.

"Might as well enjoy my engagement while it lasts." She chuckled out loud, making a sudden decision. "I'll wear it until the demanding Mr. Weston comes after me in hot pursuit!" She giggled mischievously, hoping he had spent the night without sleep for fear she would skip town.

Honey walked to a nearby shopping center, found a pay phone, and made arrangements with a local garage to charge her car's dead battery. Her steps were light returning to her dingy room to prepare her limited wardrobe for the change in employment.

Apprehensive at the long delay, Brett waited for Jordan's call. He refused to look through the mail Lillian had handed him until he found out about Honey. Tired of drinking coffee, he paced restlessly. The sharp buzzing had barely stopped when his hand pushed the intercom button.

"Yes!" he answered impatiently.

"Mr. Jordan on line three, sir."

Brett picked up the phone without hesitation, sat behind the massive desk, and relaxed, the perfect image of a prosperous business executive.

Dressed in a well-cut gray suit, the pristine white of his shirt beneath his dark tie with its small pattern showed vividly against his tanned throat. The sheen of his elegant black shoes matched the mirror brightness of his desk. Feeling capable of vanquishing any challenge, he answered without greeting.

"Did she agree?"

Amazed by his employer's about-face, Claude assured him Honey would report to work the following morning. He had never known Brett to reverse a single decision during their years together, nor had he ever sounded disconcerted, especially over a junior trainee for the company.

"I must tell you, Brett, she didn't jump at the chance to work for you."

"She didn't?" Brett responded with astonishment, remembering her living conditions and small amount of cash in her billfold.

"Your surprising offer gave her the impression you are indecisive and unstable." Claude could hear what sounded like a stifled laugh before he continued. "She insists on not meeting you until she is established in her position."

"She did what?" Brett burst forth, repeating Claude's words verbatim. Unable to contain his humor any longer, he burst out laughing.

Brett pictured her flashing eyes and uptilted chin when she complained about him to his personnel manager. She had the independence and stubbornness of a mule combined with the daring verbosity of a virago three times her age. He was also aware it was the first time in his life any woman had defied him, and the excitement of their altercations had driven thoughts of any female but her from his mind.

Laughter was still audible in his voice when he told his personnel manager, "Fine job, Claude. Take the rest of the afternoon off and charge your lunch to me."

"Drinks too?"

"Of course. Oh, and another thing, don't mention my name in the future if you can avoid it."

Brett gave no explanation for his secrecy, narrowed eyes glittering with amusement at Honey's unpredictable behavior.

"She may worry a man to death, but she sure as hell will never bore him into an early grave," he reasoned with indulgence, wondering if he'd still be able to control her when she reached his age.

Honey parked parallel to the curb in front of Happy Hearts Marriage Bureau, checking the time before getting out of her car. She had decided at the last moment to deliver Brett's payment in person. Clutching the envelope to her breast, she walked briskly into the front office.

Smiling at the pleasant face of the receptionist, she asked politely, "May I see the owner, please? It's rather important and I don't have much time."

"Of course, my dear. I don't think she's busy at the

moment." She stood, a thin angular woman whose soft blue eyes sparkled with friendliness, lighting her plain face with warmth and character.

Honey glanced with interest at the pictures, waiting impatiently until Doris returned. She motioned for Honey to enter the room she had just exited. "Aunt Gladys will be glad to see you now."

Honey walked into the cluttered room, smiling at the old woman seated stiffly before her. "Hello again. I'm Honey Bowman, Miss...?"

"Call me Aunt Gladys, love, everyone does," Brett's aunt urged kindly. "I'm surprised to see you today, though I do admit to a touch of curiosity about the wedding Sunday. Also, I must apologize for Doris or I not getting your name Friday."

"I presumed you'd be wondering what happened. I don't think I was ever so shocked in my life as when the man you sent arrived during the wedding reception."

Aunt Gladys was shrewd, instantly having an indication what might have occurred. She wisely held her tongue, letting Honey clarify the circumstances without interruption.

Honey's chin tilted proudly, her storm-cloud eyes shimmering with consternation. "He refused to let me pay him! In fact, Brett...er, Mr. Weston, wouldn't even tell me how much I owed for his services."

She handed the sealed envelope to the picturesque old lady seated in her red velvet chair. Instead of taking it from her, Honey felt the fingers of her left hand clasped in a lavender-scented palm. The grip was firm despite Aunt Glady's age.

"Where did you get this?"

"What?" Honey asked in surprise, unaware of the reason for the reedy-voiced inquiry.

"This lovely ring, my dear. It looks quite unique. A very special ring, I would imagine."

She was stunned by the sight of Brett's mother's engagement ring circling the slender finger of the young girl before her. Her mind whirled with inquisitiveness.

Handed down from father to son, the ring had been in

the Weston family for generations. It had never at anytime been worn by someone other than the intended bride
or wife of the elder son.

"It is lovely, isn't it, Aunt Gladys? I've never seen a
more exquisite ring in my life." She lowered her hand,
looking at the old woman with sudden dejection. "Unfortunately, it's not mine to keep. It was supplied by the
escort you sent me as a temporary, make-believe engagement ring. No doubt he rented it from a pawn shop. You
can tell him he can arrange to pick it up from me when
he's between jobs, since I prefer to return it personally."

"Was he what you hoped for?" Aunt Gladys questioned curiously, hardly able to contain the happiness she
felt as each mystery was explained.

"Oh, Aunt Gladys, he was...perfect," Honey whispered in a throaty murmur. Her cheeks were tinged with
pink at the memory of their passionate embraces and her
shockingly ardent response.

"Actually, he's the type of man most single women
dream of, don't you think? In looks anyway," she added
with a grimace.

"It puzzles me, though, why a man of his obvious
qualities is content with such a demeaning job."

Honey expected Aunt Gladys to be insulted and apologized, not wanting to hurt the old woman's feelings.
"Isn't it unusual to keep a man of his looks and intelligence?" Reminded of Brett's domineering ways, she
blurted out intentionally, "Of course, he is also conceited,
arrogant, and demanding when his plans are thwarted. Besides that, he had the nerve to call me—the one who hired
him—a bungling, indecisive, lying, defying, belligerent
witch!"

Honey sat on the edge of the Victorian couch, leaning
forward with hands raised in emphasis. She looked across
the cluttered desk, unaware she was being scrutinized with
admiration by the keen eyes of Brett's aunt.

She lowered her lashes, admitting honestly, "I'm afraid
that despite my desperation we didn't get on all that well.
He knew I was going to report his excessive forcefulness.
He said I was defiant and argumentative and even had the

nerve to mention that his other er ... women were more amiable. I think that irritated me the most.''

''It appears I'm going to have to talk with him today,'' Aunt Gladys reassured Honey, her blue eyes dancing with mirth. This was going to be the most exciting match she had arranged in her life. ''I hope you didn't let his words offend you, love.''

''Of course not! I think my calling him a gigolo several times evened the score.'' Honey giggled, remembering Brett's furious face.

Unable to resist the chance to find out more about her escort, Honey blurted out inquisitively, ''Does the man have many dates? I mean is he often busy escorting women at night?''

Laughing at Honey's assumption that her nephew was for hire, Aunt Gladys decided to talk with Brett before explaining their relationship to her. ''My dear, that young scoundrel is seldom home. As near as I can tell he spends nearly every evening escorting some woman around town.''

Dismayed by the candid reply, Honey looked up. ''Isn't he getting tired of all that playing around? Surely he must want to lead a more normal life sometime.'' She held her breath, waiting for the answer with deep concern.

''That's what I've been advising him to do for years now. I've also warned him that one day he'll get caught like all the other determined bachelors before him, most of whom end up devoted husbands and very happily married men.''

''Most women wouldn't want his type, Aunt Gladys. You should know better than I that women like gentle men. Life with Mr. Weston would be like living with a time bomb.''

''Even they can be defused, love.'' She wished she could have witnessed their meeting. She had never seen her nephew when he wasn't composed. Could the young woman before her have actually caused Brett to lose control of his cool mind?

''Have you known him long?'' Honey asked softly, unaware her feeling for Brett was bared to his great aunt.

Long accustomed to sensing genuine love, often before the parties involved were aware of it, Aunt Gladys leaned back with a satisfied smile.

"I've known Brett since he was a young man," she answered truthfully, watching Honey's changing expressions.

"Has he always been interested in escorting a variety of women?"

"Always!"

"You mean he's reached his age without ever being involved?"

"My dear Miss Bowman, that independent young man has been involved since grammar school. If you mean has he ever been in love, the answer is probably no. His affections are passed around like an endless supply of candy."

"Well, it's about time he realizes that a surfeit of sweets will eventually cure anyone of the habit of overindulgence!" Honey stormed back. The more she heard about Brett the more she realized how fortunate it was she hadn't fallen for his striking looks. Her first impression had been correct. He was simply an overaged gigolo for hire by the hour. Honey was thinking how glad she was to be on a tight budget or she just might be tempted to hire him again. Not because she liked him, but she did enjoy their arguments. Another kiss or two wouldn't be hard to take either!

Honey remembered her job suddenly and rose. "I'm supposed to be at work in ten minutes." She pointed to the envelope, reminding Aunt Gladys unnecessarily to give it to Brett. "I made up a statement of what I thought his time was worth. Would you believe my mother's friend Wendell and Brett knew each other and Brett didn't like the man any better than I did?"

Honey's eyes darkened with remembered pride in Brett's forceful arrogance. "As a pretend fiancé Mr. Weston was perfect. You should have seen him, Aunt Gladys."

"I wish I had, my dear. How very much I wish I had." She bid Honey good-bye, her hand reaching for the phone to dial her nephew's office before she heard the front door close.

Walking into the rear service entrance of the seafood diner, Honey heaved a sigh of relief. Her day's preparations were completed and her long hours waiting tables would soon be over.

The afternoon had been spent carefully going through her clothes to make certain every item was spotlessly clean and mended. Her meager wardrobe made it hard to match a variety of clothes suitable for her first week's work in a prestigious office. Her mind reeled with the thought of a paycheck large enough to cover a clothes-shopping spree and a larger apartment too. Two things she would insist on were a bathtub, and a refrigerator that worked in its own separate kitchen.

As Honey pinned her hair on her nape she heard her name called.

"Honey, I'm so glad you're here!" A day shift waitress ran up to her, speaking rapidly. "Mary Jane cut her hand. She won't be able to work for at least two weeks, maybe even three. She wants you to cover for her and work seven days a week until she's better."

"Oh, no, Beth! I'm going to turn in my notice tonight. I start work in the morning downtown. You know I only agreed to part-time work in the first place. The boss conned me into five nights a week and now Mary Jane wants me to work every single day. I can't possibly do it."

Honey's soft heart was touched by the dismay on Beth's face. She took her hand, asking compassionately what the matter was.

"I met this marvelous guy, Honey. He's stationed at Terminal Island Naval Station and has weekends free the rest of the month. If you can't help, I'll have to work Saturday and Sunday."

Tears filled Beth's eyes. "I know he'll find another girl. He's so handsome that no girl can resist him when he wears his Navy uniform. You remember him, don't you?" Her plaintive voice and flushed cheeks, speaking of her boyfriend, were more than Honey could bear.

She pictured the pink-faced homely young man with the gawky, youthful shape of a growing boy. His thick hair was unruly and a bright orangy red. Surely, Honey thought, Beth would never have to worry about some other girl stealing him from her.

Honey smiled, Beth's despair changing the moment she recognized the pity in her lovely eyes. "I'll talk to the boss. If he'll let me start work at six o'clock, I'll help out for three weeks. But absolutely not one day longer. What hours will I have to work on the weekends?"

Beth's blue eyes shone with relief. Honey was so kind. "You take over my hours. It's easy, really. I don't start until eleven and get off at seven thirty. You'll have Saturday and Sunday morning to sleep in and two early nights a week to relax."

"But, Beth!" Honey cried in exasperation. "I have to be at my new job by eight in the morning. I don't get off until five, have to be at the diner by six, and work until two in the morning. I'll be lucky to get four hours sleep a night." Honey shook her head, wondering if there would ever be a letup to her complicated working arrangements.

"I'll be a trainee too and need to be alert. . . ." Her voice trailed off as Beth walked away to phone her boyfriend and tell him the news.

Honey shrugged her shoulders, a habit that was beginning to irritate her with its necessity. Something was always cropping up unexpectedly. She walked to the back of the kitchen, boldly approaching her gruff boss, who was supervising preparations for the evening meal.

He watched his kitchen help closely. They nervously mixed grated cabbage in a huge stainless steel bowl. The endless supply of coleslaw that was served took his attention until he glanced sideways, forgetting everything else to admire Honey's striking beauty. He realized his fortune in hiring her. Her shapely figure, vibrant hair, and pleasant attitude were a definite asset.

"You wanta see me about something, Honey?" he asked, turning his attention back to the young man stirring the salad. "Add more vinegar to the dressing! My customers like it tart," he barked loudly.

"I have another job, Mr. Demario. I'm turning in my notice." With one waitress disabled, she knew he would be unhappy. "I've agreed to take Beth's place on weekends and Mary Jane's place on weekdays, if you'll let me come in at six o'clock. For three weeks only, though.''

"Damn it, girl. You're my most popular waitress. Most of the men who keep coming back here five nights a week don't even like fish. They come to see your legs! I could maybe consider raising your salary a little and let you keep all your tips.''

He looked at Honey hopefully, knowing by her determined face the answer was no. The fact he paid the lowest possible wages, and had a reputation of being miserly didn't enter his mind as a reason for his constant turnover of help.

"Okay, girl, get to work.'' He turned back to see the young man pouring vinegar carelessly from the large commercial bottle directly into the mixing bowl. His hands sliced the air in anger. "My God, don't they teach you to measure anything in trade school?'' His furious tirade continued as he yelled, "I said I wanted the coleslaw tart, but I don't want it to pucker my customers' mouths.''

Amused by her employer's frantic hand waving and bellowing voice, Honey knew he would be involved in one argument after another with his staff during the night. He continuously made a nervous wreck of his kitchen help and caused his waitresses to avoid him at all costs.

Honey tumbled into bed at two thirty after a busy night. She hadn't managed to take a break or find a spare moment to fix a sandwich for dinner. She slept instantly. She was too weary to be nervous about starting a new position.

Deep in sleep she dreamed, imagining Brett being her real fiancé and their love mutually shared. A tranquil love, with him as soft voiced and gentle as her father. A totally erroneous impression of his volatile personality.

Chapter Four

The shrill ring of Honey's alarm clock brought her awake with a start. With an unladylike grumble she rose, reached to the top of her dresser, and shut it off, appreciative of the silence. Another item she intended to purchase was a radio with a slumber alarm. Music would be less startling to hear first thing each morning.

She stretched her arms high overhead, leaned over to touch her toes twice, then slumped back down on the bed with a moan of disgust. Resting her forehead in her palms, she felt exactly the same as she had pulling an all-nighter cramming for a college final. She had expected life to be easier after receiving her college degree. Now she was committed to working two full-time jobs for three miserable weeks.

A grim smile touched her mouth when she stood up for the second time, walked into the closet-size bathroom, pulled her nightie off, plopped a plastic shower cap over her hair, and shoved the curtain aside. Instantly awake when the ice cold water hit her heated flesh, she began to shiver. She grabbed the wash cloth, lathered her body with fragrant soap, twirled quickly to rinse, and turned off the spray.

"Anyone who says they enjoy ice cold showers in the morning is a worse liar than I am," she complained out loud. She thought with longing of soaking in a deep bathtub filled with perfumed suds. Hot water to bathe in and ice cold water to drink were the two things she craved the most since moving into her small room.

Dressing neatly in a soft gray skirt with a burgundy print

blouse, she would be ready as soon as she fastened the narrow black belt and slipped into her black pumps. She picked up her inexpensive plastic purse, pausing long enough to add a sparing spray of perfume before walking to her car.

When she walked into Mr. Jordan's office, she heaved a sigh of relief that her car had started and she wasn't late her first day at work.

He noticed Honey's circled eyes, assuming she was nervous. "You look tired, Miss Bowman. I hope you didn't lose sleep worrying about your new job."

Smiling brightly, Honey nodded. She wasn't about to explain she was still a waitress. She forced herself to concentrate for the next hour, reading and signing the numerous forms placed before her.

Awed by the amount of her monthly salary, she looked up. "Is this correct?" She pointed to the paper before her. "I'm afraid I neglected to ask what I'd earn, but I certainly didn't expect it to be this amount at first." Her mind flitted about, thinking she would be able to afford a new apartment, start paying off her college loans, and send her old car to a garage for much-needed repair.

"Certainly you realized working for a company of this importance, you'd be paid equal to your education. Your potential worth to us will be returned when your training is complete. At that time you'll receive your first raise."

Honey was elated to learn employees were encouraged to take advanced college courses plus the series of actuarial exams that the company subsidized.

"Your employer is considered to be very generous by his employees and extremely extravagant by his competitors. That's also why we rarely have a vacancy unless there's sudden illness on the staff, which caused your being hired."

Honey rapidly signed her name on the last form before looking up with a dimpled smile. "I guess his generosity helps balance out his unusual behavior about hiring me. The poor man probably has more money than tact. I won't complain." She chuckled. "I'm receiving twice the amount I thought I would to start."

"That reminds me, Miss Bowman. I have a month's advance on your salary to give you." He searched through the papers on his desk for the check. "This will enable you to meet any unexpected expenses that weren't anticipated when you moved here and is our way of thanking you for agreeing to start immediately."

Honey's chin raised automatically, her crisp statement stunning the man across from her. "Since that is not a normal company policy, I refuse to take it." She shook her head no. "Tell my employer for me, please, that I don't want charity... only the chance to prove that I'm capable of doing what I was hired for."

A dimple appeared beside her mouth, her eyes shimmering with humor when she started to speak. "Didn't the man realize I could have cashed his check and never returned?"

Claude laughed with her. "I doubt very much if that ever crossed his mind... nor would it yours."

"Not today anyway." She laughed. "The end of the month might be a different story."

He placed the papers in a neat pile on his desk, asked her to follow him, and took her to the fourth floor to introduce her to the statistical supervisor. He explained as Honey listened attentively that the first two months would be spent working with defined contributions, complimenting her on her extensive mathematical training.

His voice was filled with enthusiasm telling her about P.P.C. "Our president and founder of the company has a fellowship in the Society of Actuaries and is a genius in this business. He spends most of his time doing public relations work now, but there isn't a facet of pension planning he doesn't know."

Honey's eyes scanned the vast brightly lit room with admiration for its well-designed interior. Expensive carpeting muffled the sounds of their steps as they crossed the broad entrance. The many offices were partitioned on three sides with walnut paneling to a height of six feet. The front was made of glass from desktop upward, giving the illusion of privacy without the claustrophobic feeling a totally enclosed room would have.

Rock music resounded from speakers concealed in the eight-foot ceiling, attesting to the youthful staff. Honey smiled, taking the outstretched hand offered palm down in greeting. Receiving a brief squeeze, she lowered her arm, scanning the woman before her as meticulously as she was being looked at in return.

In her early thirties, her pretty face was framed by a shining crown of short-cropped hair stylishly turned under. Warm brown eyes were as welcoming as her wide smile. The woman was elegantly clad, and Honey was envious of the fashionable two-piece pantsuit with its vest-style top over a gorgeous ivory silk blouse.

Honey returned her smile, knowing at a glance that she was going to get along well with her immediate supervisor. When they were better acquainted she vowed to find out where she purchased her clothes.

"Welcome, Miss Bowman. I'm your boss, but don't let my title worry you, as I'm actually here to train you. My name's Corrine Anderson, but everyone calls me Corkie."

"I'm Honey." She laughed when Corkie's eyebrow raised at her name. "In name only, as I have a reputation for having an impertinent tongue," she said, thinking of Brett's constant irritation over her outspoken comments. "Also I have a pretty short temper."

"We'll get along fine, then. I wouldn't know how to take anyone if they were as sweet as your name implies. We have a pretty lively group working here." Corkie looked at the personnel manager, her eyes twinkling with humor. "Claude will confirm that. He avoids this floor whenever possible. None of us knows whether it's the music or the average age."

Mr. Jordan flushed, good-naturedly refusing to comment. It was true, he agreed. He heard enough brain numbing music at home. How anyone could work with the noise level that high he'd never understand. He excused himself, anxious to return to the peaceful silence of his private office. At least when he was young music had a melody.

Claude was also anxious to phone Brett and chide him

about his lack of success with his newest employee. His employer would be shocked to hear Miss Bowman had refused to take his advance in salary. He hoped to be around if she ever met Brett. His position wouldn't bother her in the least if he was any judge of character.

The excitement of a new job with a prestigious company, along with the friendliness of an endless group of people anxious to meet her, made the morning hours seem to fly by. During her lunch hour, spent in the employees' cafeteria, Honey was surrounded by a string of intelligent, aggressively attentive young men, each anxious to get their bid in first for her favors. They weren't the least concerned she was needed for her education and mathematical expertise. To them, she was like a bonus and simply a lovely source of distraction.

Honey laughed, shrugging aside the numerous invitations for private late night tutoring, thanked each one, then held up her hand. Quick to spot Brett's ring, she let them assume she was unavailable.

Their youthful appearance was spoiled by the image of Brett. His forceful personality and sophistication made them seem gauche and immature.

Memories of Brett's demeaning occupation as a professional escort available for hire by anyone with the money furrowed Honey's smooth forehead briefly. A sudden inspiration brought the dimples flashing next to her soft mouth. She decided to hire him for another night out when she received her first paycheck. It seemed worth the expense to brag about her new job. He would be furious to know about her having a legitimate—that would be the word she'd use—occupation. She'd imply that he was a middleaged rentable Romeo! That was perfect. She'd have to write it down so she wouldn't forget it.

Despite her intentions to belittle him, Honey's heart beat faster picturing Brett as it had each time she remembered their tumultuous day. She knew his lovemaking had thrilled her beyond all expectations of what a satisfying male–female relationship could be. It disturbed her to acknowledge that he was the man of her dreams. With two horrifying exceptions: his volatile behavior—no gentleman like her father—and his occupation! A profession so objectional, she knew she'd never condone it or be able to put it out of her mind.

Waving goodbye to her new friends as they went to their cars at the end of a hectic, confusing day, Honey raced across the street. She slid beneath the steering wheel, praying her car would start easily. She sighed with relief hearing the unreliable motor sputter to a start, rest, then hold steadily. She checked the time, pressed the gas peddle to the floor, and held her breath. She arrived with bare minutes to spare, thankful she hadn't encountered a traffic policeman.

Changing into her skimpy uniform in the small restroom, Honey started work immediately. Waves of tiredness rushed over her as the customers thinned out and the clock neared two. Too tired to change, she gathered her skirt and blouse together and walked wearily to the back of the restaurant to her car.

She drove home slowly down the near vacant street, then parked along the darkened curb, her thoughts only on the length of time it would take her to get to bed. She pushed open the door to her room, crying out with fright when she noticed the stormy features of Brett Weston standing in the middle, hands resting on his hips.

"What are you doing here?" she berated him, her body shaking with alarm. "You darn near scared me to death! You, you... you... gigolo!"

Brett looked insolently over her revealing waitress uniform, his narrowed piercing eyes partially hidden by straight thick lashes. Her wavy hair tumbled about her shoulders, causing his breath to catch. Its glorious color gleamed in the overhead light. Her face had haunted him since their last meeting. He ached, longing impatiently for the taste of her lips and the texture of her soft curves.

Dismayed by the dark circles under her eyes, he let his glance slide over her full breasts, lingering as they rose and fell rapidly beneath the clinging black body shirt. The short plaid skirt emphasized her tiny waist and the curves above and below. Seeing her legs for the first time, he felt a quiver in the pit of his stomach at their long shapely length clad in black net hose. They were as beautiful as he had imagined.

Standing motionless, her palms flat against the closed door, Honey watched with alarm as Brett moved toward her. She stood silent, glaring at him, her eyes wide and sparkling furiously.

When his hand rose to pull her to his body, Honey cried out with shock. His long length crushed her back against the door and the rapid beating of her heart was caused by desire rippling across her nerves at the pressure of his taut form.

Fright changed to hunger. She longed for his touch, his seductive lovemaking, and his hot, sweet possession of her mouth one more time.

Brett lowered his head, paused briefly, and held her darkened, startled glance with his compelling green eyes.

Oh, God, she thought with yearning. *I love him! And I didn't even realize it until I saw him again. How could it happen so fast?*

She inhaled the smell of his sandalwood aftershave, her senses awakening to respond. The heat of his body touching hers gave her new vitality, the impetus to respond fervently. She hadn't known she was capable of missing the very essence of his soul.

"You dared to call me a gigolo again!" His mouth descended, searing her lips with a kiss so hungry and seeking, she cried out in alarm. Not heeding her plea, he cupped her face, his mouth relentlessly probing hers apart, insistent on total submission to his will.

Honey's arms rose, reaching forward to clasp his neck convulsively, pulling her body tightly against his potent physique. She returned his experienced passion with total commitment of her compassionate heart.

Tearing his mouth from her clinging lips, Brett clamped her to him, his hands running over her waist, the swell of her hip, and intimately to her lower back. He pressed her forward, wanting her to feel the touch of his aroused body, forcing her to remain in contact while he questioned her in a voice harsh with desire and shaking with wrath.

"Where have you been? I've been here since ten

o'clock. Four and a half hours cooped up in this cell-like dump waiting for you to get home. When you do drag in you arrive wearing some scanty outfit like a common hooker. I realize this is a busy seaport area, but I didn't expect you to go streetwalking at night, trying to take on the entire Navy!''

Unprepared for Honey's violent reaction to his condemnation, Brett was clinging to her hips when he felt the sharp slap of her palm against his cheek.

Twisting furiously, tears spurted to her eyes. Incensed by such gross misjudgment, she cried out, "Why, you ... you insufferable beast! I've been working. Not the streets, as you accused, but a legitimate job. Something you wouldn't understand!''

Releasing his punishing hold at the shock of her resounding slap, he stood in shock. First at her irate censure, then at her helpless look when she lowered her head.

The sight of her pitiful face covered with tears while she wept heartbrokenly was more than he could bear. He drew her to him tenderly, tucking her face against the soft cashmere of his sweater, his hands cradling her within their hold.

"Hold me, Brett," she pleaded, her slender body shaking uncontrollably. "Please don't yell at me with any more insults. I ... I can't stand your verbal abuse tonight. I'm so tired.''

Brett lowered his chin, inhaling the sweet perfume of her clean hair. He rubbed her spine, his hands circling softly around and around to ease the tightness of her straining back.

"Tell me, Honey. Explain what's happening. I had no idea where you were. I even feared you were injured or worse.''

He could feel her legs trembling in contact with his thighs. Scooping her into his arms, he stepped back to the daybed. He sat down, cradling her, his hands continuing their soothing stroking motions. As she relaxed they slid from her back to her hip, then lower over her thighs. His breath caught at the first touch of their flesh.

Honey raised her face from his shoulder. She looked at

him, her tear-drenched eyes mirroring her hurt in their charcoal-gray depths.

"I was so proud, until you accused me of...of..." She sobbed passionately, refusing to voice his deriding abuse. "I started working today at a wonderful new job. Something I've trained four years at a really tough college for."

She clung to his shoulders, her face burrowed into his neck, deep sobs racking her body. "I wanted to share my happiness with you, not get scared half to death and ridiculed."

Raining kisses on the side of her face, Brett comforted her before gently easing her away. He held her slender shoulders in a gentle grip.

"You couldn't have worn this outfit to your new job, I presume, so explain to me why you arrived home so late dressed like this?" he asked softly.

Honey cast her eyes downward, their heavy lashes spiked with tears shadowing her smooth cheeks. Talking slowly, she told him, her voice throaty and unconsciously sensual. "I wear these at the diner where I work at night."

"What are you talking about now? Isn't one job enough?" he exclaimed in disbelief. "You really shouldn't be let loose in the city alone." He shook his head. Would there be no end to the shocking tales she blurted out every other time she spoke?

"Why do you need to work two jobs? The rent on this unfit hovel or payments on the wreck of a car I saw parked here Sunday night couldn't be that expensive!" Brett demanded an explanation, angered again by her independence and refusal of his financial advance from his personnel manager. He was still rankled about that.

"I promised to fill in for one of the girls who was injured. It's only for a couple more days," she told him, knowing he would cause trouble if he thought she was committed for three weeks.

"My new boss is so unpredictable, he insisted I start work immediately. I already had a temporary job and had to give that boss notice." She glanced at his face, deciding from his fierce frown to placate him without telling a direct lie. "It's only for a...little while."

A tiny moan of delight escaped her throat as his hands roamed freely over her back and hip, his touch bringing rapture where it lingered.

Brett let his hand slide along her thigh, spreading his fingers over her net hose, able to see a tantalizing glimpse of creamy skin. Inhaling quickly, he felt the familiar ache in his loins at the feel of her exciting young body in contact with his.

"If it's only for two days, that will be all right. Not one day longer, though."

"Why did you come here tonight?" she asked him, trying hard to remain coherent while his hands stroked her sensitive leg.

"I wanted to take you to see an apartment I heard of. I'll pick you up after work tomorrow and drive you to it."

Honey shook her head no, her glance searching his, uncowed by his deep frown. "I don't want you to pick me up. I'll go with you Saturday, early in the morning." She didn't want him to know where the diner was for fear he would find out she had promised to work for three weeks instead of two nights.

"I refuse to wait until this weekend," Brett told her emphatically. "I insist you see it tomorrow after work."

Groaning with the pain of controlling his emotions, he watched her face. His hand continued its exploration of her leg, slowly stroking up and down the length. He stopped to fondle the sensitive area behind her knee, happy at the sudden dilation of her eyes. He had never made love to a more responsive woman. She visibly reacted with pleasure, allowing him access to her warmth, yet he could tell she was virtuous. With her passionate temperament if she had been sexually experienced, they would have made love the first night. She wouldn't have denied him and he couldn't have resisted her.

"Why the hell do you have on these horrible net stockings? I want to place my hands on your skin without any barrier."

Honey stretched her leg, moving it to avoid his touch. She leaned forward, hiding her head on his shoulder. She knew her cheeks were colored with embarrassment.

"Don't. Please, Brett, stop," she requested abruptly, needing to stop his intimate fondling. She reached for his hand, holding it still, feeling the heat burning into her thigh while she tried desperately, yet unsuccessfully, to control her need.

Brett easily shrugged away from her fingers. He reached into his pants pocket, then raised his fingers to her clinging blouse. His hands touched the soft, satin-smooth skin of her full breasts, inserting some money into her low-cut bra between the deep cleavage.

He felt the rapid beat of her heart as it matched his. His hand remained on the smooth flesh, staring without remorse into her wary eyes. He leaned forward, placed a hard brief kiss on her parted lips, and told her grimly, "This is another reason I'm here."

He had forgotten about his aunt's phone call. The old woman had actually gloated with delight over Honey's visit. She had had the nerve to chuckle at his discomfort while repeating each derogatory comment verbatim. His only living relative had sided with Honey, warning him it was time he had a setdown from his surfeit of clinging, adoring women.

"How dare you leave me a handful of your grubby little bills, with a statement marked paid in full in bold capital letters!"

"You deserved it!" she retorted sharply, head thrown back to glare at his handsome face before insolently throwing the money on the floor.

"Seventeen dollars? How generous of you. Fifteen dollars for *my* services. That really hit me. Eight full hours I put up with you. That isn't even equal to minimum wage. Less than two lousy dollars an hour! I couldn't believe it." Not finished, he railed on. "Then you add another two dollars to it for driving you home...in a one hundred thousand dollar car, yet. A bus would have cost you more!"

"That's all I could afford, and if you're insulted, that's your fault!"

Brett's nostrils flared as he retorted arrogantly, "My dear naive little minx, I feel I'm worth at least two or three *hundred* dollars per date. That's what my expenses usually average on a single night out on the town with a sophisticated—not a youth—companion."

Honey pulled back, squirming uncomfortably on his lap, his tantalizing fingers still cupping her breast possessively. She clasped his hand, thwarted in her attempt to remove it.

"I don't have that kind of money! I'll give you some more—not two hundred dollars by any means—when I get my first check." Pride filled her voice, the mischief in her eyes a deliberate taunt. "I'm earning far more than I expected. My boss may be extremely eccentric but he's also generous."

"Stop!" Brett interrupted grimly. "I don't want to hear any more about the man. Now listen and listen good! I told you before you don't owe me a single dime for my escort services."

"But—but—"

"I'll warn you one time only. If I hear another thing about payment, I'll lay you beneath me on this lumpy piece of granite you call a bed and make love to you until your extremely eccentric boss comes looking to see why you didn't come to work!"

Coerced into silence by the force of his declaration, Honey stared, her hand slipping from his to touch his shoulder.

Pleased with her silence, Brett tenderly stroked her breast. He could feel it straining against his palm, swelling with response. He rubbed his thumb gently across the nipple, watching awed as the enticing point hardened in instant response. His breath caught, hearing her low murmurs of excitement. His dream of the night before would soon be true. He knew within seconds his mouth would be worshiping where his hands touched.

Honey quivered, clasping Brett's nape. She threaded her fingers lovingly through his ebony hair, moving them over his well-shaped head. She made no protest when he unbuttoned her blouse and pulled the lacy cups of her décolleté bra below her breasts.

Aching with desire, Brett's head descended toward her

bemused face, forcing himself to wait before touching her nakedness. He touched her mouth, felt her lips cling during the gentle first contact. He knew the moment he kissed her deeply he would have to fight to keep from taking her innocence. Her lips were moist, her breath as fresh as a newly opened flower, and as her mouth parted it was an invitation impossible to resist.

Honey squirmed, her hands clasping his head to pull it closer, not satisfied with his tender lovemaking. She wanted him to kiss her mouth with the hunger she felt churning in her lower abdomen. He was driving her wild, his lips teasing with kisses trailing over her face. He pressed her eyelids closed, kissed her sensitive earlobes and the dimple in her cheek.

"Kiss me, Brett!" she cried. "I want you so." Unaware of the consequences of her request, she sought satisfaction from the man holding her.

Brett let his eyes rove over the flushed beauty of her face. Passion flowed between them like a magnetic force. She had asked him to love her and God knew he was ready.

His mouth took hers, deeply hungering for further contact. She felt his tongue extend inward, probing gently. He moved it slowly until he felt her tentative touch. She became bolder, excited by the havoc his stimulating kiss was raising to her senses. She inhaled, drawing his tongue deeper, instinctively sucking it.

Unaware of Brett's instant reaction to her sensual mouth, she was pulled on top of his broad chest as he lay back on her daybed, his head on the pillowed arm. He slid her body across his abdomen, until she was over his face. Losing contact with her mouth, he buried his lips between the heavenly softness of her breasts projected above. His eyes darkened, smoldering with the need to feast on the satiny fullness with his mouth as well as his glance.

"Such gorgeous breasts," he whispered in husky reverence.

With the weight of her slenderness balanced across his hips and lower chest, his hands were free. He placed them aside her breasts, cupping them with great tenderness. She lowered her back letting him enjoy the sweetness as wave after wave of physical desire burned through her limbs, torturing her with its consuming power.

Brett's mouth was warm and moist as it surrounded the peak, eagerly worshiping the hardened tip until Honey cried out with the ecstasy of it. He then moved restlessly to the other breast, his tongue rapidly caressing the erect nipple. He took the point into his mouth, sucking so gently, her body shook. She could feel the pleasure of it in her abdomen.

Whimpering at the exquisite torture, she squirmed to draw away, yet wanting nothing more than to stay within the magic of his arms until he declared a love equal to hers. She felt the exciting hardness of his body beneath her hips. He wanted her as badly as she wanted him. Moving over him, she reveled in his great body shuddering when she extended her limbs sensuously between his long outstretched legs.

He pressed her breasts together, squeezing gently with long fingers that stroked the burgeoning flesh in massaging motions while his tongue stroked first one nipple then the other. He tasted and touched, ending with a lingering caress that drew the entire bud into his opened mouth.

"Stop, Brett," Honey cried out desperately. "I...I can't..."

With startling quickness he removed his hands, placed them on her shoulders, and eased her off his body. He reached over, kissing her lips gently. He was filled with remorse for his unrestrained actions. He watched as she rose, turned her back, and buttoned her blouse. He could see her shoulders tremble, aware he was solely responsible for the uninhibited lovemaking.

Brett looked at his watch with disbelief. "It's four o'clock! I presume you have to be at work early?" He stood, took her shoulders in his arms, and turned her around, drawing her into his arms to comfort her after his assault on her awakening emotions.

"I can hardly tear myself away and don't think I would have to by the response you just showed me."

Honey pulled herself from his arms, lying firmly. She

was still trembling with the desire to beseech him to stay with her, but she would make certain he didn't know it.

"Of course I wouldn't let you spend the night with me! I happen to believe any woman who allows a man those privileges before he commits himself to her is a fool!"

Honey's small chin raised. She hoped he couldn't see its faint trembling as she tried to stop the rapid beating of her heart. It took a lifetime of pride in her own moral belief to deny his remark. She admitted inwardly that if he asked again, she'd relent.

Brett smiled, aware of the indecision crossing her expressive face. "Little liar. I could make you mine any time I like and I guarantee you'd never raise a finger to protest or make one verbal rejection."

Incensed by his arrogance, Honey frowned, admitting the undoubted truth of his words.

"Don't you know there isn't a woman in the world who can't be had by the right man, at the right time, in the right place!"

"I don't believe that at all!" she stormed back, admitting that she was on the way to becoming the world's greatest liar.

Brett laughed, his eyes filled with tenderness. He drew her forward and caressed the top of her forehead with his lips, letting her face rest on his chest. "Good night. I'll pick you up tomorrow."

"But . . . but" Honey started to interrupt, her voice muffled by the movement of his upper torso shifting beneath her mouth when she glanced upward.

Brett eased her a short distance away, his compelling glance pinning hers with obvious intent to end any protest.

"Tomorrow you see the apartment and that's final! It will only take a few minutes to look it over. Thursday night you can move in, since that will be the last night you will ever work two jobs."

Honey's eyes lowered, afraid Brett could read the thoughts racing through her mind. She was too tired to confess about agreeing to fill in for Beth. His ardent lovemaking such a short time earlier had raised havoc with her thought processes. She felt incoherent, much too weary to drive the surging satisfaction of his touch from her mind.

Her breasts still tingled from the pleasure of his uninhibited lips covering each inch over and over. His seeking mouth, the warmth of his moist tongue stroking her nipples, had ignited her passions with a fire slow to subside.

Releasing her shoulders, he walked to the door. A swift backward glance caught her standing motionless in the middle of the small room. Her obvious fatigue tore at his heart. He ached to share all his worldly possessions with her, yet she obstinately resisted each attempt to help her. He was thankful she would be vacating her dreary dump of a room without further protest. At least they had settled that argument.

"One final reminder, Honey. Not only lock this door at night but for God's sake lock it in the daytime too. I just walked right in!"

Brett closed the door behind him, leaving as abruptly as he arrived. A grim smile tugged his lips, satisfied by the sound of Honey's lock turning.

Too exhausted to make up the daybed, she slipped out of her uniform and wispy underwear, wrapped an old flannel robe around her nakedness, and sank onto the hard cushions. She was asleep in seconds.

Barely two hours passed when the alarm trilled. Honey rose, groped awkwardly to shut it off, and curled back on the daybed for another half hour's much-needed sleep. With a low moan she forced her eyes open, rubbing them like a small child in a vain attempt to fully waken. She eyed the advancing hands on her clock balefully, forced herself to stand up, and walked into the bathroom. Temporarily revived by a cold shower, she dressed carefully before driving to P.P.C. for her second day's work.

Already familiar with the fourth floor, Honey entered the broad foyer with confidence. She looked impeccably groomed and vibrantly alert, belying her lack of sleep. A light coating of makeup covered the dark circles beneath her eyes.

A brash young man named Enrico sauntered over with

an extra cup of coffee to hand her. His expressive eyes were filled with admiration as they lingered on the tiny waist and full curves of her rounded breasts.

"You look like a breath of spring. Fragrant and sweet as honey, Honey," he quipped, narrow shoulders thrown back to appear taller.

She accepted the coffee with a smile, greeted her co-workers, and made a hurried exit to the privacy of her assigned office. Her face was flushed at the loud wolf whistle that followed her progress. It would take getting used to. Even in college she hadn't received such obvious appreciation. Working and studying were foremost then. Loving Brett had heightened the awareness of her own femininity, it seemed.

Seated behind the large desk, she leaned down to place her purse out of sight. When she straightened, she was startled to see her office filled with the same men who had greeted her on arrival.

Verbal in their praise, each outrageous compliment was topped by the other. Their ridiculous bantering continued despite her reminder that she had work to do even if they didn't.

Running them off with a few well-chosen words, Corkie laughed as she greeted Honey. "I'll have no problem keeping track of your whereabouts on this floor. Just follow the parade of overly amorous, highly paid brainpower."

"Good morning, Corkie," Honey greeted her superior, pleased the men had scattered quickly at their immediate supervisor's outcry.

"Good Lord, but I'm glad my boyfriend doesn't work here. I'd hate to find him joining the crowd worshiping at your doorstep too."

"There were only three," Honey assured her, amused by the droll tone of Corkie's words. "It's only because I'm new here. In a week they won't even bother to say hello when I come to work."

Corkie threaded slender fingers through her hair in an unconscious habit, gold bracelets jangling from her wrist in various lengths. "Not so and you know it. Their minds may be in the clouds with the rest of the earth's geniuses, but believe me below the belt they're like any other insatiable male on the make. Thank heavens I'm thirty-five and beyond the terrible twenties. They seem so darn young sometimes."

"I agree," Honey said, thinking of Brett's mature features and sophistication. She held up her finger, too bemused by the beauty of gleaming jewels to guard her tongue. "Their comments don't bother me. I'm already very much in love." She placed her hand on the desktop, lashes lowered while she tried to think of a way to retract her statement.

"I noticed your ring yesterday and knew you were committed." Corkie held up her left hand, free of any jewelery, showing it to Honey. "If some man gave me a rock the size of the one on your finger, believe me, I'd be in love too."

Corkie hitched her hip on the corner of Honey's desk, her eyes filled with admiration. "He must be quite some guy. What's his name and what's he do?"

A tinge of pink colored Honey's cheeks over the embarrassment of Brett's occupation. She shrugged her shoulders noncommittally, her eyes meeting Corkie's squarely.

"Right now, let's just say I've decided to keep his identity incognito."

Surprised, Corkie agreed good-naturedly to contain her curiosity. She spent the balance of the morning helping clear up areas of confusion in Honey's mind over some of the technicalities in learning the mentally exacting work of an actuarial assistant.

Corkie was never still, her mind sharp and alert. She didn't rush Honey, though it was apparent she was impatient to return to her own desk. She straightened a cluster of gold necklaces, returning to prop her hip on the edge of Honey's desk.

"What do you know about defined contribution plans?"

Honey smiled, explaining word for word from her college notes.

"Defined contribution is a pension plan that provides for an individual account for each participant and for benefits based solely on the amount contributed to the participant's income, expenses, gains and losses, and any forfeitures of accounts of other participants that may be allocated to such participant's account.''

"Enough!" Corkie laughed, her brown eyes alight with humor. "I've heard all I can stand. Now get to work on this case and see what you can do on your own." She lay a stack of papers before Honey, returning to her office and the completion of her own case load.

Honey's weary mind reeled with the need for accuracy. She worked steadily throughout the day, aware a nap during her lunch hour would have benefitted her more than her bowl of soup and the constant conversation. She hadn't even seen the movies that her co-workers critiqued so vehemently.

At five o'clock Honey said a hurried good-bye and rushed from P.P.C. to the diner with barely time to change into her uniform. Traffic had been exceedingly heavy and she was forced to grit her teeth, stuck behind a huge bus. She didn't know which was worse, inhaling the acrid exhaust fumes or having to stop at every corner while passengers loaded or stepped off.

Stepping from the employees' bathroom, she was stopped by two older waitresses returning from days off. They had heard about Honey's ring and demanded to know each intimate detail.

She refused to answer. Going to her station, a forced smile raised her lips, highlighting the dimple in her cheek as she took the first order. Mentally marking off the days until she could relax in the luxury of only one job, she automatically took orders, filled water glasses and coffee cups, and served endless plates of fish and chips for the rest of the evening.

Feeling raw from the jealous taunts behind her back, she sped home, completely forgetting Brett would be there until she saw the sleek black Ferrari parked in front of her landlady's house. The last thing she wanted to do was look at an apartment.

Honey's door was pulled open so abruptly, she sat and stared upward without saying a word. The faint light of the moon outlined Brett, standing impatiently beside her old car. She made no protest when he helped her out.

"Thank heavens you only have one more night to work at the diner, Honey. You'll be dead on your feet if you keep this up."

He hugged her to him, his hands running up and down her back with the soothing motions she had come to cherish. She felt a brief kiss across her brow before being placed in the passenger seat of his car. He bent down, kissed her lips despite the discomfort of her being so low, raised his great height, and walked to the driver's side. She raised her fingertips to her mouth, his touch as always lingering seductively long after he drew away.

Turning on the inside light, he glanced at her dress. "You look beautiful, darling. As fresh as a bouquet of dewy flowers. Are you cold without a jacket?"

She shook her head. With him so close, enclosed in the intimacy of a sports car, she knew she would never feel the cold. His warmth reached out, enfolding her as surely as if she were wearing a sweater.

Reaching for the ignition to start the motor, Brett was stopped by Honey's hesitant voice. She could feel him stiffen, knowing he recognized the refusal she was about to blurt out.

"I can't go! I don't want to look at an apartment tonight. When I get my first check, I'll rent my own place." She refused to meet his steely glance; instead she stared at her hands clasped tightly across her lap.

"I...I have no intention of being a kept woman." She ignored his censuring gasp to continue with added emphasis. "I could never be your mistress...especially knowing another woman's money would be paying for my upkeep. I couldn't bear it when you went out at night," she blurted out jealously, her stormy eyes lifting to meet his, daring him to explain.

"My God!" Brett roared in disbelief. He leaned his head against the side of the door, looking at her for a long moment. His eyes darkened, appearing merciless as they held her glance. Laughing hoarsely, his husky voice filled the interior of the car.

"You really take the cake. Did I ask you to be my mistress? Did I even ask to keep you, for that matter? Did I ever ask you to wait around for me while I wined, dined, and bedded—that's what you really meant to ask, wasn't it?—another woman, no matter who paid for the evening?"

Honey faced forward, looking at the reflection of the black night on the windshield. She stuttered, distressed by his vehement outburst.

"No—no, but isn't that what you had in mind? The women at the diner accused me of . . . suspected I was . . ." Her voice faltered. She turned to face him, feeling she owed him an apology.

"I'm sorry, Brett. For what I said and for keeping your ring. It keeps the men from bothering me at work. I had intended returning it in a week or two. I feel so embarrassed, knowing you don't want me—"

"Not want you! I've thought of little else since I first saw you. That does not mean I'm setting you up in an apartment to be my mistress. I've wanted you from our first meeting, sweetheart. As a carefree bachelor I hate to admit I feel as if I could happily spend the rest of my life within your arms. To explore every inch of your body until I learn what pleases you most would be the ultimate bliss."

Honey's stomach muscles clenched listening to Brett's harshly outspoken desire for her. "It seems I spoke impulsively," she added contritely.

"Something that's a bad habit of yours and that you appear to do with almost every comment," Brett teased. "Now relax while I drive you to the apartment. I want to get you back to your room as soon as possible so you'll have at least one or two hours sleep tonight."

"Whose apartment is it? Why are you taking me there anyway?"

Brett slid from the curb with sudden acceleration, maneuvering through the streets smoothly. His eyes never left the highway during the lengthy explanation.

"When I told your landlady you would vacate that hole soon, I meant it. My affluent friend, the owner of this

Ferrari, won't need his place for a couple of months. He'll appreciate you staying there and protecting it for him. If any burglars are casing it, they'll see it's occupied and stay away."

Brett thought of the lies necessary to coerce Honey into accepting his help. His apartments had the most expensive, efficient electronic security system available, plus twenty-four hour patrol by hired security guards. During his ownership not a single tenant had been burglarized. If she ever found out she was being manipulated, she would be livid, he reflected, easing to a stop as the light changed to red.

"How much will it cost? I don't get paid for at least two weeks."

"It won't cost you a penny! He owns the apartment. You'll actually save him money by staying there; he won't have to hire extra security," he lied again, determined to move her from her repugnant room if he had to carry her bodily from the place.

Silently thinking over his words, Honey watched Brett ease the Ferrari into the private locked basement garage of Weston Towers. A nine-story luxury apartment building setting on valuable coastal frontage property, it overlooked the beautiful white sands of Long Beach.

"Weston Towers! But that's your name. You aren't related to the owner, are you?" She giggled mischievously, her interested gaze taking in everything as Brett slid to a stop in his numbered parking space.

"Yes, my dear, I'm related to Weston and to J. Paul Getty and the Rockefellers, also," he retorted dryly, escorting her to the exit. "Possibly even J. P. Morgan and Vanderbilt too!"

Taking a small private elevator to the ninth floor, Brett took Honey's arm, guiding her along the wide carpeted hallway to huge double doors crossing the end of his luxurious apartment building. He opened the door with his key, watching her face as she stood in the entrance.

Stunned by the sight of his broad living room furnished with long couches and massive deep-cushioned armchairs, she turned to Brett.

"But how could any man leave this? It's like a dream come true. In fact, Mr. Weston, it's perfect."

Brett watched indulgently, her expressive eyes filled with rising excitement as she contemplated the room.

"Even the bookshelves are filled. I could read for years!" she exclaimed, running forward, her slender fingers trailing over their sleek covers while trying to read some of the titles.

She twirled around, wide eyes scanning the well-stocked wet bar, elaborate stereo system, large screen television, and extensive video recording equipment.

"Good Lord, the man must be loaded," she blurted out in awe. Despite the room's basic masculine appearance, the pale gray carpeting, burgundy color scheme, and stark white walls looked marvelous. Deep wine had always been her favorite color even with auburn hair.

She walked back to Brett, still standing in the doorway, slipped her arm through his, and smiled. "Thank you for bringing me here. I've never stayed in anything like this in my life." She lay her head on his arm, noticing for the first time two vases filled with fresh flowers. "How lovely." She pulled away, inhaling the heady fragrance of velvety roses.

Brett walked forward, took her hand, and led her on a brief tour of the large kitchen, furnished with the most modern appliances available, past the full-size dining room with its sleek polished table and chairs, through the four king-size bedrooms, each with an adjoining bathroom. He paused, a smile tugging his lips while Honey lingered, eyes filled with longing at the deep bathtubs. He knew the apartment was way too big for one man, but small rooms had always made him feel claustrophobic. Besides, he used it often to entertain and house clients, its size perfect for both.

Honey's head was spinning with enthusiasm when they entered the living room. "Oh, Brett, it's gorgeous and close enough to work that I could walk."

Her eyes shimmered, a soft dreamy gray, matching the throaty murmur of her voice. "I'll give your friend five hundred dollars a month while I stay here. I'm earning a

fantastic salary now, and that should cover half his rent."
Chin tilted upward, she asked, "Doesn't a place like this
rent for about a thousand dollars a month?"

Brett thought of the four thousand dollars minimum he
could get for a top floor full-service luxury apartment in
his exclusive building. He'd been asked to sublet it for
that amount many times. Honey hadn't even seen the two
broad balconies overlooking the harbor, one with a clear
view to Catalina Island.

"You don't need to know what the rent is," he returned
harshly, thinking she had much to learn about the cost of
renting beachfront property. "You'll pay nothing. Let's
go. You look dead on your feet."

With his hand cupping her waist, Brett eased Honey
from the apartment, their feet silent on the carpeted hallway as he guided her to the elevator.

"You can move in after work tomorrow night. I'm leaving town later this morning for a business flight back East.
I'll call you at work."

Silence filled the paneled elevator smoothly traveling to
the basement garage. Honey was filled with regret after
leaving the vast rooms. The service porch alone was over
twice as big as her room and definitely more cheery.
Seated in the Ferrari, she lay her head against the seat,
bemused by the continuing changes in her luck since
meeting Brett.

"You don't even know where I work," she suddenly
remembered, her thoughts going back to his last comment.

"Give me the name of the company," Brett asked
dryly, pent-up over the constant deception.

"I'll give you the number of the phone on my desk
only. If you call the company's number, they might switch
you to my boss, who is undoubtedly a very cranky person," she said. "I have to lay low until I learn my job."

She turned to Brett, admiring his strong profile while he
waited for the traffic light to turn green. "The man didn't
want to hire me in the first place. If he finds out I'm getting personal calls my first week on the job, he'll probably
fire me without batting one of his old blue eyes."

Brett's hand clenched, shifting gears to accelerate rapidly, unbelieving of Honey's erroneous impression of his character.

"What makes you think your boss has blue eyes?" He flashed her an angry look, his strong voice sharp.

Undaunted, Honey shot back, "Well, it stands to reason. A balding head with thin fringe of gray hair, pale watery blue eyes, florid face, big paunch, and loud bellowing voice. Sexually frustrated too."

"What?" He gave a muffled growl.

"That's why he takes out all the disappointments and failures caused by his bad relationship with women on his newest employee," she continued, refusing to repeat about his sexual frustrations.

"I can't believe this," Brett moaned beneath his breath while Honey continued unabashed.

"Also why he overpays his help. It's his way of making up for his personal insecurities. I studied psychology. It taught me to size up people from their actions only."

Shaking his head in disbelief, Brett pulled to a stop in front of Honey's room. He stormed around the car, taking her rapidly to her door. He pushed it open easily, dismayed that she had forgotten to lock it that morning. *My God,* he thought, *she's driving me insane,* vowing to check for gray hairs when he got home. Surely they must be showing already.

"Where do you work?" he demanded aggressively, watching as she set her purse on the dresser top. "Maybe I know your employer. I occasionally travel in the upper circles." His personal feelings rankled by her attitude, he teased her deliberately. "That is, when my...clients... are well heeled!"

"You wouldn't know him, Brett. I figure he's an introvert too. The kind of man with a computer for a brain. One with no social graces or the poise to mingle with the opposite sex. I'm certain he wouldn't attend parties. His P.R. success would be gained in smoke-filled bars."

Brett gasped, checking his rage and the desire to explain just who her employer was. Gritting his teeth, he remained silent, furious at the thought she assumed he had no social dignity or the composure to associate with her sex. Irritating, lovable little mixed up minx!

Honey kicked off her shoes, curling up on the end of the daybed. She looked at Brett's towering figure, curious about his sudden tension. His temper was getting as short as hers.

"I work at P.P.C. They're an actuarial service. Pension planners. Very technical work. You wouldn't understand and I don't feel up to explaining it to you tonight." She looked at her clock, grimacing. "This *morning*, that is. You'd better go home, Brett." She stood up, tiny without her three-inch heels. A frown crossed her face momentarily. She looked at him, meeting his eyes boldly. "I've been thinking and I'm undecided about the apartment. If I do decide to help your friend, I insist on paying my way. I have an excellent job now, which you seem to keep forgetting."

Brett pulled her into his arms, raising her on tiptoes to quelch her constant spew of words. He kissed her furiously, his mouth hungry for hers. He probed relentlessly until she parted her lips, returning his anger with passion. Holding her face next to his heaving chest, he rested his chin on her thick silky hair.

"Me forget about your job! Believe me, that's the last thing I could ever do. You've thrown it up to me every chance you've had since you got the damn thing."

"At least it's legitimate!" she stormed back, uncowed by his outrage.

"If you think a hundred or so pounds of shapely female not even out of her twenties will shame me into changing my occupation, forget it. If there is anything I won't do, it's change my way of making a living," he warned.

She pulled back, opening her mouth to reply.

"Shut up and kiss me, damn it! I have a plane to catch later today and a flight back scheduled to arrive Saturday at eleven. By then, you'll be moved in to his apartment and that's final!"

Bending Honey's slender body backward, Brett raised her chin, crushing her soft mouth with a kiss. Moving his mouth from her clinging lips, he kissed her forehead, trailed his lips over her face to her ear. Inhaling the fragrance of her hair and skin, he took the lobe of her ear into his mouth, teasing it with his sharp breath.

"Quit defying me, you adolescent witch. You seem to delight in trying to drive me out of my mind. Will you ever obey me in a calm, quiet manner?"

His breath fanned her ear with its warmth, arousing her despite his barely controlled violence. She delighted in his anger, her hands raising to pull his head closer, her mouth raining kisses on his taut throat. She could feel him swallow, her caresses continuing undaunted by his temper. It crossed her mind that a gentle man would never satisfy her. She needed someone as volatile as she was. Someone just like Brett.

"Quit that!" Brett stormed, pulling from the deliberate excitement of her mouth. His desire to chastise her changed, his body hardening in mounting excitement. Yet he disentangled her clinging arms and turned to leave.

"Here's the key to your new apartment. Use it!" He placed it on the small dresser, slamming out of her room with the order to be there Saturday at eleven thirty or else.

The squeal of his wide tires rapidly pulling from the curb was an unnecessary reminder that her independence had ired him again. He would be even more furious when on Saturday he'd find her still working two jobs.

Chapter Five

Honey sat at her desk, arched brows furrowed in contemplation. Biting the side of her pencil, she tried for the fifth time to balance a column of figures she had been working on since morning. Embarrassed by her first quick estimate, she was recalculating the cost. The $32,000 error was an insult to her college degree.

After reworking the numbers, she lowered the mistake by eighteen thousand dollars, which infuriated her further. Scolding herself, she grumbled beneath her breath.

"A math major and I make foolish errors that drastic. I do the darn theory right but somehow the columns don't balance."

She scowled, starting the tedious process over. Her mind reeled with facts and figures as the strain of two jobs and lack of sleep took their toll.

Trying unsuccessfully to blank the disturbing sound of rock music resounding throughout the fourth floor from her mind, she shrugged in resignation. She hoped to improve her concentration by checking her computation out loud when she was further disturbed by the ringing of her phone.

"Miss Bowman speaking," she answered quietly, fearing it would be Mr. Jordan calling her to his office on orders from her employer. A direct command from the top floor to fire her for her incompetence.

"Hi, Honey. Have you missed me?" Brett asked with the confidence of a man experienced in sensing a woman's interest.

Honey's face flushed with happiness, forgetting everything but her pleasure at hearing from Brett. She forced herself to speak calmly, her reply a brash lie.

"Actually, no."

"What did you say?" he demanded, his tone teasing before laughing out loud.

"I said I didn't miss you," she returned sassily, her ready humor spoiling all attempt to sound stern. Her palm covered the mouthpiece in a vain endeavor to prevent him from hearing her chuckle.

"That's better. If you giggle after a remark like that, I know you're lying to me again."

"Actually, I'm pleased it's you, Brett. I was afraid to answer the phone for fear it was my boss."

"Why?"

"You won't understand any of this, but I'm having a little difficulty learning cost calculations and just made a thirty-two thousand-dollar error."

"You did what?" Brett's voice thundered into her ear.

"Made an error and felt so guilty, I thought the big man upstairs was calling to fire me."

"My God, he should before you bankrupt him."

"That would take some doing. I hear the Panther is disgustingly rich."

"Who?"

"The Panther," Honey chortled, each word adding to Brett's chagrin. "That's what everyone on my floor calls him. He's the Panther and his tenth-floor office is his lair. Kind of clever, huh?"

"No!"

"You sound grouchy today," Honey reprimanded him, undaunted by his clipped response. "Apparently you've never worked for anyone like him before. All the girls say he's a handsome brute. As sleek as a jungle cat with the same animal magnetism but even more difficult to capture."

"I can't believe it," Brett murmured beneath his breath, dreading what he would hear next.

"The guys say he's a womanizer—"

"An impotent womanizer?" Brett snorted, interrupting

Honey's outburst to remind her how wrong her assumption of her employer's character had been.

"Apparently not, since they all envy his sexual prowess. Dan and Enrico said he just lunges on his prey and women fall like ninepins."

"Dan and Enrico who?" Brett demanded, deciding to have a talk with two of his employees when he returned from New York.

"You wouldn't know them." Honey refused to give him their last names. A mischievous giggle preceded her next recitation.

"He shows a definite partiality to big-chested dyed blondes too. The guys really laughed when I mentioned his women probably had a waist size equal to their intelligence quotient."

"Don't say any more or you'll really be in trouble," Brett stormed. He could picture her flashing eyes and the dimple beside her lush mouth. Worst of all, he could picture his own staff fawning over her. Panther, be damned! When he returned, they would darned well hear his roar!

"Your employer sounds awful." His voice was filled with pique.

"Oh, no, that's the part that surprised me the most." Honey dismissed Brett's idea. "Everyone thinks he's the greatest. Generous, a genius with figures...no pun intended..." She laughed devilishly. "He's aloof but aware of everything that happens in his territory."

"Apparently not aware of your financial error!" Brett couldn't resist the temptation to chide her.

"I hope not," Honey whispered, suddenly serious. "I really goofed in my judgment of his image. He doesn't sound at all like I had him pictured." She wondered how she could have been so mistaken.

"Lucky for him," he retorted drolly. "I'm surprised you haven't asked for a complete description!"

"I don't have to ask. The guys drop by my office all during the day and each one volunteers a few more company secrets."

"My God, you're a menace!" Brett could see his fortunes collapse.

"No, just a good listener," Honey retorted flippantly.

It was time to change the subject. If he heard any more inside secrets about his own company, he'd have to reorganize it from the first floor up.

"I don't want to hear another word about your boss, your job, or his obnoxious staff." His voice lowered to a husky, seductive caress. "I've missed you. I'm calling to remind you that I'll be with you the length of time it takes to drive from L.A.X. to Long Beach after my flight lands. How do you like the apartment?"

"Well, er. . ." Honey hesitated, evading a direct lie.

"You've moved in, haven't you, Honey?"

"No. Sorry, Brett, but I changed my mind. I decided to wait until I find a place on my own. That way the situation won't be misconstrued by anyone."

Furious at Honey's continued refusal to accept his help, Brett roared over the phone. "You obstinate little devil, you sure *are* moving, and it will be tomorrow morning around eleven thirty. I don't care what anybody thinks, nor should you. Another thing, Miss Bowman, I guarantee you right now that as soon as I get you alone in your new apartment, you'll definitely wish you hadn't disobeyed me—"

"Why, Mr. Weston?" she interrupted, her voice dripping with sweetness.

"Because I'm damn well going to kiss you senseless. You've annoyed me to where I can't think of anything but your firm little chin tilted defiantly upward. I can't see anything but your soft mouth telling me no at every offer of assistance. To top it all, you're always bragging about having a legitimate job. . .meaning I don't! Furthermore—"

Laughing at Brett's lengthy tirade, Honey clicked the phone off with her finger. She deliberately left the receiver off the hook so he couldn't call her back.

Stimulated by her telephone confrontation with Brett, her mind was alert and she balanced the columns on the next try. For the first time she fully understood her part in figuring an employee's retirement benefits due to the mathematically projected deductions of their pension planning company.

Her ash-gray eyes glimmered with mirth. Annoying Brett was becoming her favorite pastime. She grinned as Corkie entered, an expensive leather shoulder bag slung casually over one narrow shoulder.

"Time to go home, Honey. How are you doing? Are things finally beginning to fall into place for you?"

"Good heavens, is it time to quit?" Honey glanced at her watch and put the files in a desk drawer and stood up. She grabbed her purse, painfully aware of the inferior quality compared with her supervisor's.

"Everything's much better this afternoon, Corkie. At least my bungling has lowered to an acceptable level," Honey expounded. "It's obvious I should have decided to be an actuary before the last semester of college."

They walked to the elevator together. Taking it to the main floor, their hurried strides took them through the lobby dividing spacious rooms leased by a savings and loan company on one side and a nationally known bank on the other.

Honey wished Corkie a pleasant weekend, waved goodbye and rushed to her car, trusting she would arrive at the diner in time to start her night shift. Friday nights were always so busy, she dreaded them.

Hours later she drove home, thinking how pleasurable it would be to sleep in, using the extra time to make up her daybed. She was thankful it was a weekend and she wouldn't have to work at P.P.C. for two days or go to the diner until eleven o'clock. Tugging the comical sheet over her shoulders, she squirmed into the most comfortable position, reflecting on her conversation with Brett. Her last thoughts were filled with a mixture of eagerness and apprehension over their next encounter.

The tiny hands on Honey's clock reached six thirty when she began to toss restlessly. Furious at herself for unnecessarily waking early on Saturday morning, she rolled over onto her stomach. Deliberately pulling the sheet over her face, she was determined to lay in bed until ten o'clock even if she couldn't sleep.

Brett's image entered her mind while it was still hazy. Amused by her ability to arouse his ire, she began to look forward to his punishment. His kisses always thrilled her no matter how fierce.

Despite a hurried shower, she took her time dressing, brushed her tumbled hair into flowing waves, then applied makeup. Deftly buttoning her long-sleeved white silk blouse, she straightened the square-cut hem over the elastic waistband of cool denim slacks in her favorite wine color. Both were a birthday present from Marcie and excellent quality.

Honey decided to budget her anticipated income. Taking a stack of business-size envelopes from a top drawer, she laid them on the daybed. Dumping the contents of her purse on the dresser, she found a pen, grabbed a hardback book to write on, and sat down.

Feeling smug at the thought of her excellent wages, she marked each envelope, neatly printing in large letters an estimate of her expenses. Rent, auto repair and gas, college loan, food, clothes, and with a touch of whimsy, Chanel No. 5 perfume and gold chains. She underlined the last two in bold strokes, feeling she was the only woman in the world who wanted and didn't have either. Last was an envelope with Brett's name, the seventeen dollars returned, plus minimum balance due.

She propped them boldly on her dresser, returned the scattered items to her purse, and left for work, making certain to lock the door behind her. Refusing to leave Brett a note, she knowingly chose to further aggravate him by not disclosing what diner she worked at. That would anger him as much as hanging up the phone while he was talking.

Smoky eyes dancing, the dimple in her cheek was as visible as her soft red mouth turned upward with a mischievous smile. She lazily settled behind the steering wheel. A brief glance at her wristwatch brought forth a disgusted moan. She had dawdled over her budget too long and didn't have a minute to spare.

She turned the ignition with her key, groaning at the familiar tick followed by a lifeless-sounding whirr repeated sluggishly until there was no sound at all.

"Darn! My battery would decide to give out today of all days," she grumbled to her car, furious it would let her down again. There was nothing to do but rush to the bus stop two blocks away.

Arriving at the diner forty-five minutes late, she undressed, pulled on her uniform, and hurried to serve the weekend tourist trade.

As her day shift neared an end a large family in the middle of the room took her attention. She pleasantly waited as they argued back and forth about what each was going to order. She felt a tinge of sympathy for the mother. Five sons under ten would be hard on any woman.

Honey kept her face averted from the outside booths. She could feel the intense gaze of four young men trying to attract her attention. They had been persistent with their unwanted admiration for the last hour. They deliberately tarried, refusing to vacate their booth. Each had motioned for Honey repeatedly in order to stare more closely at her figure or to make suggestive remarks.

Ignoring her cold eyes and sharp warning of a powerful, extremely jealous fiancé, they continued to gaze insolently as she walked back and forth to the other tables. She was becoming increasingly uncomfortable. Their loud voices carried across the room with comments about her shapely legs and curvaceous figure. Honey was openly annoyed and near the point of asking her boss to intervene when she returned from the kitchen, arms loaded with a large tray of fish and chips.

Honey hesitated briefly, scanning the room to make sure that her other customers were well cared for. Her face paled, breath catching in her throat as she spotted Brett. He sat in the far corner, his broad shoulders held stiffly against the back of a large booth.

Ignoring his violent expression, she forced a smile on her face, placed the plates expertly before each member of the family, and returned to the kitchen. She picked up a bottle of ketchup, requested by the young boys to pour in a thick, smothering red mass over their French fried potatoes, and returned. After setting the bottle, an extra basket of bread and butter, and a pitcher of ice water on the table, she walked over to pick up a menu.

Held like a shield in front of her breasts, Honey approached Brett. Slender chin tilted independently, smoky eyes shining with humor, she walked forward with unconscious grace.

Raucous comments from the four men sitting near Brett did not go unnoticed, evident by the raging fury in his narrowed eyes and tightly clenched knuckles resting on the tabletop. Honey stopped in front of his table, one hand outstretched.

"Your menu, sir. Our specialty is deep fried fish and chips." Her voice was filled with playfulness, the enticing dimple appearing as a deep mark in one smooth cheek.

Brett's brilliant green eyes met hers, one hand knocking the menu to the other side of the table. He studied the delightful curves of her enticing figure as boldly as the four strange men, his glance lingering on the rapid rise and fall of her voluptuous breasts. Returning his gaze to the alluring impertinence on her face, he spoke. His voice was low, each word enunciated crisp and clear for her ears alone.

"I do not want a menu, nor do I care what the specialty is in this ptomaine parlor!"

Pulled unexpectedly into the booth against his hard body, Honey returned his glare. His taut thigh touched the curve of her exposed leg, causing a tremor of excitement to course through her body.

"You're hurting my hand, Brett," she whispered, her widened eyes pleading for him to release his harsh grip. "How did you find out where I work anyway?"

She tried to pull free of his clasp, looking quickly around to see if anyone had noticed her sitting next to a customer. With the exception of the four bothersome men staring at her with astonishment, her other customers were busy stuffing their mouths full of fried fish.

Brett ignored her question, hissing, "You said you were only going to work two more nights. You seem to think I don't have your mathematical background—which you delight in throwing up to me—but at least give me credit for being smart enough to figure out that two more days working at this diner would have ended Thursday.''

"So?" she stormed back, several strands of auburn hair falling free of her chignon.

"This is Saturday! The day I told you I would meet you at eleven thirty. The day you should have been moved into your new apartment. You'd better be prepared to give me a good explanation when we're alone!"

Honey squirmed to get away from his side before her boss came storming out of the kitchen to see why she didn't pick up her orders. She glared at Brett, her stormy eyes sparkling with glints of charcoal black, breasts heaving with her rising temper.

"Let me go, Brett! I only have twenty minutes more to work, then we can talk."

Ignoring her words, he pulled her hand forward, his grip tighter. His piercing gaze held her glance, mirroring the heightened fury coursing through his body.

"Who are those four revolting creeps in that booth?"

"Admirers!" Honey pointed out impudently.

"Some of the horde of ardent ones that surrounded you that you taunted me about the first day we met? I suppose this"—he looked over the interior with disgust—"is the...luxurious...restaurant you idled your nighttime hours away in too?"

"Glad you like it." Head thrown back, she tugged her hand free, at the same time stomping the top of his shoe with a pointed heel. She was glad when he winced. She glanced at the four men, lashes fluttering, sickened by the coy smile she gave them just to prove to Brett she wouldn't be intimidated.

"They are rather cute, aren't they?" Her stomach definitely clenched over that lie.

His knuckles strained, fingers splayed on the tabletop, his mouth thinned in distaste while muttering close to her bowed head.

"I have never in my entire life seen a more ridiculous group of males. They haven't taken their leering eyes off your body since I sat down. I promise you, if I hear one more wisecrack about your well-endowed feminine curves or sexy bu—er, derriere, I'll knock their teeth so far down their throats, it will take a urologist to find them!"

"Hush, Brett. That's uncouth," Honey censured him.

"So are they," he shot back grimly.

As Brett returned his attention to her, Honey smiled mischievously. Her eyes danced with amusement, unable to stop a soft teasing giggle. The dimple in her cheek emerged when she raised her eyes innocently.

"You aren't jealous, are you, Mr. Weston? They did mention they had good jobs at the shipyard. You know, some nice legitimate type of work?"

Honey swept from the booth. Brett's sudden intake of breath warned her the tight hold on his temper was near an end. She rushed into the kitchen to pick up her next order, calling impishly to the cook.

"Fix me a big plate of your greasiest fish, cooked extra brown. I have a special friend out there who just loves fried food." Balancing a third plate on her arm, she looked at a tray of potatoes. "Add an extra large helping of those hard-looking French fries you're going to throw out later, please."

She returned to the dining room, deliberately sauntering toward the booth where Brett sat brooding. Wiggling her shapely hips seductively, she gave him a broad wink, passing by with her chin tilted at a sassy angle.

Handing the plates to her customers, she rushed to the kitchen to pick up his plate. It was filled with fish, scorched and covered in a thick greasy batter and a heaping serving of cold French fries. She grabbed their largest bottle of ketchup as she passed the counter. She walked to Brett, laid the plate before him with a grand flourish, broke into a playful grin, and pointed out in a sugary voice, "Your order, sir." Honey chuckled, spoiling all attempt to keep her expression serious.

"You're going to pay for this tonight, Honey," Brett hissed beneath his breath.

"Why, thank you, sir. I can hardly wait." Deftly avoiding his outstretched hand, she spun away toward the privacy of the kitchen.

Serving ice cream to the five boys at the center table,

Honey was dismayed to observe Brett storming from the booth, his untouched plate still where she had placed it.

He stopped at the booth occupied by the four boisterous men. His voice was too low for her to overhear the heated conversation, but his words were obviously effective. The men threw some money on the table, rushing from the diner in great haste after a single furtive glance in her direction.

Honey felt a tremor of intuition that serious trouble was brewing, confirmed by Brett storming by her without a glance. He boldly pushed through the swinging kitchen doors with one outstretched palm, slamming them back with a resounding bang.

With trembling hands she helped the busboy clear the tables, expecting to be called into the back any moment. Finished with her customers, she sped into the employees' restroom. Her fingers were shaking so bad, she could hardly remove her uniform. She had never seen anyone so enraged. Brett's eyes were filled with revenge.

The door burst open as Honey was slipping into her slacks. She pulled her blouse on, fixing the buttons, her eyes scanning her coworkers' expressions.

"Wow! Where did you ever find that gorgeous hunk?" the oldest waitress asked, her heavily made up eyes flashing with excitement.

"Man, but he is really tall, dark, and then some!" a younger, dyed blonde cooed, fanning her face as if Brett were the hottest man she had ever encountered.

Honey straightened the crumpled hem of her blouse, readily agreeing with their remarks.

"I thought what your man told those young guys was something, but when he lit into old Demario, I couldn't believe it," the third exclaimed enviously.

The blonde spoke up, eyebrows raised in awe. "He actually told him you were leaving tonight and he didn't give a damn if the boss didn't have a single waitress to replace you. He even threw up the fact he shouldn't have a restaurant anyway if the poison he'd been served was an example of his culinary expertise."

"It was really something, wasn't it?" the older one interrupted. "When I left, he was telling the boss what he thought of him allowing a sweet, innocent girl like you to be subjected to the vile abuse of four oversexed, pimply-faced perverted young hoodlums."

Honey was communicative, momentarily forgetting her fear of Brett's wrath and her coworkers' previous jealousy.

"My...man...does have a way with words and the strength to back them up." She enjoyed the possessive sound of calling him her man. It had rather an avant-garde connotation. Quite with-it at least.

After handing her uniform to the waitress closest to her size, she excused herself and left. Sneaking out the back door, she intentionally avoided the front entrance and the kitchen area. She held her purse with a tight grip, ducking behind a large pungent trash bin. She waited, contemplating the best time to rush to the bus stop as fast as she could run.

She crouched down, wishing it were dark. As soon as she was certain Brett wasn't around she would bolt for the corner. She slowly stood up, peeking cautiously over the smelly bin.

Perfect, she thought. Not a single person in sight. She twirled around to start her escape. She yelped with surprise, feeling her shoulder clasped in a hard lean hand, and she knew instantly who held her.

Honey looked at Brett. Waiting for his angry abuse, she was shocked to see an unexpected calm look. His jaw was taut, mouth sensuous, eyes brilliant, his thoughts well hidden. Only the tight grip and slight flare of his nostrils indicated he wasn't totally composed.

Without a word he guided her to the front parking lot. He shoved her unceremoniously into the passenger seat, slamming the door with unusual force.

Aware it was time to remain silent, Honey bowed her head, refusing to glance his way while he started the car. She clasped her purse on her lap, using it to hide her clenching fingers. Her eyes closed as he roared out of the lot, tires spinning when he sped around the corner. Without uttering a single statement he drove at top speed to his destination.

Honey glanced covertly sideways through her fringe of lashes. Brett didn't look quite so cool now. There was a rigid set to his firm jaw and his fingers clenched the steering wheel in such a stranglehold, the knuckles were white. Breathing in a tightly controlled manner, his cold eyes were so dark as to look black when he turned into the private entrance of Weston Towers.

"Why are you pulling in—"

"Shut up!"

Brett eased into the basement garage, braked to a sudden stop, and climbed out. He slammed the driver's door, stormed to the passenger side, yanked the door open, and dragged her none too gently out of the Ferrari.

When he gripped her arm, she couldn't speak, his touch such a sensation of pleasure and pain, her heart beat erratically. She was held so close to his side, she feared he could hear it pounding in the silence of the elevator.

Arriving at his apartment, he unlocked the door, pushed her inside, bolted it securely, then turned back around. His stormy eyes pinned hers, one hand raising to nonchalantly slip the key into an inside pocket of his suit jacket.

Honey was swept off her feet. Held in a crushing grip, she was carried into the master bedroom, each long stride carrying her closer to the king-size bed.

She lay sprawled, thrown onto the pale gray quilted spread, heedless of her plaintive outcry. Sudden realization of his intent filled her body with anticipation. His punishment would be her pleasure. She felt sickened to know she wanted him. She was actually trembling with desire for a man whose temperament was stirred to the point that his control was gone.

"You thought you had things all going your way, didn't you, witch?" Each word was articulate, cutting across her nerves like sandpaper. He loomed over her, standing at the edge of the wide bed. "For your information, *fiancée,* it's my turn now!"

Honey's smoky eyes widened with intrigue watching Brett shrug off his jacket. His deep hypnotic voice held her mesmerized as he continued to peel off his clothes one by one. His silk tie, long-sleeved white shirt, polished Gucci shoes, nylon socks...

"Are you so naive that you actually expected to get away unpunished for hanging up the phone, then leaving it off the hook? So foolish that you work longer than the two days you said at that damned diner? So stupid you think you can refuse to move in here?"

"If you're perturbed, that's your problem," Honey blurted out, trying to ease imperceptibly to the opposite side of the bed. Why was it so wide? She knew she'd never make it without his noticing.

"Stay still!" Brett yelled, aware the moment she tried to get away. "*Perturbed* is too mild a word for how I feel. If what I said before wasn't bad enough, you had the nerve to flaunt your sexy little buttocks, barely covered by that plaid mini skirt, at me tonight."

"Only once and you deserved it," Honey said childishly.

"Did I deserve that revolting plate of grease and grits with a king-size bottle of ketchup?"

"Don't you like fish and chips?" she asked guilelessly. Her eyes devoured his naked chest. God, but he was sexy! His wide shoulders glistened in the light. Dark springy hairs covered his chest, veeing to his slim-fitting slacks. His deep-timbred voice brought her out of her reverie quickly.

"I abhor any greasy food. I abhor ketchup. But... most of all, I abhor being made a fool of by some little adolescent who is too damned irresistible for her own good!"

"Would you like to hear a good explanation now?" she sassed.

"No!" he grated, reaching for the buckle on his belt.

Honey swallowed convulsively, watching as Brett undid it, pulled it from his slacks, and threw it carelessly on the rug.

"Brett, stop! Can't you take a little joke?" Honey pleaded when he casually unzipped his slacks and slid them off his hips. "Please, Brett, no—" Her voice faltered, unable to take her eyes from the sight of his lean hips clad in black low-cut Jockey-style briefs.

"Look at me, Honey! See what little I've got on? That, sweetheart, is *one* more item than you're going to be wearing in exactly one minute!"

Honey stared at Brett, her eyes drawn to the magnificence of his near-naked physique. His lithe, muscular body was tanned. He was fit as a youth of twenty with the added appeal of maturity. Her eyes dilated, entranced by the flatness of his abdomen. She could see his hipbones and the hair travelling downward from his navel. She swallowed, wetting her lips with her tongue, wishing instead she could run it all over his body. She was filled with questionable desires. Sensuous ideas so wanton filled the core of her being, she shook her head, trying to clear her mind. She thought only men could ache with unrequited needs. The erotic trembling in the lower part of her abdomen proved a woman could feel equally unfulfilled.

Determined to teach Honey a lesson she long remembered, Brett lowered his body to the spread, drawing her to him when she attempted to roll off the far side.

Pinned to the soft mattress, he easily held both palms in the clasp of one hand. His other went to the waistband of her slacks. Her slender body squirmed desperately in a vain attempt to get away from his touch. Placing one long leg over her knees, he subdued her effortlessly.

Honey was silent, her widened eyes dilated with feverish excitement. She lay passive when he slid the slacks from her body. A soft flush tinged her cheeks seeing his heightened expression. His narrowed eyes obviously relished the sight of her long legs and rounded hips barely covered by stretchy black bikini panties.

Brett took his time, sliding his free hand possessively upward across her smooth thigh, letting his palm rest on the black material until she moved sensuously, a soft moan escaping her throat. Spreading his fingers, he slid up onto her flat stomach, feeling a deep quiver as her silky body began to tremble with ecstasy.

Slowly Brett unbuttoned her blouse, his fingers deft, amazed she offered no resistance. He had expected her to fight like a wildcat, yet she lay back, shifting luxuriously. His need to chastise her was being met with the most fundamental passion he had ever witnessed. He pulled her silk blouse aside, looking fixedly at her breasts rising and falling with the beating of her heart. Barely contained by the scalloped cups of her lace bra, they took his breath away with their voluptuous beauty. He raised her up, expertly slid her blouse from her shoulders, and threw it with her slacks onto the deep-piled rug alongside his own discarded clothing.

The impact of her flawless skin covered by brief sensual underwear caused the familiar ache to flood his loins. He let his glance linger on each exquisite curve, knowing her beauty would be imprinted forever, completely erasing any woman who had come before.

Shocked by Brett's hungry expression, Honey worried that her eyes would reveal the same cravings. Her passionately molded mouth parted in anticipation. She waited, wanting both his drugging kisses and intoxicating touch.

His anger subsided, overcome by passion tightly controlled. His unique green eyes were unfathomable tracing her nearly naked body. A groan escaped his lips, the words coming unbidden.

"You're gorgeous. The most beautiful female I've seen in my life, though you have far too much on."

Before Honey could object, Brett had removed her remaining lace. She lay back, hair spread across the pillow in silky waves. Her breasts rose and fell, their full beauty creamy mounds of delight, the dainty nipples a delicious pink. She reveled in her nakedness, ecstatic her innocent femininity could make an experienced man tremble at the sight of it.

"I don't think I'll let you out of this apartment until I've made you mine in every way physically possible," Brett warned her, his voice filled with seductive urgency.

Acutely aware of him, her body yielded, moving with natural suppleness until her limbs nudged his. Her hands raised, lingering on the velvety hardness of his naked shoulders.

"How many ways are there?" Honey questioned in a throaty murmur.

"An endless variety, my love." Brett reached one hand

to cup the side of her face, his fingers touching her ear and the sensitive area behind. He cradled her face tenderly, his husky words bringing a soft flush to her dreamy features.

"Shall we read my friend's copies of *Kama Sutra* and *Joy of Sex* together, or will you let me improvise? I feel innovative tonight."

Honey was filled with indecision. There was nothing more in the world she wanted than to let Brett make love to her. A nagging voice at the back of her conscience warned her of the consequences of her actions. If she became Brett's lover without a commitment to the future, she had everything to lose but the pleasure of the moment—a craving escalating each second she lay with him above her.

He was an admitted sophisticate. Though his desire for her now was obvious, it was highly possible her naiveté would bore him within weeks. Possibly sooner. His occupation brought him in constant contact with lonely women. How long would it be before one of them had more to offer? How could her innocent passions hope to compete with a woman closer to his age, a woman of experience?

She squirmed, withdrawing from his tenderness in a desperate attempt to quell the flame inside. Her hands that had moments before caressed his shoulders began to hit him.

"Don't, Brett. I...I can't!"

"Shut up and lie still!" He was astounded by her mood change. She had given him every indication she welcomed his lovemaking. His shoulders still tingled from her touch, his body still hard with desire from the touch of her hips pushing into his and her silky limbs soft against his legs.

"I'm not going to let you off this bed until I've taken your resistance and defiance and turned them into yearning and passion equal to mine." He placed his palms each side of her smooth face, cupping her chin to hold her still. "What's with you? What causes these hot and cold moods?"

"It's your fault. Because you're a—" She had to bite her inner cheek to keep from calling him a detestable name.

"A rentable Romeo?" he grated, thinking of the paper on her dresser.

"Where did you see that?" she demanded, attempting to shake her head free of his confining hold. Did she drop the note somewhere?

"You talk too much."

"I . . . I . . . do not."

His head swooped down, mouth taking her lips in a fierce kiss, chest muscles crushing her breasts, lean hips pressing hers into the deep innerspring mattress.

"Now, my delectable witch, give me your love."

Helpless beneath his strength, Honey opened her mouth to plead.

"Please . . . don't . . ."

Clamped hungrily over her parted lips, Brett's mouth smothered the protest before she could complete it. His statement of intent to make love to her echoed through her mind as she succumbed once more to the expertise of his drugging kisses.

She received the relentless persuasion of his probing tongue, welcoming it with the memory of their last passionate encounter. She remembered exactly what pleased him the most, drawing his tongue into the moist warmth of her mouth with soft sucking motions.

Helpless beneath the havoc of his emotional reaction to her deep kissing, Honey let her tumultuous receptivity encompass them. The fervent magic of his touch caused her mind to reel, all desire to stop him forgotten the moment he took her lips.

She clung frantically, her slender arms clasped around his iron-hard shoulders. His body felt like steel sheathed in velvet to her searching hands. Her sensitive fingers explored from the nape of his neck to the rippling width of his back and shoulders. Caressing the taut biceps of his powerful arms, she slid her hands to his chest. She could feel the rapid beat of his heart as his body shuddered above hers. She buried her fingers in the springy dark hair, clenching convulsively. Her power to cause the low groans of pleasure were exalting, urging her to greater daring. Exploring even lower, she trailed one hand along his side. Refusing to stop when she reached the waistband of his briefs, she slid her fingers beneath it, unconsciously knowing where to touch him to bring him the most satisfaction.

Brett pulled away sharply, his body trembling with the effort of checking his intensified passions. The feel of her soft hands roaming freely over his torso had taken him to the brink of losing all control. He had been too long without a woman and the one beneath him was unbelievably responsive. He had dreamed of taking her innocence and showing her the exquisite joys of making love. Instead she was so damned naturally passionate, she'd be giving him lessons!

"No, Honey." He checked the progress of her hand. "Hold my shoulders. I want you to touch me . . . to touch all of me . . . but not tonight."

Obediently Honey clasped his nape, arching her pliant body beneath him, instinctively raising her curved hips against the taut muscles of his aroused body. Their lack of clothing brought an exclamation of heightened desire from her throat when she felt his hairy chest brush the satin smoothness of her breasts and the soft skin of her trembling abdomen.

She lay back, letting him decide the limits of their loving. Her wantonness would haunt her. Even more would be the thought of all the things she wanted to do but hadn't.

Brett kissed her deeply, his lips leaving her mouth to trail with hunger over her thickly lashed eyelids, along her jaw to her small ears. He circled her inner ear, probing with his tongue before burying his face in the glorious abundance of her hair. The auburn strands spread like silk over the pale gray spread, the fragrance as clean and sweet as her body pressed beneath him.

He raised his chest, his hands sliding from her shoulders over her arms, down the satiny length of her bare legs. Without haste he stroked the curve of her thigh before moving upward across her femininity . . . forcing himself to repress his innermost desire to linger . . . upward across her hip. He spread his long fingers over her stom-

ach, fondling the flawless skin in a slow circular motion.
Lips hungry for the taste of her scented body, he kissed
her neck, teasing the delicate hollow of her throat.

Honey placed her hands on his ebony-black hair, pressing his head toward the erect peaks of her breasts. Her
body arched, giving him easier access to the full curves.
When his mouth took one nipple into its warmth, she
cried out with pleasure. The sucking motions were followed by the rapid motion of his tongue across each
nipple. She thought she would die with the feel of his lips
tasting, lifting, and returning to stroke again. Every inch
of her breasts felt the sensuality of his caresses until she
moved beneath him, trying to entice him to the warmth
between her limbs.

Her soft murmurs of passion broke the silence of the
room. She was completely quiescent to his every need,
eagerly obedient to each erotic wish and responsive to his
most blatant desire. His conquest was complete.

He raised his hand, whispering intimately against the
side of her neck. One hand tenderly caressed her throbbing breast.

"Love me?" His tongue probed her sensitive ear, teasing her sensuously.

"Yes...yes...oh, God in heaven...yes!" Honey tried
to hold his head still to stop the torture of his seductive
mouth. He was licking her neck, the sensation driving her
wild.

"Say it!"

She inhaled, the heady aroma of his heated body per-
meating her brain forever.

"Say it, Honey!" Brett commanded tersely.

"I love you, Brett," she groaned, her shaken voice
barely above a whisper.

Clasping her shoulders, he rolled onto his back, pulling
her slender length over his. Shimmering auburn hair tumbled about her passion-flushed face in a mass of silky
waves.

She twisted to get away, feeling the heat of his desire.
Shocked by her body's instinctive motions, she shifted,
shivering with the desire to get even closer. She had a

desperate need to become one with the powerful man beneath her.

With strong arms he pulled her upward, kissed the erect tip of each projecting breast, then eased her down, cupping her tenderly along his side.

"Still love me?" he questioned softly. He was satisfied by her reaction despite the difficulty of trying to cool the heat in his loins.

"Yes." Her voice was muffled by the strong column of his throat.

"Will you let me make love to you?"

"Y...ye...yes." Her lips moved involuntarily, pressing hot kisses into his shoulder.

"Anytime I want?"

"Yes."

"Are you through defying me?"

"Uh...huh."

"What?"

"Yes."

"No more lies, no more protests?" His hand cupped her breast, the thumb rubbing across her raised nipple.

Honey held his palm still. "Please, Brett, stop teasing me," she cried out. "It makes me want you so much."

Brett pulled away, speaking with confidence. "Good. You're finally the way I've wanted you since I first saw you." He removed his hand reluctantly from her breast. All of his anger was gone. His dominant male ego was placated. His strong sexual desire for her was unsatiated. That part of their relationship would come later, despite the fact she lay along the length of his body utterly naked.

Brett reached down, kissing the softness of her passionately shaped mouth before easing her from his side. He sat on the edge of the bed, resting his head in his palms. His chest heaved with unreleased emotion. A twinge of conscience crossed his mind. He had deliberately set out to seduce her in order to quell her defiance, yet forced himself to reject the invitation of her body. His blunt comments were muffled.

"Get up, Honey. I proved my point, I think. Remember when I told you any woman could be had by the right man at the right time? Don't you agree that tonight was the right time for us?''

"Obviously," she nodded in awed agreement. It was useless to ever deny her response. She lay staring at the bare muscles of his tanned back. Still bemused by his love-making, she silently watched the dampness of his powerful shoulder muscles ripple when he turned to look at her. His lean body was fit and straight, the spine ramrod stiff as he casually turned from the poignant yearning in her face.

Honey pulled herself into a sitting position, clasping her arms around her knees to watch Brett. She was un-ashamed of her nakedness. It didn't bother her as much as the complexity of his personality. She waited in silence, hoping for an explanation of his sudden withdrawal.

Brett stood up, slipping his slacks on. He made no move to turn away, casually zipping them before fastening the belt buckle. He let his eyes roam over Honey's flawless figure as she sat in the middle of his broad bed. Her eyes were wide, filled with inquiry, though she didn't ask for a justification of his actions. He pulled on his shirt roughly, buttoned the front and cuffs, then tucked it neatly into the waistband of his slacks.

"Come on, Honey, get dressed now," he prompted, handing her her slacks and blouse. Her underwear was at the foot of the bed. He turned to leave the bedroom, looking over his shoulder when she questioned.

"Did you deliberately make love to me just to see if I would let you?" Her voice rose from a painful whisper to a husky entreaty, escalating with her rising temper.

"Yes, more or less."

"But why?"

"I warned you I'd control your impudence when I returned. At the sight of your skimpily clad figure sashaying around the restaurant, making love seemed the most logical, if not the most gratifying, way to do it."

He spun around, her muffled outcry tearing like a knife through his heart. She looked beautiful in her nakedness, her momentary vulnerability giving way to the force of her strong character.

"Well, of all the damned nerve!" Gray sparks flew from her eyes, her glance boldly holding his. "Who gave you the authority to keep me in line?"

"I didn't need anyone to give me any authority. This conflict is just between you and me."

"Well, Mr. Weston, I hope you're satisfied with the results!"

"Hardly, my love." One dark brow raised in disbelief. "If it's any consolation, my plan backfired in the worst possible way. I feel like hell now. I want you with every breath in my body, yet I found myself not taking you tonight because my damned conscience wouldn't let me. Your virtue is indeed your best protection."

At the door, he turned to give her a lingering glimpse. His hands were clenched tightly each side of his hips, his voice suddenly weary.

"As a man who always picked his women from an ample list of sophisticates eager to satisfy his every whim, I suddenly find myself beaten at my own game. Thwarted by an innocent young woman whose chastity should be guarded. From her own passionate nature as much as mine. I'm determined to protect you, if it kills me."

"Protect me! From whom? From other men or from yourself?" Honey cried out, her voice shaking with the depth of turmoil in her heart. She loved him but had no intention of allowing any man the liberty of quelling her impetuosity without an argument.

Honey clasped her clothing to her trembling body, her slender chin upraised to give him a final retort. Silken strands of auburn lay around her shoulders and framed her proud little face in wispy disarray.

"Both," Brett admitted, his deep voice grating across her nerves. He knew he could easily kill any man who dared touch Honey. She was his woman. He felt it in his heart as deeply as if they had already exchanged vows of marriage. A sudden thought of Wendell Foster crossed his mind. He shook his head, his brows drawn together in a sudden unconscious glower.

"Both?" Honey chided, curious about the sudden look of rage crossing Brett's face. "You're the *only* man I've ever let touch me. The *only* man to see me undressed and the *only* man I've ever responded to."

Each word echoed with such clarity, Brett had no doubts Honey was speaking the truth.

"So, no thanks, Mr. Weston," she continued proudly, a brief glimmer of unshed tears shimmering in her expressive eyes. "I don't need your help in guarding my virtue. As long as I avoid your arms, I'll have no problem at all!"

Brett gave her a lingering smile filled with indulgence for her verbal daring. He doubted if there was a man alive who would ever be able to restrain her speech. He knew he didn't want to.

He left her alone to dress, walking slowly to his bar. He had an endless night ahead of him. A restless night he well deserved and one of his own making. Dear God, how he loved her.

Chapter Six

Honey entered the living room. She had taken her time dressing, hoping to regain her former composure. She felt wounded, her tumultuous passions awakened, then bruised—laid bare by Brett's strong personality.

"Please take me back to my room now, Brett. I...I want to go home." She stood across from him, her chin arched upward proudly.

"You are home."

"What?"

"You heard me," he told her nonchalantly, setting his whiskey glass on the bar top.

"But—" she spluttered. "You can't just move someone else out without getting their permission."

"I did." He stood in front of his bookshelf, watching as Honey's hands rose to her waist, casually telling her.

"I paid your dragon-faced landlady a month's rent, removed your meager collection of clothing and personal items, and brought them here before I came to pick you up at the diner."

Brett could feel her rising fury across the living room, knowing his meddling into her affairs would not go unchallenged.

"You had no right!" Honey snapped, her eyes shooting gray sparks his way. "I had decided not to move and purposely made certain you didn't have the diner's name."

Ignoring her counter, he made clear what had transpired. "Your...ex...landlady was eager to tell me where you worked and couldn't have acted nicer. The hypocritical old witch," he mumbled under his breath.

"What about my car?" she blurted out, her mind reeling with the speed of Brett's actions when he made up his mind to do something.

"I had it towed to a junkyard. As soon as you mail them the pink slip, they'll send you twenty-five dollars. Which is more than the thing's worth," he informed her with firm conviction.

There was no need to tell her he had ordered her a new burgundy-colored sports car until the delivery date was near and she knew what his intentions for her future were.

"I won't tolerate it, Brett! You absolutely had no right. Furthermore, I'm leaving this instant." She started to move into the living room, his words stopping her like a solid barricade.

"You'll stay here and that's final!"

"I most certainly will not! I'm emphatic about—"

He held his hand up, halting her next comment in midsentence. His eyes were brilliant, a deep forest-green just daring her to defy him.

"Who knows," he continued suavely. "Your eccentric, indecisive, womanizing boss might end up thanking me for seeing you have no excuse for being late to work." He hoped that mentioning P.P.C. would help to overshadow his tyrannical move. "You said it's only a short walk away."

Honey's brows drew together in contemplation. Her car was a wreck and had been causing her problems for years. It had never been reliable, always refusing to start when she needed it the most. Perhaps Brett was right, though his audacity rankled. She doubted if there was another man in the world who would transfer a woman's belongings without seeking her permission first.

She looked around confused, uncertain what to do next or how to handle the awkwardness of the situation. If Brett had moved her from the room, she had no choice but to stay in the apartment. She didn't have enough money to rent a room in the cheapest motel for even one night. Until she received her first paycheck, she had to budget every penny even to afford a bowl of soup for lunch. At least at the diner she had been entitled to one free meal a day. Walking to work would be a big saving.

Brett watched her closely, his eyes filled with tenderness. Sympathetic to the trauma of his near seduction, he reached out to her.

"Come to me, Honey." His deep voice coaxed, husky with understanding. Hands outstretched, he beckoned her forward.

She rushed into his arms, clinging to his waist with a sure grip. Her flushed cheeks pressed into the cool silk of his shirt. Enfolded close to his heart, her world was secure. His presence had become the most important thing in her life.

"Are you mad at me?" Brett whispered, kissing her tenderly on her smooth forehead. Nuzzling her tumbled hair aside, he inhaled her sweet fragrance filling his nostrils.

"Furious," she told him, enjoying the caressing motions of his hands running along her spine. "You're the most arrogant man I've ever confronted. Unfortunately, it's not all your fault," she whispered, burying her face closer into his shoulder.

"What isn't?" he prompted curiously. She molded to him like a second skin, each feminine curve responsible for his mounting desire.

"That I'm putty in your hands," she admitted truthfully. There was no reason to act coy. It was obvious. Brett only had to touch her and she would consent to anything he wanted. Any battle with morality was a mental conflict she had to fight alone. Her constant verbal defiance was a ploy, the only way she could retain a semblance of her own personality until she learned to deal with his.

"Did you mean it when you said you loved me?" His fingers stroked her back, sliding gently up and down in massaging motions.

"Yes." She looked at him, her eyes deep pools of slate gray. "I couldn't have let you make love to me if I didn't." She lowered her heavy lashes, adding without shame, "I enjoyed your...love...your touch."

"Good. That's as it should be, as you'll undoubtedly be

subjected to it every time we're together." He kissed her brow tenderly, his breath ruffling her hair with each serious declaration. "You've known from the first I find it impossible to keep my hands off you."

"I won't let you live with me," Honey warned him, holding her breath that he might attempt to coax her into letting him stay the night. She didn't know if she could deny him despite cognizance it would be a violation of her principles. She prayed he cared too much for her to ask.

"Relax, my love." He raised her chin with his thumb, placing a lingering kiss on her quivering lips. "I'm not going to move in with you." He dropped a kiss on the tip of her nose, warning gravely. "A month from now you might find me in your bed permanently, but not tonight. You're much too weary and still bewildered about my motives."

Honey extricated herself from Brett's arms reluctantly. She walked across the room, needing to get away from the disturbing contact of his body. It was impossible to think clearly when he held her. She looked over her shoulder to see him leaning casually against the edge of the bar, his eyes scanning her slender body. What were his future plans? When would he confide them to her? Could she stand the wait?

"Will you be working nights, Brett?" A tinge of pink touched her cheeks. Thoughts of his occupation revolted her.

"Of course," he said calmly. "I work almost every night. You won't be jealous of my job, will you?"

Honey shrugged her shoulders, walking around the room nervously. Her hands stroked the smooth furniture, picked up a book, and laid it back down before touching the rose petals in the nearest vase. They were a deep velvety burgundy and filled the room with a sweet perfume.

"No. I'm not the jealous type," she lied, refusing to meet his glance. Her mind reeled at the thought of him escorting other women. "Will you make love to another woman while you're working?"

If he said yes, she was leaving if she had to stay at the Salvation Army until she got paid. *No* man would subject her to that type of humiliation. Some things weren't meant to be shared and Brett was first on the list!

Brett laughed inwardly at her mutinous expression, thinking of his long hours involved with company problems. "I guarantee you I'll not make love to anyone while I'm working." Heading a company the size of P.P.C. had curtailed his pursuit of pleasure many times. Until meeting Honey, the challenge of his work had proved far more interesting than his most stimulating date. His eyes sparkled, trying hard to contain his mirth. She was becoming livid again and he'd never loved her more.

"It's not funny!" Honey censured him firmly. He looked far too amused considering the seriousness of her question. She turned to stand before him, hands braced on her hips, expressive eyes flashing with impatience. Because he was imperturbable didn't mean she wasn't easily angered. Nothing she did seemed to penetrate his self-possession since she had admitted she loved him. Arrogant beast!

He walked forward, gathered her close, his hands cupping her face. His glance lingered, knowing her acquiescence was only temporary. Already she was openly resuming her former impertinence.

"You're a constant delight to me, little spitfire," he crooned.

She placed her hands on his chest, starting to tremble as his fingers fondled her ears and sensitive neck. He was so much taller, so mature and experienced with women. Had her innocent response really made his great body shudder with passion? Had her kisses actually drawn forth unbidden moans of pleasure from his throat?

"Do you think I could ever be satisfied now with a complacent woman, no matter how willing or sophisticated?" He framed her face between his palms, raising it up to hold her glance with eyes soft with indulgence. "You've forever spoiled me, my darling."

She stared at him, the dimple in her cheek appearing when she deliberately gave him her sweetest smile. "Can't you change occupations? I hate what you are." Her voice was soft, filled with plaintive appeal.

"Sorry, Honey. I told you I would never change my way of making a living." His mouth twitched, the effort of holding back his laughter almost more than he could bear. Darned, if she wasn't trying to cajole him using the strength of her feminine wiles.

Honey's glance turned suspicious. Brett looked too smug. It was apparent that fluttering her eyelashes wouldn't work either.

"Don't, then! I couldn't care less how you earn your money," she lied, refuting her previous dislike. "I'm too involved with my own job now to worry about yours anyway."

"Good," Brett agreed readily. "Now maybe I'll no longer get called a gigolo or receive snide little remarks scribbled on office letterhead. A rentable Romeo yet!" he reminded her mischievously.

Embarrassed at the thought of Brett looking through her scant things and inexpensive clothes, Honey flushed. "I'll stay, though I intend to pay your friend a share of the rent while I'm here," she insisted independently.

"The hell you will," Brett threatened, his voice brooking no argument.

Understanding immediately that he was serious, Honey walked to the long couch. She sat down, gracefully tucking her legs beneath her on the deep comfortable cushions. It was like sitting on goose down in comparison with her unyielding sofabed.

She looked at Brett through her thick lashes. He stood braced, anticipating another verbal attack. She shrugged a shapely shoulder.

"Fine with me. I won't offer *you* any money, but when I meet your friend, I'll insist that *he* take it."

That should end that argument, she surmised, hoping to placate Brett for the time being. Before he could object her mood changed to one of sheer exhilaration. She had never been one to stay mad for long.

"Frankly, Brett, I should be furious with your audacity." Her eyes shimmered with happiness, her dimpled cheek moving as she put her head to one side, slanting him a pert glance. "I'm so anxious to take a long, luxurious bath in a deep tub that I'll stay until the owner returns."

Slapping his forehead with the palm of one hand, Brett cried out in disbelief, "You mean that all my persuasive powers... my moving you in without your permission... my stealing your transportation, had nothing to do with you staying here?"

"Not a bit," she said amused. She shifted comfortably, already feeling pampered by the unaccustomed extravagant affluence.

"One damned bathtub was all it took," he growled, eyeing her humorously.

"That and the icemaker in the refrigerator," she chuckled. "I dote on frosty drinks also."

A sudden sense of devilment filled her voice with a sassy lilt.

"If I had any idea what your talents were... your legitimate ones"—she flushed—"I'd see about getting you a job with my company. Unfortunately, it takes a keen mathematical mind."

"I know enough arithmetic to know you *add* up to trouble!" Brett stormed back, miffed that she assumed her Bachelor of Science degree was superior to any education he had. He was inclined to show her his doctorate. Knowing he had earned a Ph.D., graduating summa cum laude by the time he was her age, should curb her impudent tongue for a day or two at least.

"I was told that years ago." Honey smiled happily. She stood up, walked to Brett, and grabbed his hand. She leaned into his shoulder, her glance quickly surveying each beloved feature of his handsome face.

"Show me around again, please. I want to look through all the cupboards and drawers, study each book, search through the tapes and records. It will help me decide what your friend's like."

"Since when do you need physical evidence to form an opinion of anyone's character?" he teased, threading her slender fingers through his affectionately.

"Touché, Mr. Weston." She smiled, all anger at his

dominance forgotten with the excitement of living in such splendid surroundings.

On impulse she teased, "Is your affluent friend a bachelor?"

Brett pulled his hand free, giving her a sharp slap on the round curve of her buttocks before clasping her with both hands behind the back. His arms held her the length of his body, forcing her to stand still.

"Yes, he's a bachelor," he answered wryly, his narrowed eyes locking with her wide-eyed glance. "Not for long, though. He has plans to marry in the near future."

Uncaring of Brett's attempt to stifle her saucy remarks, Honey gripped his lean waist, bending back to cut in playfully, "Too bad."

"Why?"

"Because he sounds like my kind of man."

"How's that?" Brett said, touching her cheek where the dimple appeared before sliding his hand around to cup her tender nape.

"He's the marrying kind." Honey squirmed closer, bending into the arousing touch of his hand gently caressing her neck. "He appears to be considerate too. A tough kind of man to find among today's cynical, supermacho studs...wanting only to please themselves."

"Meaning whom?" he growled deep in his throat.

"Before I get into any more trouble, you'd better take me on a grand tour."

"Great idea." Brett leaned forward, drawing Honey up to meet his face. Deliberately keeping his emotions controlled, he took her lips, kissing her tenderly without seeking the heady sweetness of her inner mouth. He released her reluctantly, taking her hand to guide her through his apartment.

"I know this place as well as if it were my own," he said in a deep voice, pulling her into his room, where they had made love earlier.

Honey drew away. Avoiding the mussed bedspread, she scanned the elegant suite before opening the many dresser drawers. The king-size bed was made up with sleek satin sheets in a deep rich silver-gray. The linen cupboard held dozens of thick, velvety bath towels and washcloths, soft quilts, and extra bedding of the finest material she had ever seen.

She rushed from bedroom to bedroom before reentering the master suite. A soft rose tinged her cheeks as she looked from the tumbled spread to Brett. He leaned against the doorjamb, an indulgent smile on his face, patiently watching her look over his guest rooms.

"Which room will be yours, Honey?" Delighted by the happiness shimmering in her lovely eyes, he was satisfied that she had finally agreed to let him help her. She looked up, her wide smile causing his heart to increase its beat dramatically.

"This one, of course!"

"Care to explain why?" he asked smoothly, thrilled that he would be able to imagine her sleeping in his bed. Picturing her soft form slithering beneath his sheets brought a momentary twinge to his loins. She was becoming an obsession. One no woman in the past could remotely claim being.

"Er...it has my favorite bathroom." Honey backed off, pointing toward the door beside her. She had no intention of inflating his ego by telling him the sole reason was the desire to sleep in a bed that would always remind her of her near surrender and just how close she had come to losing her virginity.

She swept into the bathroom, her feet sinking into the deep pile of soft pale gray carpeting. The darker gray double oval sinks matched the deep oblong sunken tub big enough to hold three or four adults easily.

Sliding the mirrored doors of the medicine chest open, she stared in awe at numerous bars of expensive, exquisitely scented soap, jars filled with bath salts, boxes of powder, small vials of perfume, and large bottles of cologne and hand lotions.

Her eyes widened, their smoky depths dark and mysterious as she turned to find Brett behind her. "I can't believe this!" Her face expressed disbelief. "How could anyone afford so much Chanel No. 5? I've seen beauty counters with less stock."

Spinning around, she went to him, both hands grabbing his arm. She looked upward, unbidden tears forming deep pools in her eyes. He would never dream how she had hated hoarding cologne, afraid she would not have the money to replace it once the bottle was empty. Never in her wildest dreams had she imagined seeing a medicine chest literally filled with her favorite scent.

"Do you think I could use some of this until I get my first check?" Honey asked breathlessly, her voice husky with wonder. If he said yes, she knew she would absolutely wallow in it. "I promise to replace it."

Hugging her squirming body, Brett smiled fondly, his strong white teeth vivid against the tan of his face. "Little Miss Innocence, this is all yours."

He recalled the stack of envelopes marked in anticipation of her wages. A phone call to his apartment manager requesting he send a maid to the local department store with orders to fill the bathroom cabinet with her favorite scent was all it took. The natural aroma of her body would always be far more heady to him than the finest man-made fragrance, he concluded with a shudder.

"Mine?" Honey whispered, not understanding. It was hard to believe what was happening. She was beginning to feel like royalty.

"Yours, little one," he assured her lovingly. "A gift from my friend for helping him out by apartment sitting. Do you like the scent?"

"Like it?" She could hardly speak she was so astonished. "I adore it. In fact, that was one of the first things I intended to buy when I got paid. Not this much, though."

She hugged Brett around the waist, laying her face on his broad chest. She could feel his lips caressing the top of her hair and hear the steady rhythm of his heart beating beneath her ear—a sound she would revere the rest of her life.

"Remind me to give your friend a kiss of appreciation when I meet him." She could feel Brett's chest heave beneath her face, hear the deep rumble of his laughter before he spoke.

"You're a greedy little devil. Apparently all it takes to

arouse your interest is a fancy bathtub and an endless supply of perfume.''

"You're not aware I lived in a crowded college dorm, sharing a boxlike concrete shower for four years. An apartment like this was only seen in the glossy pages of *House Beautiful,* and Chanel No. 5 was something furtively sprayed on my wrists from a tester bottle on a drugstore beauty counter.''

She wiped her brimming eyes, deciding it was best to leave the intimacy of the bathroom or she'd become positively maudlin.

"Time to inspect the kitchen.'' She glanced over her shoulder at Brett, following close behind. "Do you know where the nearest supermarket is?''

Her eyes softened, shadowed with pain at the abrupt thought of her beloved parent. She turned away, her voice barely above a whisper.

"I haven't cooked a complete meal in a full-size kitchen since my father... died.''

Honey thought of the long days caring for her father. He had never allowed his illness to dampen his humor or positive outlook and always praised each carefully prepared meal she served him.

"Tell me about your father, sweetheart,'' Brett coaxed with sincere sympathy. It was obvious Honey had given and received love equally from her favorite parent.

Her eyes shimmered with unshed tears. After all this time, she still felt overcome with sadness to know she would never see her father again.

"You would have liked him, Brett. He was so kind and loving. He knew from the first he was dying, yet always assured me that each day should be met with happiness.''

She rushed into Brett's arms, her voice breaking and so sad, it nearly tore him apart. He couldn't bear for her to be desolate. She had borne so much alone. Bitterness filled him thinking of her selfish mother daring to encourage her to marry Wendell Foster and then coldheartedly withdrawing until Honey felt compelled to move out. He knew the imminent confrontation with her would be marked with bitter words. He was determined she learn of her daughter's financial hardships and how bravely she faced the world alone.

Honey avoided Brett's eyes, not wanting him to see how very much his concern meant to her. "I loved him so much."

"I know, darling. I know," he crooned, his large hand cupping her face to the warmth of his chest. He ached to declare his intentions but was too stubborn, wanting to wait until he could leave his work and devote long weeks undisturbed to her. She was in need of love and deserved a full-time husband. Not one whose case loads were the heaviest they had been since he started his company. Long hours and late nights of work would enable him to catch up on work he alone could handle. For the first time in his life he was willing to delegate authority to others in his company. Four more weeks should clear his obligations.

Honey withdrew from Brett's arms, bravely giving him a wide smile. His tenderness had nearly been her undoing. Later, when they had more time, she would tell him more about her youth.

"This is not a kitchen to act gloomy in." She smiled warmly, successfully overcoming her momentary sadness. With light steps she walked around the spacious, well-lit room before turning to face him.

"Time to inspect the inside of the refrigerator, though I dare say it will be awhile before I can afford to fill one this size."

"Look inside, Honey," Brett urged, pleased that he had thought to ask his manager to see it was stocked.

Honey pulled open the wide door eagerly. She was dazed to find it filled, her eyes quickly studying the packed interior. It brimmed with pleasing gourmet selections of food, some she hadn't enjoyed in years, if at all.

She reached for a jar of imported caviar, read the label, then replaced it, unaware that Brett watched her adoringly. There were canted wines, thick steaks, fresh fruit equal to that sold at Hollywood's Farmer's Market, imported cheeses she had never heard of, and creamy dairy products.

"No TV dinner for me," she burst out, eyeing a choice

pair of tender lamb chops. She shut the door reluctantly, facing Brett with one brow raised in inquiry.

"Who, for heaven's sake, is responsible for all this?"

"I'll take blame for this," Brett explained. "I left that box of discount garbage for your landlady."

"Thank you, Mr. Weston, though you used the wrong word. You take credit. Anyone this charitable can't claim taking blame." She rose, giving him a wide appreciative smile. "I'll love you forever, or ... er ... until I can afford to restock the refrigerator myself."

Honey turned from the refrigerator, pulling open the stocked cupboards and drawers.

"Your friend is becoming more like my ideal man all the time." A twist of amusement pulled at her mouth, highlighting the impish dimple. Ignoring Brett's sudden warning look, she continued unabated. "He's not a gigolo too, is he?" Amused by his sudden intake of breath, she asked daringly, "He does have a good, legitimate job, doesn't he?"

Honey shut the cupboard door with a bang, moving back step for step as Brett moved forward, relaxing when he stopped in the middle of the room.

"Unfaithful little wretch!" he growled, flashing her a censuring look. "An hour after declaring you love me, you start seeking personal information about my friend."

He gave her a roving appraisal, his glance lingering on her full breasts outlined by the thin silk of her blouse, before lowering to trace every inch of her body. His look was that of a man who knew the woman before him as intimately as he did himself. Pleased by the sudden tinge of rose on her face and the nervous fluttering of her curling lashes, he continued grimly, each word unknown to her as the truth.

"I told you previously, he's met the woman he loves. He did admit she still causes him problems, although he's definitely pleased with his recent progress. As to his occupation, he's a prosperous business executive with a well-known, totally legitimate company."

"When can I meet him and what's his name?" Honey taunted, looking over her shoulder while retreating into the service porch area.

"Never and none of your business," Brett retorted, glaring at her with a glimpse of humor in his narrowed eyes.

"Spoilsport." Honey giggled, her smoky eyes sparkling with mirth. As if any man but the one before her could arouse a hint of interest. Her heart was committed to the towering man before her. So totally, he would be staggered at the rapidity of his conquest.

"Obviously you equate money with success," Brett hastily.

Honey's expression changed instantly. Her arched brows drew together in a serious frown. "No, Brett, I don't," she replied calmly.

She straightened, still as a statue, while meeting his eyes squarely. "My mother does and she made my father's life hell because of it."

Deliberately forcing the bitter difference between her mother and herself from her mind, she smiled at Brett and returned to the kitchen.

Honey pictured in her mind how attractive the room would be with a few homey changes.

"Now what's the matter?" Brett inquired, watching her dreamy expression while she ran her eyes around the room.

Honey moved forward, placed her arms around Brett's waist unselfconsciously and burrowed her head into his chest.

"I was thinking how I could improve your bachelor friend's kitchen with a feminine touch here and there."

Brett lowered his lips to her hair, kissing the silken strands between each exclamation. "You just arrived and already want to redecorate."

His hands stroked her back, controlling his escalating excitement as she squirmed closer, her hips moving in ways that always drove him to the brink of restraint.

"You're even complaining about its masculine facade. It looks fine to me."

Honey pulled back, arching her throat to stare at his face. He was so tall, he towered over her even when she was wearing her high heels.

"It's going to take a few days to adjust to living in high society. This apartment is on the ninth floor, isn't it?"

"Now whose jokes aren't funny?" Brett said, putting his arms around her in a comforting hug. His voice changed, suddenly serious. "I had planned to take you out for a late-night dinner."

"Are you hungry?" Honey looked at him, her fingers threading through his lovingly.

"Only for you," he answered, gripping her hand to raise it to his lips. He kissed the palm, nibbled her fingers one by one, and waited for her reply.

Honey's face flushed slowly. If Brett didn't stop, she was going to collapse. Already she could feel the churning starting up in her lower abdomen. It had been bad enough forcing laughter when they were in the bedroom and his body lay full length over hers. The man was making her insatiable for his lovemaking.

"I'm not very nourishing." She tried unsuccessfully to pull away.

"Am I complaining?" Brett husked, kissing her inner wrist, aware of the rapid beating of her pulse beneath the fine skin. Sympathetic to the sudden fatigue in her eyes, he quit caressing her fingers, clamping them gently in the palm of his hand.

"Walk me to the door, Honey. With regret, I'm going to let you sleep in solitary *dis*comfort tonight."

"*You're* going to let *me* sleep alone?" Honey chided, her chin raising with annoyance at his conceit until she noticed the devilish gleam in his eyes. "You'd better be teasing, Brett. If there's anything I intend to have equal say in, it's making love. Maybe your friend had a good idea after all," she pondered seriously.

"What about?" Brett quizzed, slow to catch her meaning.

"Staying pure until the age of thirty-four."

Brett drew her against his chest, murmuring into her tumbled hair.

"By the time you're his age, you'll be a roly-poly wife with a brood of obnoxious children and a devoted husband with a head full of silver hair."

Honey looked at Brett's raven-black hair. Not a single strand of gray showed in the ebony strands.

"You're safe, then. With hair as black as yours, it would take more than eight years to turn silver."

"Good! It would ruin the reputation I've built as a rentable middle-aged Romeo. Besides, I never offered myself to you anyway." He ducked out the door rapidly, laughing when Honey slammed it shut with a loud bang.

Brett whistled loudly, uncaring he was out of tune, striding with confidence to the elevator. It was the first time he had ever exchanged puns with a woman. Honey made him feel like a young man one moment and an aged, jaded womanizer the next.

Nevertheless, she always intrigued him with the effervescence of her tumultuous personality. Without cessation the heady excitement of her responsiveness to his caresses had him so bemused, he couldn't imagine life lacking her companionship.

He was a totally happy man. A sexually frustrated one, but that would end soon. The image of how was enough to make him lose his sanity in the interim.

Chapter Seven

The large rooms suddenly appeared lonely and unfamiliar without Brett's presence. Honey glanced around on her way into the kitchen to get a cool drink.

She sat down in the booth, feeling as if she were swallowed up in the plush comfort. She scanned the impeccable room while sipping the fruit juice. Cupping the frosty glass with both hands, she knew she would never again be satisfied living in the substandard conditions Brett had removed her from with such arrogance.

Her aspirations didn't include the luxury of his friend's apartment, but she should be able to find a lovely one-bedroom unit. It would take getting used to to have a regular income the size she was earning at P.P.C. Every penny earned had, of necessity, been scrupulously budgeted for years.

Bemused by the unexpected and abrupt changes in her life-style, she relaxed. Her eyelids began to droop from lack of sleep, her dark lustrous lashes shadowing her cheeks. Finishing the juice, she sighed, got up, rinsed out the glass, and set it upside down on the countertop.

She walked into the master bedroom with heavy steps. Working two full-time jobs had caught up with her, and nothing sounded better than trying out the softness of the deep innerspring mattress in the tranquilly silent apartment.

Sliding open the closet door, she looked at the pathetically small bundle of personal items and clothing stacked in one corner, haphazardly crammed into the orange cartons she used for lack of a suitcase. She imagined what Brett had thought.

Honey hung up her dresses and other clothing, amused at how out of place they looked in one small corner of the twenty feet of vacant closet. She found her faded flannel robe, ignored the pink baby doll nightie, and walked toward the bathroom. There was nothing that could prevent her from a long, luxurious bath in the wide porcelain tub. How could she have forgotten that despite her need for sleep?

Hot water gushed forth in a steady flow, gradually cooling as she adjusted the temperature to her liking. She opened a jar of bath salts inhaling rapturously while pouring them into the tub. For someone used to hurried warm showers on hot days and cold ones when the weather was cool, she felt absolutely wicked using such an overabundance of water and scent for one bath.

Slipping into the silken warmth, she eased down until she lay submerged to her shoulders. Resting her head on the contoured edge, she sank lower, uncaring that several strands of hair got wet.

"Brett's friend, I love you," she whispered to the empty room. She held her left hand up, enthralled by the gleaming beauty of Brett's ring. "Almost," she added softly. "But not quite as much as I do your aristocratic, devastatingly appealing acquaintance."

She sighed, overcome by the languorous feeling spreading through her limbs. But the relaxation was not for long, she realized, when the bedroom phone rang with startling clarity.

Wrapped in a hastily grabbed velvety bath sheet, she rushed into the room, its thick carpeting absorbing the water from her bare feet instantly.

Perplexed that she would be receiving a call, Honey responded hesitantly. "Hello..."

"Hi, sweetheart. Were you asleep?"

"Brett! Where are you calling from?"

"My home, of course."

"Oh, my gosh," Honey spoke gravely. "I don't even know where you live." She suddenly realized she actually knew very little about the man who had become the most important person in her life in a matter of hours.

"Where do you live, Brett?" Honey questioned seriously. Wrapping the towel more securely around her damp body, she clambered onto the wide bed. With both legs tucked beneath her, she leaned back against the padded softness of the elegantly simple headboard, waiting for his reply. She was filled with eagerness, wanting to know everything about the man she loved.

"In a house," Brett answered simply, aware of her curiosity though not wishing to satisfy it yet.

"I imagined that," she scolded. "I mean where in a house?" She frowned. His voice was filled with amusement and she knew full well he was knowingly refusing to allay her inquisitiveness.

"In the hills."

"What hills?" Darn the man. She could feel her temper start to rise and they hadn't even conversed five minutes.

"Palos Verdes Hills."

"I've heard that's pretty high-class real estate." Marcie had told her some of the estates equalled any in Beverly Hills or Bel-Air.

"Most of it, although that needn't concern you tonight. What took you so long to answer the phone? There's one right by your bed."

"Actually, I wasn't in bed." His deep voice never failed to thrill her. Even on the phone it caused a tremor to run up her spine and her heart to beat in rapid staccato.

"Let me guess. You were either greedily guzzling an ice cold drink, soaking in the tub, or filling the room with the scent of Chanel No. 5. Am I correct?"

"I had finished a glass of boysenberry-apple juice on the rocks and was dozing in the bathtub."

"Shall I return and join you?" he suggested boldly, his voice filled with sensual undertones. "I know the tub could hold both of us easily."

Honey's face flushed softly, his suggestive words bringing a sudden vision of them naked in the tub. She could picture his wide hair-covered chest and muscled shoulders glistening with drops of water. She shifted uncomfortably, her thoughts in a turmoil again.

"Cat got your tongue, love...or aren't you up to imagining our bathing together yet?" His voice softened, lowering to a husky murmur, the hunger in it running across her heightened nerves as if he touched her. "Believe me, Honey, that's something I've envisioned several times already."

"Not clearly you didn't, Mr. Weston. I was covered with bubbles from head to toe."

"Not in my vision you weren't, Miss Bowman!" His deep laughter was filled with sensuality, convincing her his imagination was as erotic of her as hers had been of him.

"Hush, Brett," she chided, hoping her voice showed at least a hint of distaste. "Why did you phone me tonight? If it's to talk about your fantasies, a psychiatrist could help you more than I could."

"Don't be naive, you seductive beauty. How could anyone help me when all I need is a—"

"Brett!"

"A good night's sleep. Now who has the naughty mind?" he teased. "I hate to change the subject, since I can picture you blushing from here. I forgot to warn you I'm taking you out Sunday at—"

"But the diner!" she interrupted, still not certain what had transpired between her boss and Brett other than what the waitresses had told her.

"Honey, that damned diner is a nightmare from your past. You'll never serve a single plate of that abominable seafood to a customer as long as you live."

"But—"

"Drop it, woman." Brett's voice was filled with warning. "In ten or twelve years we'll talk about it. By then maybe I'll have settled down enough to forgive your impudence and forget your four horrendous—admirers."

"Okay," she agreed, pleased that he'd resolved everything at the diner. She had hated the work from the first. "What time?"

"Twelve noon."

"Too early. I'm exhausted." She slumped down, stretching lazily on the soft mattress. The phone was cradled to her ear, held by one hand as the other spread out over the quilted spread. It was velvety soft to her sensitive fingers, a direct contrast to the lumpy daybed with its faded cotton cover that she had dozed on the night before.

"You can't imagine the relief I feel knowing you'll be safe at night," Brett told her sincerely. "Sweet dreams, sweetheart."

"Good night, Brett," Honey whispered back, her throaty voice filled with sudden fatigue. It would be so heavenly to only work one job and get a full night's sleep every night of the week.

The sound of Brett making an exaggerated kiss over the phone brought a smile to Honey's lips as she leaned over to place the receiver on the cradle. Brett had brought more pleasure into her life in the short time since she'd known him than she ever dreamed existed.

She held the towel to her dry body, stood up, and lay the spread back, remembering that he hadn't agreed to coming for her later. It didn't matter, she thought, yawning sleepily, she'd be awake long before noon anyway.

With casualness belying the fact she had never slept that way before, she eased naked between the satin sheets. The slippery feel of the luxuriant material sliding over her soft form was unexpectedly sensuous. She was asleep within minutes, her head pressed deep into a soft goose down pillow, her body relaxed in peaceful slumber.

Exhausted mentally and physically, unused to absolute quiet, Honey slept on in the soundproofed apartment high above the city's noise.

Brett knocked on the door, waiting impatiently for Honey to let him in. An indulgent glimmer shone in his deep green eyes. He assumed correctly that she was still sound asleep.

Inserting his key in the lock, he let himself in, shutting the door quietly behind him. His footsteps were muffled as he walked across the heavily padded carpeting. He went straight to the master bedroom, pushing the door wide with an outstretched hand. A smile softened his firm mouth, one glance taking in the small mound of femininity snuggled comfortably in the center of his wide bed.

Honey's face was hidden beneath tousled waves of gleaming hair, one hand resting between her cheek and the pillow as she lay on her side. The bath sheet was carelessly draped across the foot of the bed next to a well-worn cheap flannel robe.

Brett stared at her for a moment, his expression filled with loving tenderness. He knew the silence of the room would be broken abruptly when she found him in the room. He sat on the side of the bed, bending toward the middle, his hand gently shaking her shoulder.

"Wake up, sleepyhead." Shaking her a little harder, he heard a tiny murmur of protest, muffled by the satin sheet tucked around her chin.

"Come on, Rip Van Winkle. It's time to get up," he called louder.

Awake the instant she heard Brett's deep-toned injunction, Honey pulled the sheet over her head. She clutched it frantically for protection before rolling onto her stomach, facedown on the pillow.

"Get out of here, Brett! It's not even daylight," she cried out in a muffled voice. It seemed only minutes since she had fallen asleep.

"You're much too early," she scolded, glad to feel him pull away.

"Early!" Standing at the edge of the bed, he exclaimed in rebuttal, "It's exactly twelve noon and we have a date. Now raise that delectable mound of womanhood out from under those covers and get dressed, or I'll dive under there with you."

"Don't you dare!" she warned, turning her face sideways. She lowered the sheet to reveal one sparkling gray eye shooting frosty sparks at his face.

It took all her willpower not to roll onto her back and welcome him into the warmth of the bed with outstretched arms. Just a glance at the reckless mischief visible in his dancing eyes, the upward tug at the corner of his sensual mouth, and the fire seemed to rush through her bloodstream. She closed her eye, hoping that blotting out his image would stop the mounting excitement caused by his unexpected appearance.

"Shutting your eyes won't help, you sexy witch. The invitation to join you was clearly visible in that one gorgeous smoky glance."

"You're ridiculous." Honey chuckled, turning over to stare upward. Brett's chin was taut, his arms folded casually across his chest, his face expressing masculine arrogance.

His keen eyes lazily explored her tumbled hair, vividly contrasting with the deep gray pillowslip. She was like a flame in his bed, her face aglow with a haunting beauty. The passion in her glance reached out to him with compelling insistence.

Honey pulled herself into a sitting position, hugging the slinky sheet about her body, momentarily forgetting she was undressed. A bright flush tinged her cheeks, aware the moment his eyes darkened, lingering on her full breasts. His glance moved over her body, taking in the smooth shoulders and sudden trembling of her fingers.

"Why didn't you tell me you sleep raw?" Being a bachelor held less appeal by the second. She didn't even know the power of her personality on his senses. God help him if she ever found out how much. It was a constant challenge to his intelligence to keep her suspicions sidetracked. Once aware of his capitulation, she'd utterly revel in his changed life-style.

"I don't." He didn't need to know it was her first time.

"You prevaricating woman. There's nothing between your gorgeous figure and my needs but a thin layer of satin sheet," he taunted with provocative intent, at the same time sitting back down on the mattress.

"Get out, Brett. You talk like a maniac," Honey ordered anxiously. "Get off the bed, leave this room, and make certain you slam the door behind you."

Brett ignored her demand, leaning over to cup her chin with his palm. He took her parted lips so quickly, she didn't have time to slink beneath the covers.

The instant she felt his hungry mouth cover hers she was lost. Both hands left their hold on the sheet to clasp his nape, drawing his head closer. She shifted, attempting to get closer, unaware when the sheet slipped down. It wouldn't have made any difference anyway.

Nothing mattered other than the magic of his passionate mouth continuing to possess hers. She could never get enough. A throaty murmur of dissatisfaction left her parted lips when he refused to deepen the kiss and raised the sheet without caressing the warmth of her upthrust breasts.

Brett pulled free of her fingers, reluctantly forcing himself to stand. With slow deliberation he warned her, "I'll leave you alone to dress this time, Honey. You're temporarily secure, though I'm certain you've surmised by now it's too late for both of us."

Honey's eyes shimmered with a questioning look. She stared at Brett through a fringe of curling lashes, the seriousness of his words leaving her temporarily speechless.

He looked so appealing, she felt mesmerized. His short-sleeved knit shirt exactly matched the color of his vivid eyes and emphasized the deep tan of his hair-covered forearms. Narrow-legged white slacks outlined the taut muscles of his long legs. He was stunning. Her heart set up a familiar tattoo against her breast.

"Too late for what?" she questioned, wanting him to explain exactly what he meant. Was it what she thought? She felt wary, uncertain if he was teasing or not.

"You have a college degree. You figure it out," he answered, his long strides carrying him to the door. With one hand on the knob he turned back to her, waiting for a comment. He was beginning to understand that when her chin raised, she always had to have the final word. The angle now meant she had several caustic remarks flitting through her mind just waiting to spill forth.

"The only thing I'm certain of is your libidinous behavior."

"Mine? Your memory is slipping, my love. Just seconds ago *I* pulled away from *your* eager hands and clinging mouth."

He ran a hand through his glistening hair, his eyes lazily studying her. Amused, he watched her squirm beneath his bold survey.

"It's too dangerous to prove my statement with you in that delightful state of undress. My control isn't up to par yet after the strain of leaving you intact last night."

"Apparently you need to practice celibacy like your friend," Honey blurted out impudently, pulling the covers up to her raised chin. Her sparkling gray eyes swept over him with mischievous intent.

"Celibacy is a result of *not* practicing," Brett shot back with emphasis. "What I need is self-restraint. Something I defy any man to have who sees you sitting in the middle of a king-size bed with your lush breasts clearly outlined beneath a thin sheet."

He flashed her a dazzling smile and left the room, closing the door with a sharp bang. For once he had had the last word.

Honey sprang from the bed, fumbling in her haste to wrap the robe around her in case Brett returned. With disgust she looked through her limited wardrobe.

She grabbed a pair of white slacks and a vivid kelly-green blouse. Rooting through an unpacked box, she found a pair of cross-band slides with high cork wedge heels. The shoes and canvas purse were showing signs of wear, but the black matched the belt tightly cinched around her petite waist.

She delighted in the luxury of sitting in front of a brightly lit mirrored wall to apply makeup. Her eyes were reflected back, shiny and clear of fatigue for the first time in months. Long hours of undisturbed sleep had worked miracles on her frayed nerves.

Adding an excessive amount of perfume, she took a last look at her mirrored image, raised her chin, and walked to the front room in search of Brett.

Soft lips covered sparingly with glossy red lipstick were raised in a shy smile, causing the elusive dimple to appear as she approached him. She stopped, placed both hands on her hips, gazed upward saucily, and spoke.

"What's the holdup? It's been years since I've looked forward to a day of relaxation and I don't want to miss a single minute of pleasure."

Brett stood motionless, hands raising to his hips, copying her stance. His eyes made a slow survey of her rounded curves, nostrils flaring as they caught the heady scent of perfume.

"Well, in that case I think your first pleasure for the day should be this."

With relaxed dexterity he reached for her, his strong arms gathering her to his body. One hand cupped the nape of her neck, the other curving around the lower part of her back. Pulling her close, he didn't stop until they were touching from thigh to breast. He bent down, stopping a breath away from her upraised mouth.

"Quit wiggling closer." He kissed her forehead, the dimple in her cheek, and the tip of her straight nose. "I thought you were a shy maiden."

"Shy maidens went out of style years ago."

"Apparently, since you're bravely playing with fire by pushing your hips close and rubbing my spine with eager little hands."

"Shush, Brett. You make me sound, er..." Honey hesitated, unable to express the reaction she felt each time he touched her. He would never believe that she was normally cold to any man's sexual overtures.

Rapidly comparing her past escorts, the reason was easily understandable. Brett was a bold, virile lover and so appealing to her senses, it wreaked havoc with her poise just thinking of him. Pressed the length of his body, she had no control at all.

"I make you sound just like you are," he told her tenderly. His hands ran up and down her spine, lingering on her nape in a loving clasp. His face lowered, placing a series of kisses across her brow.

"What's that?" she murmured, raising her mouth to seek his.

"A passionate, sensuous woman begging to be loved."

"Umm," she whispered, her eyes turning deep charcoal with love. "I sound awful."

"Awful nice," he husked, raising her chin closer to his. "Now kiss me so we can be on our way."

Obediently Honey raised her arms, her fingers twining in the thick pitch-black hair on the back of his head. Hypnotized by his charisma, she stood on tiptoes, her parted lips seeking the tantalizing touch of his mouth. She let her lips soften, teasing with fleeting caresses on his firm clenched mouth and taut chin.

She gloried in the ability to ignite his ardor. His experience was light-years away from hers, yet she could feel his body trembling.

Brett groaned, the surge of desire flowing through him prominent in his thoughts. Her tentative embrace became bolder, her ardent mouth parted beneath his in a kiss filled with hunger. Her touch was sheer bliss.

Drowning with the need to assuage her newly aroused passions, Honey probed his teeth with her tongue, breathless when he accepted it into his mouth. The burning magic of such intimacy made her cling. She sought to give and take at the same time, dreading the moment Brett would end their embrace.

Awe-struck by her overture, Brett lowered his hands to Honey's spine, bending her pliant body unconsciously while searching her mouth. His tongue played with hers, teasing it in the sweet warmth of her mouth until her legs trembled against his taut thighs and soft whimpers of love escaped her slender throat. Each moan mingled with his own sounds of intense frustration.

He pulled himself abruptly away, ignoring the appeal of her enticing femininity. He shook his head, his eyes dark with desire. Looking at her dazed expression, he stood riveted, sensitive to her mood.

"Your magic is too much for mortal man," he purred huskily.

Emotion hung thick in the air as they stared at each other. A life force flowed between them. His words were spoken with the depth of feeling only a passionate man could express. He fondled her shoulders, careful to hold her an arm's length away.

"It appears it's impossible to kiss you casually when we're alone."

Needing to break the power of his nearness and the effect of his provocative speech, Honey blurted out urgently, "It's your fault, Brett."

"Mine!" he exclaimed, one eyebrow raised in question.

"Certainly." Her gray eyes sparkled, bright with devilment. "After all the practice you've had as a professional escort, you should be in control of any situation with a woman." Chin raised, she added, "Either in cooling ardor or at causing it."

She withdrew from his hold, walked to the front door, and stopped. With a mischievous taunt she glanced over her shoulder and asked sweetly, "Today's services won't cost me anything, will they?"

Brett moved forward lazily, his eyes warning her to hold her tongue from further sarcasm.

"Nothing but a day in my company." He opened the door, one hand on her waist to ease her from the room. Closing it firmly behind them, he guided her to the elevator, his nostrils flaring as he inhaled in an exaggerated manner.

"Now what?" she asked, looking at him out of the corner of her eye. "Are you out of breath already?"

"Hardly! I'm almost overcome by your heady scent," he teased, one hand pressed over his heart. "Wallowing in Chanel No. 5 should be illegal in the middle of the day."

Taking her hand in his broad palm, he pulled her quickly down the hall. "We'd better get the hell away from the apartment while my willpower's still holding."

Their laughter filled the elevator, breaking the powerful physical attraction between them. The echo of their footsteps reverberated loudly in the empty garage as they walked across the concrete to Brett's Ferrari.

Honey relaxed comfortably, sinking into the glove-soft leather bucket seat. She lay her head back, unashamedly looking at Brett. She admired his taut biceps and strong hairy forearms, watching entranced when he changed gears. He backed out expertly, shifted, then pulled forward with fluid smoothness. The dark hairs looked so sexy against his deeply tanned skin, causing her abdomen to quiver uncontrollably. She flushed, remembering their abrasiveness pressed over her bare skin when they lay entwined on the wide bed. Turning to hide her telltale color, she reached for her purse, delving inside for a lipstick.

Brett pulled from the basement garage, easing into traffic on the wide coastal highway while she applied fresh gloss to her mouth.

Honey relaxed. She didn't care where Brett took her. The freedom of being away from the diner was exhilarating. Rested after a full night's undisturbed sleep, she had never felt happier in her life. Love shone from her eyes when she glanced sideways lingeringly, a look easily recognized by the man at her side.

Smug with confidence that everything was going as planned, Brett reached over to squeeze her knee affectionately.

"Love me, sweetheart?"

Honey gave him a dimpled smile, one shoulder raising in a vain attempt at nonchalance, her expression deliberately enigmatic.

"I'll tell you at the end of the day. After I find out what kind of an escort you turn out to be." Her eyes swept over him boldly. Trying to keep her voice from breaking into a giggle, she taunted further. "When all is said and done, Mr. Weston, I don't have much experience of your capabilities outside the bedroom."

Brett gave her thigh a sharp slap, his deep laughter resounding in the enclosed interior. "You're getting sassy again, Miss Bowman."

He waited patiently for a traffic light to turn green, using the time to run his eyes over Honey's exquisite features. It was the first time he'd seen her eyes free of fatigue. She positively glowed, her mischievous defiance clearly warning he would have to keep alert the entire day.

"Not me." She clasped both hands in her lap, giving him a guileless peek. "Why, I'm perfectly innocent—"

"Not for long, you won't be," Brett interrupted, intentionally misinterpreting her meaning. Amused by the tinge of color on both cheeks, he chided, "You keep forgetting you're an unfledged young woman who appears to have taken on more than she can handle, so curb your tongue today or I won't feed you. You don't have enough experience yet to try to get the better of me and soon you'll admit it."

Honey chuckled at his serious insistence and the preposterous notion that she would ever obey each of his demands.

"What's the matter, old man? Didn't you get your twelve hours of sleep last night?" She turned, letting her liquid gray eyes linger. Deep inside she felt a trembling awareness totally overshadowing her flippancy.

Brett pushed on the accelerator cautiously, the powerful motor surging while he zoomed around a lumbering truck and trailer. He spoke out of the corner of his mouth, his tone threatening.

"Old man! You're in trouble now. Since I can regularly manage with five or six hours sleep, that leaves me at least eighteen hours daily trying to figure out what trouble you're going to cause me next."

Without comment he pulled off the highway, braking to a stop in front of a doughnut shop. Before Honey could remark he had eased from the car and had gone inside the small building and returned carrying a paper sack and balancing two Styrofoam cups.

Handing them to her through the opened window, he walked around the sleek jet-black hood and settled into the driver's seat.

"It suddenly occurred to me you haven't eaten breakfast."

Opening the sack, Honey realized how famished she was. The aroma of fresh-baked pastry assailed her nostrils.

"Hot apple fritters," Brett told her with a hungry gleam in his eyes. "Squishy soft, filled with bits of fruit and cinnamon seasoning and dripping with sweet glaze frosting."

"All calorie free, I suppose?" She laughed.

"Who cares? Dunk up, woman, this is it until dinner."

His hand dove into the sack, removed a fritter, wrapped it in a napkin, and handed it to her before getting his own.

In companionable silence they each consumed two fritters and drank the bitter hot coffee with complete satisfaction.

Honey started to wipe her sticky lips when Brett leaned over, kissing her mouth free of both lipstick and sugary glaze. He was totally unconcerned that a group of young men were eyeing him enviously, undecided whether they were more jealous of his date or his sports car.

Handing him the crumpled paper napkin and empty cup, she watched as he took them with his to the curbside trash can, then returned.

"Okay, that should give you enough energy to enjoy the next treat."

With a muffled roar he backed the Ferrri out of the space, made a hasty turn, and pulled onto the main highway heading north. He drove across the high Queen's Way Bridge, maneuvering through the heavy stream of traffic before approaching the parking lot of his intended destination.

Honey looked around, excitement mirrored in her radiant smoky eyes, one hand reaching out to touch Brett's arm.

"The *Queen Mary*! How wonderful. Are you taking me aboard?"

Brett turned toward her, cupping her shoulders to draw her forward. He kissed her mouth tenderly, his desire to give her a day of pleasure exceeding his need to satiate his mounting frustrations. The excitement shining in her eyes filled him with the sudden longing to cater to her every whim. A task he anticipated doing at each opportunity throughout his life.

"A cruise awaits you, Honey. A cruise into the past history of this grand old lady."

He touched a tanned fingertip to her mouth, outlining its shape. "Something keeps happening to your lipstick. Any ideas what?"

"Plenty." She chuckled, reaching into her purse for the second time in a matter of minutes.

Brett watched in fascination while she carefully outlined the passionate-shaped contours of her mouth, then blotted it with a Kleenex.

She fluffed the ends of her hair with her fingertips, slanted him an amused glance, and sprayed a light touch of perfume on her throat. She didn't care if he did think it was overpowering. She wanted to smell like a walking advertisement for Chanel for one full day anyway. Time enough later to use it in subtle amounts.

Too enthused with the opportunity to explore, Honey scrambled out of the Ferrari. She ignored Brett's gasps and snide remarks about not being able to breathe for the perfume polluting the air, walked to the driver's side, and waited while he locked the car securely.

Brett pocketed his keys, grabbed her hand, and cupped it in his broad palm. He took her toward the ticket window and long boarding ramps.

Honey stopped him, wanting to stare at the three stacks painted a glistening red and black in vivid contrast with the bright azure sky. Its powerful engines were quiet, huge bow pointed inland. The gentle swell of the sea against her steel sides didn't cause a ripple of movement as she rested motionless, waiting for the day's crowd to throng aboard.

Brett moved closer to Honey, one hand curving around her waist to protect her from the jostling people impatient to get on ship.

The smell of salt in the air was strong, carried by a soft breeze blowing across the harbor. Immense granite rocks formed the long breakwater keeping destructive waves away from the inner harbor of the busy port. The only motion was caused by the rising and ebbing of the tide or the wake left by numerous ships and boats that passed along the starboard side of the massive luxury liner nestled in its own inner protective barrier of rock.

Brett leaned toward Honey, his voice filled with interest. "I'm glad this great lady is finally able to repose with a modicum of serenity in her retirement."

"I agree," Honey enthused, excitement shimmering in her intriguing eyes. "Can't you just imagine black smoke belching when she plunged across the oceans during her productive years? My father told me when I was a child, she had carried the wealthy, titled, famous, and infamous in style from one continent to the next."

"Is this your first tour?" Brett asked, hoping she said yes. It would be more enjoyable knowing he could show her around on her initial excursion.

"Yes, and now that I'll have more free time I intend to

explore all of Long Beach. I'll probably concentrate on its boutiques and department stores first.''

"Shopping, I suppose." Brett smiled indulgently. From what he had seen of her wardrobe so far she needed to. One of his personal friends was a known designer who would delight in trying to bankrupt him with her future wardrobe. His jeweler would insist her flawless skin was the perfect foil for his wares too. She'd never dream many of his plans for her happiness were already set in motion.

Honey glanced at Brett's face, shadowing her eyes with a thick fringe of lashes. His expression was hard to read, softened somehow yet disgustingly enigmatic.

"Window-shopping mostly." She shrugged. "Come on, Brett. I'm dying to see how the thousands of troops crowded deep within her hulls managed to survive when her regal interior was converted for wartime use during World War Two. Dad had an uncle who deplored the narrow hammocks.''

Honey tugged at Brett's hand, urging him to hurry.

"Slow down, woman. We have all afternoon and I don't intend to let you rush me," Brett scolded, drawing her back to his side.

True to his word, Brett escorted her throughout the ship: into the giant engine room for a view of one of four thirty-five ton propellers, along the catwalks with a tour guide into the depths of her hull, then upward in and out to the Captain's Bridge. Brett, wanting a last glance, insisted they stroll once more around the teakwood deck.

Honey clasped his arm, laughter in her voice while pleading, "Can we stop for a while? I had no idea the *Queen Mary* was *this* big." She took hold of the railing with one hand, leaning into its strength while slipping one shoe off at a time to wiggle her sore toes.

Brett slid a roaming glance over her flushed features and thick glossy hair tousled by the breeze blowing up from the vast harbor with increasing briskness.

"We can rent a stateroom on the R.M.S. *Queen Mary*. Have room service bring us a bottle of champagne nestled in a bucket of ice and a tray of hot and cold hors d'oeuvres. You can relax on the king-size bed with your shoes off, and..."

Honey checked his words, strikingly aware of the difference in Brett's outlook than that of her college friends. To them, crowding together in an economy car and driving to a pizza parlor was a big night. A mature escort with means definitely had its advantages.

"Though your suggestion sounds immensely appealing, I think it far safer to suggest we head for the Observation Lounge."

"I figured you'd say no," he chided, taking her fingers and leading her up the stairs into the bow, where the lounge invited with its comfortable seating and wide view windows.

Honey pointed to an empty couch in front of the bar, sinking into it with a happy sigh. She watched silently as Brett ordered drinks, then turned to see if she was at ease before sitting close beside her.

Their cocktail waitress returned immediately, setting the order on the small table before them. She smiled provocatively at Brett, placed his tip into the vee of her tight blouse, and undulated away.

Honey enjoyed the attempted interplay. Brett never even noticed her sweeping glance or lush curves, which added to Honey's contentment tremendously.

Two hours passed in companionable rapport. Brett skillfully guided their conversation away from himself, hearing a condensed version of Honey's life without her realizing how revealing she'd been.

"Time to leave, Honey. Before we have dinner, I thought you'd enjoy browsing through Mary's Gate Village shops."

Brett remembered the stack of envelopes on the cheap dresser in her previous room. He had given each one close scrutiny, correctly assuming it was her youthful way of budgeting her first paycheck from his company. That they were her personal papers hadn't bothered him at all.

"Great!" she exclaimed with enthusiasm. "They're supposed to be an exact duplicate of a small English village."

She accepted his hand with pride. He was so handsome and self-assured, he attracted seductive feminine glances wherever they went. She gave him a warm smile, her look of love partially concealed by the length of her lashes. His undivided attention was giving her ego a firm boost.

Brett wrapped her hand in his broad palm and pulled her through the opened doorway, his long strides making her trot to keep up. Honey reproached him, drawing back until he slowed and matched his steps with hers.

The air was soft on her skin when they left the ship and walked outside. The ocean's pungent smell of salt lay heavy on the cooling breeze and was one she never tired of.

Attracted by the clever window display in a leather goods shop, Honey stopped. Unaware of Brett's intentions, she paid no heed as he walked into an adjoining store.

Brett, knowing what he wanted, had the full attention of an expectant salesman who laid his black velvet lined display case on the glass counter. Looking at various gold chains from hair-fine chokers to heavier pendants, he decided to purchase three lengths.

He took a herringbone chain from the salesman, felt the delicate weight against his opened palm, and placed his order.

"I'll take three. A sixteen-inch choker, eighteen-inch necklace, and a twenty-four-inch necklace." He pointed to another display, adding casually, "I want that charm holder also." Envisioning the gleaming jewelry resting on her flawless skin, he knew his possessive nature wouldn't be satisfied until she was encircled with more symbolic pieces of the precious metal.

"Would you place it on the appropriate necklace with these three charms?" Brett picked up an open heart, LOVE spelled out in capital letters, and a fat little cupid with bow and arrow, handing each gold piece to the pleased merchant.

Observing Honey from the corner of his eye, Brett paid the clerk, asking him to gift wrap the jewelry in one of the handpainted boxes displayed in the front window.

He walked to Honey, observing her widened eyes with amusement while she imperturbably checked the price of each imported item that attracted her attention. He waited patiently, letting her browse until she had circled the shop twice.

She raised her face, whispering so no one else could overhear.

"Brett, did you see how much everything is? I can't believe so many people can afford to travel and still have enough money left to purchase high-priced souvenirs too."

Brett reached a hand to her hair, smoothing a wayward strand off her forehead. His voice was filled with indulgence, delighting in her naiveté.

"See anything you want, love?"

"Heavens, no," she spoke softly. "Despite your elegant wardrobe, even you would gasp at these prices."

Brett took her elbow, grumbling beneath his breath. Her opinion of his financial situation was so erroneous, it was disconcerting. To imagine he would have to think twice before buying the entire inventory seemed unreal. It was becoming more apparent each time he saw her that his deception would have to end soon.

Passing the front counter, he took the waiting package from the beaming saleman without saying a word. Holding it in one hand, he guided Honey with the other to the parking lot, entertained by her covert glance.

Seated in his Ferrari, he hesitated before starting the motor, the small box surreptitiously placed behind his seat.

"What type of food are you hungry for? French? English? Italian? Spanish?"

"American!" she retorted blithely.

"Such as?" he returned with a lingering smile.

"Steak."

"That's man food," Brett chided humorously, willing to take her anywhere she wished.

"I've dreamed of a thick, succulent steak cooked medium rare for weeks." She eased her shoes off, wiggling her toes in the soft carpet covering the floorboard. "Of course, it has to be smothered in mushrooms with a side order of fresh asparagus spears in hollandaise sauce."

"With a can of beer, I suppose?" he probed, engrossed with her choice.

"Heavens, no! I'd expect a bottle of Dom Perignon at least."

She sighed, her head resting on the leather seat back.

"Any particular reason for your tastes?" It was a continuing delight to learn the reasons for her likes and dislikes.

"Definitely." She laughed, turning to watch as he inserted the key in the ignition. His lean, long-fingered hands always intrigued her. They were shaped so beautifully for a man. So tanned and capable looking.

"Well, continue," he prompted, the car's motor humming at the flick of his wrist.

"Everything I ate during college was either chopped, ground, minced, or mashed, consequently I have an insatiable appetite for meat in one piece."

"Your refrigerator meat tray's filled with steaks and chops."

"I know." Honey hesitated briefly to watch a family trying to keep track of five boys. They reminded her of the people she was serving when Brett came to the diner. "I intend to chew my way to the bottom of it the first week. I've lived on Hamburger Helper without hamburger or plain packaged macaroni and cheese since I came to Long Beach."

"No fish?" Brett interjected gruffly, irritated just thinking of where she had worked.

"Not after the first week. It didn't take me long to abhor greasy fish and chips as much as you loudly proclaimed to."

"Don't remind me of that revolting plate you served me," he groaned, pulling from the lot. "Those French fried potatoes looked hard enough to use as railroad spikes."

He headed back to Long Beach and his favorite steakhouse. He knew the owner would be discreet about his identity and would serve Honey anything she wished.

Within minutes they were parked, had washed up in the restroom, and were shown to a private booth away from the main dining room.

Honey listened to Brett order. He was at ease in any surrounding it appeared. Despite her age, she had had little opportunity to enjoy many of the activities he took for granted. While her college friends dated, attended movies, dances, and college planned events, she had worked or studied.

Between glasses of Dom Perignon, ordered despite a swift kick under the table, Honey relished each bite of her meal. A fresh spinach salad tossed at their table with bacon bits and a smooth oil and vinegar dressing was followed by a tender filet mignon grilled to perfection, brown on the outside and succulent and pink in the middle. Tiny whole button mushrooms were sautéed in butter, the asparagus steamed and covered with a creamy sauce.

Honey's eyes shone opalescent in the dimly lit room. She dipped her fork into the final piece of sinfully rich cheesecake, making certain she scooped up the remaining raspberry that added the grand finale to the most delectable meal of her life. With a contented sigh she gave Brett a mute appeal.

"Had enough, darling?" His deep voice expressed equal satisfaction, one hand raising a cup to his mouth for the last swallow of excellently brewed coffee.

"Hmm, yes," she moaned, looking helplessly across the table. "I feel stuffed."

Brett laughed, returning smoothly, his devilish gleam clearly visible, "You carry it well, my love. Extremely, curvaceously, and exceedingly well, in fact."

Too replete to denounce his comment, Honey made a face in displeasure, remembering how wonderful her day had been, and instantly changed it to a wide, tender smile.

She walked from the restaurant in a daze, not the least surprised it was dark as pitch. It seemed a lifetime instead of a day that they had been together. They had talked for hours in the restaurant, sharing interests, arguing good-naturedly when they disagreed over a book's qualities or the abilities of a recording artist.

A feeling of deep lassitude overcame her during the drive to her apartment. The silence was comfortable, their rapport complete, when Brett eased to a stop in his private space.

Honey lay her head on the seat back, turning sideways when Brett switched on the overhead light and made no attempt to leave the car. Tension mounted, their glances locking, his enigmatic, hers open and filled with love.

Brett reached behind the seat, handing the gilt-wrapped box with its puffy bow to Honey. He watched her changing expression as she hesitantly took the package. Raising her shining eyes, she surveyed his beloved face.

"I...I don't need gifts to make me happy." She fondled the package, running her fingers around the bow, undecided what to do. Her eyes met his squarely. "The dinner must have cost a fortune, though you wouldn't let me see either the menu or the bill."

Astounded by her reaction to his gift and dinner, Brett frowned. Her sympathy for his funds was becoming more than he could tolerate.

"Quit worrying how much I should or should not spend and open the damned thing."

My God, he thought, he had to end the charade soon. He could never remember a woman concerned about his spending too much. Usually they greedily attempted to pressure him for more despite his renown generosity. Honey's attitude was primly archaic.

"That wasn't very gracious and I apologize," she told him, aware he was plainly irritated by her reproach. He was quite unlike any man she had ever known.

Unwrapping the small package, she lifted out an exquisite cloisonné jewelry box. She opened the hinged lid, gasping when she observed the glimmer of heavy gold against a black velvet lining. Bemused that he had purchased an expensive necklace for her, she glanced up. To her dismay tears welled in her smoky eyes, blurring her vision. No man had ever treated her so lavishly.

"This is the most lovely gift I've ever received in my life. You...you seem to know everything that I like."

She slid the chain from the velvet, crying out softly, "Three chains plus charms! I can't believe it."

Her heart overflowed with happiness, removing the charms to cradle in her palm. Touching each one with a dainty fingertip, she hoped the symbols meant as much to him as they did her.

"Put them on me, please," she whispered tenderly.

Brett turned her back to him. "Hold your hair off your neck or I'll never be able to fasten these tiny clasps."

Honey swept her hair high, exposing her nape to Brett's ministrations.

He completed the task, bending forward to place a featherlight kiss against the vulnerable skin, pleased by her responsive shudder. With gentle hands he smoothed her lustrous hair before turning her around to face him.

Bold green eyes lingered on the center necklace nestling over her cleavage. Entranced, he watched the charms rise and fall with her quickened breathing.

Honey stared silently, emotional tears trickling freely down her smooth cheeks.

Brett reached forward, taking the drops into his mouth. The intimacy of his tongue licking her face brought back memories of the taste of her flesh. He ached for the time he'd have the pleasure of her entire body lingering on his taste buds.

"Thank you," she said simply, words of love longing to burst free.

She could hardly control the urge to ask him to spend the night, desperate to express her feelings by giving him her body.

"Gold enhances the flawless beauty of your skin," he told her calmly. "This is only the first of what I intend to swathe you with."

He hugged her tightly, resting his chin on the scented strands of hair brushed back from her brow. "I think I prefer the cupid. He looks rather smug settled on the satin of your breasts. As if he alone were responsible for our meeting."

Honey placed her hand on Brett's arm, reminding him in a throaty whisper, "He is, Brett. If it wasn't for that sweet old lady, Aunt Gladys, I'd never have met you. Her Happy Hearts Marriage Bureau is filled with cupids just like this."

Completely enthralled by the man she had given her heart to, she never hesitated to shield the adoration shining in her eloquent dove-gray eyes.

Brett was joyous, thoroughly convinced Honey loved him without reservation. He was filled with heady power, holding back his passion with extreme self-control. He had decided earlier it was necessary to keep their relationship innocently affectionate for the time being. He fought back his hunger, refusing her unconscious plea for his love.

Bewildered by Brett's sudden reticence, Honey remained silent, biding her time. She yearned for his fierce, turbulent kisses, eagerly looking forward to closer physical contact.

In silence she followed him to the elevator, reluctant at leaving the closeness of the car. Her head swam with the thought he was no doubt waiting until they were in her apartment to express his sophisticated passions.

Her body throbbed, she wanted his loving so badly. She could feel her limbs start to tremble with anticipation while her heart beat erratically just contemplating his approach.

Brett hesitated, giving Honey a long, unreadable look when she paused in the doorway.

She raised her face, mutely beseeching him to stay.

"Good night, darling," he husked, taking her into his arms.

His kiss devastated her, the hunger in his mouth flaring to life immediately and over much too soon. The heady warmth lingered on her lips long after his brief farewell ceased to echo in the lonely room.

"I love you, Brett," she whispered tearfully, staring at his retreating back. His surprising rejection was clearly visible in her brimming eyes. She shut the door, suddenly listless, each step heavy on the way to the bedroom. She didn't understand the man at all.

Removing her necklaces, she placed them carefully in-

side the colorful jewelry box set on the nightstand beside
her bed.

Automatically preparing for bed, she dreaded having to
go to work in the morning. A lengthy, luxurious bath
failed to ease the hurt of Brett's unexpected departure,
nor did the expensive cosmetics compensate for his absence. The satin sheets, which the night before lay against
her skin like a lover's caress, failed to soothe. Nothing
could compare with Brett's touch, a contact she craved
more with each breath until she drifted off into a fitful
sleep.

Chapter Eight

A bedside radio's slumber alarm awakened Honey. She rolled on to her back, listening to the wistful words of the song. Brett's image entered her mind, creating a vivid picture. His abrupt departure was still puzzling. He was such a passionate man, she had expected him to demand to stay the night. Instead his kiss was a fleeting touch.

Sitting up, she forced all pensive thoughts aside in the sheer exhilaration of being rested. Two nights of undisturbed sleep had worked miracles. The disc jockey's humorous banter and switch to upbeat rock music was a welcome change from the sharp trill of the small traveling alarm clock she had used all through college.

Moved by the need to reacquaint herself with the lavish apartment, she scooted out from under the sleek sheets and downy quilted comforter. Like a young child she wriggled her bare toes, delighting in the luxuriant touch of soft wool carpeting. Arms stretched high over head, she leaned alternately right and left ten times each. Every morning she was determined to start a strict regimen of exercises. She walked into the bathroom, disgusted with herself for lacking the discipline to continue beyond a few halfhearted executions.

"There's always tomorrow," she spoke out loud, much more interested in taking another unhurried bath. The soft water's silken warmth was so heavenly surrounding her body amidst the heady scent of perfumed bath salts, she couldn't possibly resist it.

Wrapped in a voluminous bath sheet, she wandered into the dining room. Sunlight filtered through a wide glass patio door opening onto a broad sheltered balcony furnished with plush cushioned patio furniture. Sliding the door open, she inhaled the cool air, heavy with the scent of the sea. She walked to the edge, drawing in her breath fearfully when she realized how high up the apartment was.

Nearby taller apartments failed to block the beauty of the view before her. She had a clear panorama of the convention center and, after walking around the corner of the double patio, an unbroken glimpse of the breakwater, the immense ships anchored offshore, and the *Queen Mary*.

Peering straight down, she could see an awning-covered rear exit opening right on the sands. Numerous people were even now spreading out blankets and knapsacks, removing terry robes and smoothing suntan lotion into their skin, preparing for a leisurely day sunning on the crowded beach.

With reluctance she forced herself to leave the intriguing height. She couldn't believe her sudden fortune. House sitting for vacationing professors had been an enjoyable way to earn tuition assistance, but none had homes with views equal to the one spread before Brett's friend's patio. It was superlative in any direction.

Back in the bedroom, she dressed carefully, pulling a deep russet nylon short-sleeved shell over her shoulders. She had found it rooting through used clothes at a local thrift shop. Washed and mended, no one dreamed it had only cost her fifty cents. She zipped up the side of her khaki A-line skirt, slipped into the canvas slides, and reached for the dainty box holding the necklaces Brett had given her.

She picked them up with care, clasping them around her neck before entering the bathroom to finish her preparations for work. Brett's ring glimmered in the indirect lighting, drawing her attention as her hand raised to brush her tousled hair. She stopped, staring at her finger for a moment before lowering it to fondle the gold cupid with a lightly polished fingertip.

Vivid against the dark color of her blouse, the dainty charms lay over her breast, moving up and down with each breath she took. It was the first time she had owned quality jewelry and she marveled at the difference between its slinky, heavy character and brass plate. Giving a final survey of her makeup, she walked to the kitchen with the subtle scent of perfume around her.

She couldn't resist the temptation of shrimp cocktail—the only seafood she craved or could tolerate after the diner—a bottle of apple juice, and a tiny foil packet of creamy Muenster cheese imported from Finland. She returned to the balcony, set her impromptu breakfast on the wide ledge, and ate her meal without haste in solitary splendor.

A casual glance at her watch broke the tranquil silence.

"Darn! First time in my life I've lived two blocks from work and I'm late."

Hastily gathering the trash, she returned to the kitchen, picturing in her mind all the changes she intended to make in its utilitarian look. She removed a nectarine from the refrigerator fruit tray, slipped it into a paper bag, grabbed her purse, and rushed from the apartment.

Taking the elevator for the first time, she exited into the mezzanine floor and walked through the carpeted lobby to the Ocean Boulevard entrance. A wide smile dazzled the old man waiting to open the opulent glass door.

"Good morning, sir," she greeted him, her cheerful voice filled with friendliness. "I'm Honey Bowman. I'm staying temporarily in Mr. Weston's friend's top-floor apartment. Are you the manager?"

He appeared to be a nice man, though his intense scrutiny seemed overly curious. Probably just careful who wanders in and out of the building, she surmised silently.

"Yes siree, Miss Bowman. I'm Bernard Bryson. Been manager here now for little over two years. Is everything to your liking?"

Honey stopped, thinking five more minutes wouldn't matter, since she was already late. He seemed much too nice to brush aside with an abrupt departure.

"Everything's perfect." Her glance swept the plush lobby, one hand outstretched in emphasis. "I'm quite unused to living in anything this elegant. You should have seen my last room in comparison." He wouldn't believe how awful it had been if she described it to him in explicit detail.

Honey returned his gaze, her dimple highlighted by an impish smile when she mentioned she was overdue at work. She waved good-bye, her rapid departure followed with the lingering scent of Chanel No. 5.

Arriving forty minutes late, she offered Corkie a breathless apology before rushing just as the phone rang. She picked up the receiver, making a vain attempt to answer in a calm voice.

"Miss, er, Miss Bowman speaking."

"Hi, Honey. You sound out of breath."

"I am," she explained, pleased that it was Brett. "I just arrived."

"I thought you started work at eight o'clock?" Brett asked, knowing full well when she was supposed to be in her office.

"I do."

"You're forty-five minutes late," he admonished her, glancing at his watch. "Your new apartment is five miles closer to where you work. That doesn't make sense." His brows drew together in a frown, wondering what possible explanation she would come up with.

"Actually"—she chuckled, knowing he would think her crazy—"I spent too long in the bathtub first, then spotted the gorgeous balcony and had to look over the area. After that I ate breakfast."

"So?"

"So, I dawdled around until I was late."

"Sounds like you need a keeper again." He leaned back, a smile tugging his mouth. Nothing seemed to daunt her.

"It's all your fault," she told him, shoving her purse into her desk drawer.

"My fault! How the hell could your being late be my fault?"

"Simple! You're the one who moved me—without my permission, remember?—into that splendid apartment. I was never late before."

Her voice lilted, filled with bravado at knowing they were separated and he couldn't effectively chastise her impudence.

"You've only worked there four days. It was just a matter of time, I'm sure." Damn little devil, he thought lovingly. He wanted her so badly, his body hardened just thinking of her impudent face and exquisite figure.

"That's probably true," she admitted reluctantly, adding as an afterthought, "the big man upstairs won't know I was late and that's all that matters."

"What he doesn't know won't hurt him is your philosophy?" he queried, his brows drawing together in a deep scowl.

Honey looked up, shifting the receiver from her mouth, as three young men who had been giving her the heaviest rush entered her office. She placed her palm lightly over the mouthpiece, one eyebrow raised in a questioning look, completely ignoring Brett's angry outcry.

"Hi, doll face," they greeted her in unison, uncaring at interrupting her telephone conversation.

"We thought we'd check to see if you needed our expert help this morning," Danny asked hopefully, propping his narrow hip on the edge of her desk. His beard and long hair were perfectly groomed.

Leaning both hands on her desk, Enrico flared his nostrils in an exaggerated manner as if overcome by her heady perfume. "Corkie took off to the fifth floor for at least an hour. We figured after a long, lonesome weekend away from this mathematical madhouse, you'd be needing some brushup training. We're all eager to share our vast, er...knowledge," he teased. He knew he was good looking and couldn't understand why Honey hadn't tumbled for his line thus far.

Kevin intruded, easily shoving Enrico aside to stand closest to Honey. He had no intention of being left on the sidelines if she decided to choose between them. "Our—mine, anyway—diverse education encompasses many talents." He splayed his legs, crossed both arms over his chest, and let his eyes boldly linger on her full breasts. "Not all of which are confined to this job."

"What he's trying to say is, we also want you to join us for beer and pizza after work," Danny blurted out, deciding to stand in case she hadn't observed his new Calvin Klein jeans and expensive velour shirt. He'd spent Saturday morning buying good clothes, thinking a date with Honey would be worth any expenditure.

Enrico's pulse raced watching Honey's snug blouse rise and fall with each breath. "Man, baby, I like that set of gold rope around your neck." He looked at his two friends for confirmation before returning his lascivious glance to her figure. "That's one swell resting place for that fat little cupid. Never thought I'd envy a charm," he declared.

Brett heard the conversation clearly. A sudden rush of anger at his employees was followed by hot jealousy coursing through his body. He could hear Honey's soft greeting, her good humor adding to his torment. She didn't even sass them like she always did him.

Damn the little witch, he thought. *She'll take over my life, corrupt my work force, bankrupt my company, and change the decor of my apartment if I'm not careful,* he surmised grimly. Phoning from his tenth-floor office, he had to control the impulse to storm to the fourth floor and drag her away from the attention of his reckless young statisticians.

Honey shook her head that she didn't need help, amusement coloring her voice as she told them to leave.

"Go away, please. I'm doing fine with my own work. Excuse me," she explained briefly to Brett before looking at the three men. "I'll talk with you during my lunch hour."

"Why the brush-off, doll?" Enrico demanded with a rolling drawl.

"I haven't accomplished a single thing today," Honey told them seriously. "Since I'm the newest employee of P.P.C., I don't want the Panther stalking down from his lair, gripping a notice to fire me in his fangs."

"Right. See you in the cafeteria." Enrico motioned to his friends. They followed reluctantly, returning to their own offices and the work set aside to greet Honey.

"Damn you, Honey Bowman!" Brett roared into the phone, unable to stand another second listening to their foolish banter. "What the hell are you doing? Running a dating bureau like old Aunt Gladys... with you the only female client?"

His voice roared over the phone, the tone irate after being subjected to each word interchanged in her office.

"Touchy this morning, aren't you, Brett?" Honey questioned, her voice filled with mocking sweetness. "It was only a couple guys wanting to help me with my work." Her throaty whisper taunted, the suppressed impudence barely held inside.

"There were *three* distinctly different immature voices," Brett stormed back, wondering whether he'd get an ulcer or develop heart trouble first, before his heavy case load of work was completed and his intentions were declared. He knew it would be a full-time occupation controlling her impertinence until she became resigned to her fate as his woman. When that eventful time came, he would damn well make certain nothing interrupted, neither his work nor staff!

"How could you tell?" She detected jealousy in his voice and reveled in his irritation. It would do him good to wonder about her. Despite her repeated declarations that she loved him, it didn't hurt him to realize that other men found her desirable too.

"I heard them clearly and they weren't there solely to help you with addition and subtraction! They'd damn well better get on with their own work or the Panther may lunge down on all of you before the day's over."

"Are you a snitch as well as an eavesdropper?" He was absolutely livid. How wonderful!

"I couldn't help overhearing their obnoxious voices," he shot back, ignoring her first question. "Why the hell didn't you tell them you were engaged? You're still wearing my ring, or don't you remember?"

Honey glanced at its fiery beauty smugly. "Oh, yes, I'm aware I still possess your jeweled band." She thought of it constantly, dreading the moment he'd demand she return it.

"Well, then, since it was good enough to fool that menace Foster, your foolish mother, and numerous girlfriends, it should be suitable for fooling three oversexed statisticians.''

Honey's eyes shone. Brett was getting more perturbed by the moment. She could imagine his dark brows drawn together and the inherent arrogant chin she loved to kiss jutting out stubbornly.

"How was I to know you'd let me use you as an excuse to avoid their attention? How long are you willing to continue this masquerade of being my fiancé, Brett?'' It was time to settle that problem right now. "Doesn't it cramp your style?''

"You're the only one who cramps my style and I'll soon remedy that. In the meantime, I intend to act as your fiancé until every male in this entire county is aware you're not free!''

"You're not free either!'' Honey shot back. "As I recall, you told me you spend about three hundred dollars each date and your woman all have to settle the bill!''

"I don't charge you, so forget about what I do for a living. Since meeting you I've been too busy trying to get your life in order to escort another woman anywhere anyway.''

He couldn't even think of someone else, he reflected with disgust, annoyed by his vulnerability to Honey's personality. His thoughts were constantly consumed with her haunting image.

"Good!'' Honey told him oversweetly. "At your age you need the rest.''

Hearing Brett's gasp at her insult. Honey gleefully hung up the phone, careful to leave it off the hook a second time. She anticipated their next meeting with some trepidation. Exhilarated by their sharp exchange, her fingers flew over the small calculator and pages of figures.

Unaware of the passing time, Honey looked up as Corkie came into the room. "Honey, you must have knocked your phone off the hook.'' She picked up the receiver, replacing it on the cradle. "Ready for lunch?''

She glanced at the gold necklaces, correctly pricing them within a few dollars. "Apparently your mystery man broke his wallet open for some expensive trinkets." She reached forward, lifting the necklaces in her well-groomed hand, fingering the delicate weight with some expertise. "These set him back quite a bit. They're much finer quality than mine and I still owe three payments on the darn things."

Honey picked up her lunch sack, getting up to walk with Corkie to the company cafeteria. Why did Brett spend so much money on her?

Sitting alone in hopes of conversing undisturbed, Honey and Corkie were soon facing Danny, Enrico, and Kevin. Despite their supervisor's censuring look, they set their trays down and begin to direct their conversation to Honey during their meal.

Honey was used to them now and found it easy to ignore the constant flirting. She remained silent, smiled when necessary, and thought of Brett. In comparison the younger men looked almost effeminate. She could feel her stomach start to churn with remembered passion. Brett was so sensual, so undeniably appealing to her senses, no man could compare favorably. With firm resolve she forced him from her mind and concentrated on the juicy sweet nectarine, then returned to her office and the completion of her first Monday's work.

Later Honey entered the apartment foyer, both hands laden with a massive ivy plant. She set it down, relieved she had managed to carry it that far without breaking her arms, her back, or the pot.

"Here, Miss Bowman, let me help you," the apartment manager volunteered, rushing from his office to assist Honey. He picked up the heavy plant, followed her to the apartment, and set it inside.

She scanned the room, her eyes soft velvety gray. "If you won't tell anyone, Mr. Bryson, I'll admit I love this unaccustomed luxury." She turned to him, smiling. "It must be a big responsibility managing a magnificent building like this."

"It is, miss," he admitted proudly, telling her to call him Bernard and asking to call her Honey. "I love it, though. I can't do the menial tasks I used to, but I make certain everything is kept in tip-top shape. Not bad for a seventy-three-year-old man, I'd say."

"Seventy-three! I can't believe it. I didn't think you were a day over sixty-five," she added sincerely. He stood so straight, his narrow shoulders held back proudly.

She asked him to share a cold drink with her, amused when he asked for a soda pop. She enjoyed his company while they sipped tall iced-filled glasses of 7-Up. He was a kindly old man, somewhat how she imagined her father would have been if he had lived to the same age.

"I'd best be getting back to the office and see everything's locked up for the night."

Honey closed the door behind Bernard, placing the tall plant along the wall near the end of the long couch. She stood back, admiring the added color and the breaking of the severity of the plain white wall. Her mind whirled with the thought of the things she could buy when she received her first pay check.

Opening the patio doors, she enjoyed the balmy sea air and vast panoramic view before going into the bedroom and changing into cut-off jeans and a well-worn cotton T-shirt. Suddenly tense, she wondered if Brett would drop in for dinner. Undecided whether to fix enough for two, she walked back to the kitchen, preparing to remove two lamb chops from the meat tray.

The unexpected ring from the kitchen phone made her jump. She picked it up, vowing to keep the need for his company from her voice if it was Brett.

"I shouldn't phone you tonight, since you've hung up on me twice."

"Why did you call?" She could feel her heart thumping wildly, his voice playing havoc with her nerves from the first word. It was so deep and sensual, just like he was.

"I wanted to let you know I'll be working tonight."

"You are?" she whispered, biting her lip to stop pleading with him to forget his detestable job and share dinner with her instead.

"Not that work," Brett assured her, aware of her indrawn breath. "I told you I had other interests. In fact, I'll be extremely busy for a month at least, which won't give me the freedom to be with you as much as I'd like."

Honey's spirits fell. She was miserable knowing Brett wouldn't be around each evening. Overwhelmed with curiosity, she stubbornly refused to give him the satisfaction of inquiring into just what his other interests were.

"That's perfect," she lied, pleased he couldn't see her tear-filled eyes. "I want to snoop through the owner's library tonight. It will be heaven to read for pleasure. I have four years of my favorite author's best-sellers to catch up on." Lord, she'd miss Brett.

"You're prevaricating again, Honey," Brett admonished her. He'd caught the break in her voice and knew she'd miss him almost as much as he'd yearn for her. Their relationship was so volatile, a stranger could determine the electricity generated between them.

"I'm, uh—" she stuttered, pleased when he interrupted another lie.

"It will do us both good to avoid any emotional conflict in the weeks ahead. As long as you guarantee me you're in bed with a good book and not entertaining one of those revolting fools from your office, I can rest easy."

"Danny, Enrico, and—"

Brett cut her words off sharply. "Forget it!"

Honey could feel her temper rise, reminding him peevishly, "Those *young fools* earn a good salary, have had a college education and—"

"Say no more, woman," Brett checked her chastisement, annoyed that she constantly brought up her impression of his character. "I still remember each word of this morning's conversation, including my great age."

"Hit a sore spot, did I?"

He ignored her comment, his voice lowering with the huskiness of desire. He continued slowly, each word an explicit warning.

"Fix yourself a good dinner, pick out a book, and go to bed...alone!" He hung up before she could comment, uncertain whether she had made out his whispered words of love.

Honey reluctantly forced Brett's image to the back of her mind, hoping her heart would listen too. It was still pounding. Had he really declared he loved her beyond all others? It had been murmured so faintly, it was possible she'd imagined the words.

Darn the man! she scolded silently. His physical interest was obvious, but he was taking his own good time to make a verbal commitment. She ached for some tangible assurances he wanted her for all time. She was twenty-six and sleeping alone in a king-size bed was becoming more boring each night.

She slid two chops under the broiler, deciding to fix a large green salad while she waited for them to cook. Deftly slicing, peeling, and chopping, she stopped to admire her handiwork. Crinkly red lettuce, tomato slices, alfalfa sprouts, creamy avocado, and cucumber were tossed with Russian dressing in a wooden bowl. A tall frosty glass of instant iced tea, the crispy salad, and succulent browned lamb chops made a scrumptious meal.

She cleaned up, wrapped a sweet nectarine in a paper towel, and went in search of the book she would read that night. She felt positively decadent stretched out on the cushioned lounge chair, eating the chilled fruit and reading until the light became too dim and she was forced to move inside from the patio.

Her clothes, few personal items, the new plant, and fragrant scent of perfume, powder, and bubble bath had already changed the apartment from its masculine simplicity. There was no doubt the new tenant was highly feminine and making herself at home.

The balance of the week was spent engrossed in her job. She fended daily invitations from the single stats, reminding them she was engaged. She had no desire for masculine company other than Brett's.

Eagerly anticipating his appearance, she spent each evening relaxing. She read from the vast library, listened to albums, strolled the beach in front of the apartment, or watched movies on the large screen TV.

Guilty that she had waited so long, she wrote her mother a long letter, explaining with difficulty about her job and giving her her new address. A shudder shook her narrow shoulders when she underlined with bold strokes that she was never to give Wendell Foster her address or telephone number. Just writing his name brought back all the terrifying memories of their one encounter alone. She stamped the envelope and set it aside to mail.

She tried a new polish on her nails, didn't like it, and went back to her favorite colorless gloss. After washing her hair, she set it in small rollers, hoping to like the intended new style. She hated the kinky curls also, rewashed her hair, and brushed it back into the familiar waves. All were unsuccessful attempts to kill time and take her mind off Brett.

Dismayed by her inability to adjust her moods to his continuing absence, her overactive mind was filled with possibilities. Each tore at her heart. She pictured him with an endless parade of wealthy sophisticates, their beauty and money blinding him to the fact that Honey was waiting impatiently for him to call or come by.

Her ready temper would take over and she would berate herself for being foolish enough to fall in love with an admitted gigolo who told her repeatedly he would never change his repugnant occupation. She was in constant turmoil.

She observed an obviously uncared-for cat lurking in the bushes at the entrance to the apartment building. Each morning she would take it meat scraps, making certain Bernard didn't see her feed it. He had warned her that pets were not allowed in the apartments. After Bernard closed his office and retired to his room to watch TV, Honey decided what no one knew wouldn't hurt them.

Sneaking through the lobby, she hunted through the landscaping until she found the cat. Coaxed with choice steak pieces and soft words, it worked it's way cautiously closer until she could grab it. The cat held tight to her chest, she ran inside, took the elevator to her apartment, and took the animal inside.

Obviously unaccustomed to such elegant surroundings, it prowled around each room, its lopped-ended tail held straight up. Satisfied that it was finally getting the life-style it deserved, it lapped up a bowl of rich cream and settled itself for the night on the long couch. Each morning a half hour before Bernard opened his office, Honey gathered its soft body in her arms and placed it outside. A routine that was pleasing to both.

The furry feline became her confidante. It heard arguments in favor of, followed by more lengthy discourse in disapproval of, Brett. In return she named it Beauty, despite its unsightly appearance.

Friday came slowly and with it her first pay check. Honey opened an account at the main floor bank, pocketed two hundred dollars, and headed toward the nearby department store.

The following three hours were spent in a flurry of shopping. The bags began to weigh heavy on her arms, piling up as she purchased item after item. Engrossed with the thrill of spending money at will, she was taken aback when the friendly clerk told her the store would be closing in five minutes.

Time had slipped from her mind as easily as money from her purse. She knew Beauty would be waiting for her bowl of cream and soft cushion to sleep on. She took the escalator to the street floor, walked out into the darkened street, and headed home.

Juggling boxes and bags for the short walk to Weston Towers, she managed to get through the main doors in time to drop everything in a heap in the middle of the lobby.

Bernard rushed forward to assist, amazed to hear a soft giggle and see her intriguing gray eyes dancing with humor.

"This is what happens when a person gets greedy, Bernard. I received my first paycheck tonight and went absolutely wild. I spent every dime in my purse and if the store hadn't closed, I would probably have tried to open a charge account too."

"Well, I agree you do have a lot of packages," he scolded with amused indulgence. "Much too many for a little thing like you to carry by yourself. I'm surprised you didn't hail a cab."

Honey laughed softly, smoky eyes filled with playful humor. "I couldn't afford one. I meant it when I said I spent every single cent in my purse." Bending over to gather the most fragile item in her arm, she looked up at Bernard. "Will you help me carry them up, please?"

"You don't need to ask, Honey. I've been wanting to talk with you some more anyway." He picked up two more large shopping bags, taking care not to crush them. "I've been thinking over what you've been telling me during our long talks each day this week and decided to take your advice."

Honey added another sack to his outstretched arms, hoping he didn't see Beauty, who had slipped inside during all the confusion. The hairy creature was waiting at the elevator as arrogantly as if she had ridden upstairs on it to plush apartments all her life.

"That's fine, Bernard," Honey told him, pushing the open button while Beauty slithered inside, making certain to stay behind both pairs of slack-clad legs.

Honey had reasoned the apartment manager was lonely and told him about Happy Hearts Marriage Bureau. She knew the softhearted old lady would be sympathetic to his needs for companionship.

"I'll phone Aunt Gladys tomorrow and arrange an appointment for you. You're a fine-looking man and there must be droves of women who would be thrilled to meet you."

Bernard was intent on balancing Honey's packages and never noticed the cat trailing after him down the hallway. When the apartment door was only inches open, Beauty scooted through, heading straight for the kitchen until its mistress was alone. It was a survivor and knew instinctively how to watch out for its own well-being.

Honey took the packages one by one from Bernard's arms and laid them on the long couch. She had become well acquainted during their morning and evening talks, and sensed intuitively he was a lonely man, missing the company of women his own age. She had learned he had only been a widower for two years and was finding it hard to adjust to the solitude, admitting begrudgingly he missed his wife's cooking most.

She thanked him, knowing he was anxious to watch TV.

As soon as the door closed Beauty sauntered into the front room, rubbing its fat body against Honey's legs. It pawed at a sack until she opened it, removed the kitchen towels, and let it climb inside, where it circled twice and lay with its head down, yellow eyes peeking out the narrow opening.

"Crazy, Beauty," Honey chuckled. "I wonder what Brett will say when he sees you. You're not the most glamorous creature I've seen."

Beauty reached a paw out, batting at Honey's foot. Honey kicked off her canvas slides, curled her legs under her, and opened the sacks to inspect each item carefully. She had forgotten just exactly what she purchased, she was in such a hurry to brighten up the rooms.

By midnight Honey was exhausted. Beauty, bored with inspecting the inside of each sack, was curled on her cushion sound asleep. The main rooms were changed by Honey's personal touch. During an indolent bath she planned what to purchase with her next check. In bed she tossed restlessly, unable to drift off to sleep. Determined to cross Brett from her mind, she rose early, wanting to enjoy the weekend away from the responsibility of an exacting job.

Skimpy cut-off jeans snugly outlined the rounded curve of her buttocks, emphasizing the long length of shapely leg exposed beneath. She rarely went without a bra, but it seemed so comfortable, she pulled her college T-shirt over her naked breasts. She glanced in the mirror, pleased they were formed high and full. No one would see her anyway, luckily, since the soft cloth clung rather wantonly.

She left the bathroom in a cloud of teasing perfume, walking barefoot into the dining room. She opened the drapes and patio doors, drawing a deep breath of tangy sea air.

Scanning the front room, she admired her additions. Ruffled pillows settled casually against the corners of the couch, their vivid material bringing out the colors of the surrealistic paintings hanging on the stark white walls. Several women's magazines were placed on the coffee table along with an imitation cut-glass candy jar filled with chewy toffees.

A wandering Jew plant trailed its abundant leaves over the smooth surface of the polished table, its woven basket container a unique shape. She walked into the kitchen after placing a stack of records on the stereo. She loved the owner's taste in music. His vast collection included all her favorite recording artists.

With the ingredients gathered together in order of use, she was eager to mix up the batter for her favorite cake. She dipped into the new metal cannisters for sugar and flour, one hand gripping the fat wood knob. She scanned them, thinking the kitchen looked warmer, their Early American design adding color on the tiled counter. Along with the bread box, she could use them when she moved into her own apartment, which helped justify their expense.

Within minutes Honey was totally absorbed in recalling the correct amounts. She grated carrots, beat eggs, sugar, and oil, added the pungent cinnamon and spices to the flour. Plump raisins and tender walnut meats were stirred in before pouring the thick, spicy batter into a round tube cake pan. Last, she placed it in a preheated oven and set the timer as a reminder.

By the time Honey had the kitchen straightened, the smell of spices permeated the room, wafting into the large apartment invitingly. It was probably the first odor of home baking to invade the rooms since construction, she thought.

While the golden-brown cake cooled on the waiting rack, she whipped up cream cheese frosting and cut perfect walnut halves, then walked into the front room.

Dropping down onto the couch, she remembered that she had promised Bernard to call Aunt Gladys. She gave up after repeated busy signals, thumbing through a *Vogue* magazine to kill time.

The sight of statuesque, ultraslender models prancing about the sleek pages in slinky couturier garment after garment filled her with envy. She was determined to spend her next check on clothes, maybe even withdraw money from her newly opened savings account to purchase something after work Monday. She definitely needed a good purse, at least.

She dialed Aunt Gladys for the fourth time, hanging up when she found it still busy. Returning to the kitchen, she carefully removed the cooled cake onto a crystal plate, centering it perfectly top side up. With deep artistic swirls she spread the thick frosting, standing back to admire her work while licking the spatula. She lined plump walnut halves in even rows around the top of the cake and standing on their sides around the bottom, each nut meat spaced identically the same distance apart.

"That's what comes of having a precise mathematical mind," she said out loud, placing the delicious-looking confectionary in the middle of the kitchen table. Sniffing the mouth watering aroma appreciatively, she returned to the front room.

A surge of restless energy prevented any hope of relaxing with a book or sunbathing. Deeply introspective, she knew only Brett's presence could stop the nervousness. She missed him terribly, the exigency to share her life with him fast becoming unbearable.

"Aunt Gladys, this is Honey," she spoke up automatically, pleased she had finally made the connection.

"Hello, dear," the old woman answered. She was curious about the situation between her nephew and Honey. He had become as closemouthed as a clam, refusing to answer a single question about their relationship. She wasn't even certain they had seen each other after the wedding. It was the first time he'd refused to allow her to pry into his personal life and she didn't like it one bit.

"How can I help you, love?" Aunt Gladys prompted, dreading the social nicety of having to bide her time until asking what was foremost on her mind.

"I have a client for you," Honey extolled sweetly. "The most wonderful old man you can imagine. He's intelligent, a hard worker, very lonesome, and quite pleasant looking."

Breathing a sigh of relief that that was Honey's only reason for phoning, she took down the details and arranged an appointment, asking, "Do you know his address, Honey?"

"I should." She laughed softly. "He manages the apartment building where I'm living."

"Have you moved, dear?" One thing Brett had complained bitterly about was the horrible room he'd returned Honey to on their first meeting.

"Actually, I think I've moved to heaven," she teased. "Much closer than before anyway, since I'm now living on the ninth floor." A sudden inspiration prompted her to ask, "Will you come have dinner with me some evening?"

"I would love to." That would be perfect. If Brett wouldn't satisfy her curiosity, then she could delve into the situation through Honey. The fact he was being so secretive made her more resolved to see her. "Give me your address and telephone number and I'll phone you when I'm free."

"I'm living in Weston Towers," Honey said proudly, giving her the information.

"The ninth floor of Weston Towers!" Aunt Gladys winced, one plump hand raising to her ample bosom in shock. She was totally unprepared for this news. What was Brett doing with the child? Before she could register her amazement, she was cut off as Honey explained the doorbell was ringing.

The excitement of Honey's voice increased audibly. "I have to hang up now, Aunt Gladys. It might be Brett."

Honey ran to the door, forgetting everything but her eagerness to see Brett. She jerked it open abruptly, uncaring she hadn't taken time to apply makeup or check the mirror to see if her hair was still reasonably neat. Nothing mattered but being with the man she loved.

Chapter Nine

Honey stared at Brett in dismay. Her breath caught, blocking the flow of words waiting to spill forward. The planned catechism would have to wait. He looked so incredibly suave, nonchalantly standing in the doorway, as if he didn't have a concern in the world and they had only been apart for hours instead of long frustrating days.

Tears of emotion filled her stormy eyes. He towered above her. She felt small and defenseless standing in bare feet, wearing skimpy shorts and a thin T-shirt.

"Miss me, woman?" Brett broke the silence, reaching to enfold her in his arms. God, but he loved her. The time away had filled him with agony.

Honey's arms moved around his waist, clinging tightly. She lay her cheek on his sport shirt. She could feel the warmth of his chest and his overpowering strength. It filled her with the security only he could give. She was overcome, shuddering at the pleasure of having him close.

Her head raised, shimmering gray eyes surveying his face bent to scrutinize hers with equal concentration.

"I don't have any makeup on, my hair's terribly mussed, I'm barefoot, and you should have called," she spoke feelingly in one long rambling outburst. For a long time she could only look at him.

She tensed as his hands sought her face. He cupped it tenderly, his thumbs raising her chin upward, long hard fingers buried in the heavy weight of her hair. His thumbs moved deliberately, stroking her lips, watching entranced as her mouth softened, then parted in preparation to receive his.

"Such warm, sweet passion awaits me. Curved so beautifully to accept our first intimate exchange today."

He exuded leashed virility, drawing her slender body the length of his. The instant their mouths touched she was entirely transformed. Altered from a young woman with normal feelings to a woman who could never get enough of the man she loved. She answered his hunger, straining toward him, full breasts crushed to his chest, hips moving back and forth seductively. She felt devoured. His lips transmitted his hunger, moving over hers until she thought she'd collapse if he didn't deepen the kiss.

Aware of her ability to incite him equally, she took the initiative. She let her tongue enter his mouth, seeking his tongue as he had sought hers in the past. At the first touch he moaned, returning ravenously to explore the sweet warmth offered without restrictions. His kiss was so perfect, she wondered how the ultimate act of love would compare. Could anything create more devastation than what she was experiencing?

She cried out, trying desperately to stop the chaos heightened by their days apart. Released from his hold, she burrowed her flushed cheeks against the comfort of his heaving chest, breathing in the intoxicating scent of his body. His hands had lowered, running up and down her spine, always giving her pleasure while keeping her close. She could never believe the tingling awareness he engendered.

"I love you, Brett," she admitted fervently. "I love you so much, I don't think I can bear another week being apart."

Moving for the first time since Honey answered the door, Brett easily guided her into the living room, kicking the door shut with one elegantly clad foot. Her response had been astonishing.

"Now, that's the kind of welcome that brings a man eagerly home at night." He kissed the side of her forehead, one hand still holding her waist while she regained self-possession. She was so volatile it always took her a few moments to calm down. He dared not imagine her response when he made love to her. It was nearly impossible to control his urge to possess her, he had fantasized about it so long.

"Did you really miss me, sweetheart?" He scanned her face, his glance filled with loving indulgence.

"Every minute," she whispered honestly, the dimple forming deeply at the first hint of her lovely smile.

"That's good, as I distinctly recall you hung up the phone on me for the second time last Monday." Hugging her squirming body to him, he inhaled, his nostrils filled with the spicy fragrance of cinnamon and nutmeg. "What smells so delicious?" He lowered his head, sniffing along her brow. "Besides you, that is?"

"Your cake."

"My cake? How could it be mine, since you didn't even know I was coming over today?"

"It didn't make any difference. I still baked it for you." She drew away from his hold, walking before him toward the kitchen. "Come see it. If you promise to forget my hanging up the phone, I'll cut you the first slice."

"Get a move on, woman," he prompted. "I'm a hungry man."

She swept forward daintily, laughing at his boyish look of impatience for home-baked cake.

"My God, you've taken the place over completely," he exclaimed, scanning the room in disbelief. "I see woman stuff everywhere."

"Do you like everything?" she asked eagerly, anxious to show him around. Following his glance, she observed him scrutinize the huge potted plant at the end of the couch. "That came from work. I asked my supervisor if a salesman I met at the diner could come by twice a month. Everyone interested takes time off to make a selection. Quite reasonable too."

"Don't say any more, Honey. Each time I talk with you, you're involved in a new scheme to cheat your boss," he chided, openly vexed.

Honey suppressed a lengthy explanation. It seemed ludicrous that Brett should think she was taking advantage of her employer. The poor salesman had a large family to support and needed money to pay hospital bills for his aged mother. At least that's what he had told her, admitting reluctantly he was an incorrigible flirt.

"Don't worry about it," she said evenly, walking into the kitchen.

Brett stood in the doorway, contemplating the many changes. Every touch added a bit more of Honey's own vibrant personality. Each new item pleased his eye, making his apartment look like a real home. She had added a warmth that the functional rooms had never had.

"Coffee or milk?" She reached for a plate, removed a knife and fork from the drawer, and carried them to the table.

"Coffee," he responded, enjoying the sight of her relaxed manner in his apartment. "Black," he added, anticipating her next question.

With a dimpled smile she handed him a cup of coffee before slicing a large wedge of cake. He picked up the fork, pierced the moist cake, making certain it had ample frosting, then raised it to his open mouth. His eyes shone, filled with devilry while he chewed. He took another bite, deliberately making her wait for his praise.

Aware of Brett's intent, Honey turned her back on him, taking another cup down for her own coffee. She moved to the booth, scooting in beside his Calvin Klein-clad hips. She couldn't help but compare how much better they looked on Brett than they did Danny.

"Brett Weston!" Honey stormed, unable to hold her tongue.

"It's delicious, you impatient witch," he responded quickly. "You're getting harder to resist all the time. It's a good thing I'm a wary man or you'd probably seduce me today. I've heard the way to a man's heart is through his stomach."

He drank the last drop of coffee, scraped a scoop of frosting off the edge of his plate, stole a walnut half from the cake, rose nimbly, and patted his flat stomach.

"As you can see by my lean frame, I've avoided womanly wiles and home cooking with extreme cunning and shrewd ingenuity for thirty-four years!"

"How disillusioning," Honey scoffed. "I presumed your lack of avoirdupois was from chasing after, not running from, women."

She slid from the booth, placed both hands on her hips, and scrutinized him with lazy insolence. "And all the time I thought you were a superstud."

With a sudden burst of speed she fled into the living room, barely able to avoid Brett's outstretched arms as he unexpectedly lunged forward in pursuit.

Unable to quell her laughter, Honey collapsed in his sinewy arms. Braced within his hold, she stared, head thrown back, eyes shimmering with mischief.

Both hands clasped behind her back, he growled deep in his throat, lips thinned with the pretense of being angered.

"Superstud huh?" His fingers spread, leisurely running up her spine, exploring the delightful feminine smoothness. Reaching the middle of her back, his hand moved back and forth, one eyebrow raised in question. "You're really asking for me to prove my worth today, aren't you, woman?" His hands swept under her shirt to caress her warm skin.

Honey squirmed, enjoying the touch of his muscled length touching her bare limbs. "I asked for nothing," she told him curiously, her fingers rubbing his waist in a vain attempt to ignore his hands' journey.

"Nothing but trouble," he shot back, one palm running around the side to cup a full breast. "I know enough about women to realize you forgot to dress in all your underwear."

"One little piece of lace," she whispered, her voice breaking as his thumb stroked the nipple into a taut bud. She could feel her stomach lurch as his fingers squeezed tenderly, the taunting thumb continuing its insidious rubbing. She should have realized he would notice there was no bra beneath the tight material of her T-shirt.

"An important piece of protection between your provocative shirt and my bare hand, which I noticed the moment you flung open your front door."

"You...you did?" she questioned breathlessly, unable to tear her glance away as he studied her expressive face.

Tenderly he lifted each plump breast, cupping them alternately in the trembling warmth of his palm while his thumbs stroked back and forth, manipulating the rosy soft tips to keep them sensuously erect.

"God, yes, I did," he groaned. "You have such beautiful breasts."

He withdrew abruptly, furious with himself. He had vowed to keep his hands off her, yet within fifteen minutes he had fondled her naked breasts—had ached to take them into the warmth of his mouth.

Damn it to hell! He shuddered, miserable with the effort of trying to restrain his aroused manhood. It seemed all he had to do was think of her and his body betrayed him, straining against the tautened cloth of his slacks.

Honey moved shakily, adjusting her shirt, then reaching down in a vain attempt to pull the ragged edges of her shorts over the swell of her bottom. Brett offered no reason for his withdrawal or week's absence. Filled with a momentary feeling of insecurity, she was afraid to question his whereabouts, concerned his answers might spoil the tranquil mood of their afternoon. Possibly later, she thought, walking forward.

She sat down on the couch, her eyes on Brett as he turned once more to face her before settling into the corner beside her, his right arm snaking out to draw her next to his side.

"Do you mind if I watch the Los Angeles Dodgers play the San Diego Padres this afternoon?" He had had no intention of watching the game, but baseball seemed as good a way as any to tamp the tension between them while enjoying her company. He hadn't even intended on seeing her, knowing he was playing with dynamite to do so. He had missed her so much, it had been impossible to keep away. He had even driven up and down the coast for hours before speeding back to see her.

He reached for the remote control unit on the end table, asking once again if she minded. "Well?"

"Of course not," Honey answered truthfully. "My father liked baseball and I always watched the games with him."

Brett switched on the TV set, stretched his broad frame comfortably into the cushions, kicked off his casual loafers, and placed both stocking-clad feet on the coffee table, having to shove several magazines aside to do so. He was drawn, curious to read the titles. *Ms.* Magazine. *Vogue. Cosmopolitan.* All women's magazines and apparently well read, noticing a turned-back page in *Ms.* marking where she had left a story.

Honey tucked her legs beneath her, snuggling into the curve of his arm, her tousled head cradled against his chest. She felt like purring, it was so wonderful having him with her. His thumb unconsciously stroked her shoulder, then stopped, the tanned fingers moving to her nape to rub and twine through the unruly tendrils of hair.

Reaching over, Brett kissed her on the forehead. "You really do like the game, don't you, Honey?"

She raised her head, a vivid smile bringing the elusive dimple into sudden life. "Naturally! I don't lie...er, not often anyway." A soft flush touched her creamy cheeks, remembering the vast number of untruths she had told since moving to Long Beach. Before he had time to refute her statement, she said gaily, "I forgot. I have to make a phone call."

Starting to get up, Honey was pulled backward, held close to Brett's side. He pushed the mute button on the remote control unit to shut off the sound of the TV, reached for the phone resting on the side table, and placed it on her lap.

About to object to his high-handed attitude, she frowned in censure, then dialed without comment. She was well aware he was unashamedly going to listen to her conversation while pretending interest in the ball game.

Brett leaned forward, grabbed a toffee candy from the cut-glass dish next to his feet, unwrapped it, and chewed thoughtfully. He caught on immediately, unbelieving at what Honey was up to, more obvious with each sweet-spoken word.

"Bernard? This is Honey. I talked with Aunt Gladys and your appointment is for two o'clock. I forgot to call you earlier, so you'll have to rush to get there on time."

Honey turned her shoulder away from Brett, annoyed by his raised eyebrow and the sideways shaking of his head. It was none of his business what she arranged for his friend's apartment manager.

"Don't worry about closing the manager's office. The owner won't even know you've been away."

Brett's muttered obscenity was totally out of line, Honey thought. She turned to face him, her chin raised defiantly, unconcerned now that he might understand what she was up to. It certainly wouldn't be of any significance to him.

"Don't forget to wear that nice powder-blue suit you had on the other night." Her voice softened, tender with the thought of how happy Bernard would be. "The color enhances your blue eyes and makes you look very handsome. Tell Aunt Gladys hello and don't forget to call me tonight when you return. I'll be anxious to find out if you found any ladies that made your heart beat faster."

Brett deliberated, wondering how on earth he had managed to conceal his astonishment at Honey's words. It was impossible to think she had talked old Bryson into going to his aunt's in hopes of finding a mate. His former manager had been depressed, unable to adjust when his wife died. He'd wanted to raise his pension but had been begged to return to the job he'd retired from eight years earlier. Brett had agreed, making certain he had plenty of help and didn't overdo. The last thing the old man seemed to want was another woman.

Handing the phone back to Brett, Honey explained matter-of-factly, thinking it best to ignore his sudden ill humor.

"That was Bernard."

"Bernard?"

"The apartment manager," she returned defensively. "I sensed at our first meeting he was lonely and missing the attentions of a woman. It took me a week but I finally talked him into seeing sweet little Aunt Gladys. I made him an appointment today before he could change his mind."

A wistful look changed her eyes to gentle dove gray and

shaped her mouth to a sensuous fineness. "Poor Bernard.
Can you imagine, Brett, he was afraid to leave the building
since it isn't his day off? I soon assured him it would be
okay. There's never any business on Saturday afternoon
anyway." She shot Brett a sidelong glance through heavy
lashes. "At least I don't think there is."

Brett stretched, his long arms extended overhead before lowering to clasp her naked thigh in one tanned hand.
"My God, I can't believe you, Honey," he complained,
trying to keep his mind off the silken skin beneath his
wandering fingers.

"How?" Her voice came out in a breathless murmur.
His touch had ignited her need for closer contact. "Er . . .
in . . . what way?"

"Your taking over everyone's life you meet. Do you
always manage to convince people it's okay to leave their
jobs on your assurance alone?" She looked like an impudent angel and all the time created havoc like the devil's
own advocate.

Honey placed her hand over Brett's, uncertain whether
she wanted to stop his fingers wandering up her thighs or
guide them to greater exploration.

Brett knew Honey had forgotten his question. Forcing
himself to keep his own desires under control, he gripped
her thigh to stop her movements.

"Anything besides cake left to feed a starving man?"
Her hand was trailing inquisitively up his leg. If it got any
closer to his pocket, she'd realize how desperate he was
for physical release. "Cat got your tongue?" he prompted, breaking the long silence.

"No," she answered abstractedly, trying hard to remember if she had put Beauty out when she first got up.
Her brows puckered. "I haven't forgotten any of your
leading questions. You sounded so much like a grumpy
boss, I thought it unnecessary to comment on my supposed meddling."

"Supposed meddling?" He reached down to place a
hard kiss on her upraised lips, both hands having a time
holding her squirming body still. "You're a full-time men-

ace!'' His breath wafted across her forehead as she twisted to get away.

Springing up, she stood alongside the couch, hands raised each side of her rounded hips provocatively. ''Just for that derogatory and totally false comment I'll make the lunch, but you have to do the clean-up chores.''

She swept into the kitchen, bright auburn curls bouncing on her shoulders. One quick peek over her shoulder showed him staring boldly, both hands linked behind his neck.

Brett watched her long shapely legs and rounded bottom with narrowed eyes. He could feel his stomach muscles clench with hunger. Hunger for his woman, not for food, he grumbled. He berated himself angrily for having the lack of control of an overzealous teenager.

Honey stood in the kitchen, both hands clenching the rounded edge of the counter. She took several deep breaths, needing a few moments to compose herself before fixing their lunch. Brett had created havoc to her self-possession from the moment he stormed into her life and drew her into his arms for his first heart-stopping kiss.

Dreamy thoughts of a blissful future swam through her head as she prepared a lunch tray. The tranquil silence was dispelled the moment she heard his loud roar.

''Honey! Get the hell in here immediately!'' Brett reiterated fully.

Her heart lurched, the sandwiches forgotten during her rush into the dining room. ''What's the matter?'' Her eyes widened, pursed mouth twitching as she tried to suppress the desire to laugh out loud.

''This hideous feline is the matter!'' Brett's lips were compressed. He looked furious, his glowering face filled with chagrin as Beauty wound her unsightly body around his nape, her face nuzzling into his neck with complete disregard for the owner's distaste.

Honey walked forward, trying vainly to control her sense of humor. Brett looked so funny, his back stiff, proud head held away from the cat's persistent affection. Obviously she had failed to put her out.

One large tanned hand reached up, gripping Beauty's back, the other cupping her weight with the hind legs resting on his palm. He looked at the cat with aversion, annoyed he was being studied as intently by its yellow eyes as it was by his darkened green gaze.

"This is the ugliest cat I've ever seen," he complained in horror, frowning as it burrowed its head against his thumb. "What's the thing's name?" He lowered it to his lap, even more disconcerted when it turned around several times before settling comfortably.

"Beauty," Honey said sweetly, her voice filled with mocking compliance.

"You're kidding? This is the most revolting feline created, with its chewed ears, lopped-off tail, skinny frame, and fat gut."

Honey walked forward, bending to remove Beauty from Brett's lap. With both hands cradling the cat's body gently, she pulled, stopped by his sudden yell as ten claws sank through brown trouser legs into the tanned skin beneath. Yellow eyes glared balefully upward, having decided her mistress's visitor was to her liking and wanting to stay put.

Brett removed it without a qualm, scolding sharply when it batted a widespread paw at his taut wrist. He set it on the rug, looking at the hairs on his slacks with disgust.

"The damned thing's shed all over my slacks too! Do you have a brush?" He stood, trying ineffectively to remove the numerous multicolored hairs from his expensive slacks. When Honey returned with a small clothes brush, he took it, sweeping across his pants in swift, angry strokes.

"I suppose harboring this abhorrent creature in a pet-prohibited apartment complex is your idea too, and what the owner doesn't know won't hurt him?"

"Yes and yes," Honey declared, answering both questions at once. A grin tilted the corner of her mouth, the dimple deep in one cheek. Beauty was busy rubbing against Brett's legs, twining her body in and out, shedding hairs faster on the bottom of his pants legs than he could brush them off.

"This thing's determined to shed on my new slacks."

He bent down, picked up the cat, and stomped to the front door, jerked it open, strode to the elevator, the cat still held in his firm grip, and disappeared as the doors slid shut.

Within moments Brett returned, slapping his palms together as if one problem was solved. He kicked the door shut, storming forward to loom over Honey, annoyed further by the devilish lights dancing in her expressive eyes and the saucy tilt of her shapely chin.

The moment was static. She watched him swallow, fascinated by the Adam's apple in his lean throat as it moved up and down. He was furious at her defiance of a few minor rules. She waited for his denunciation, her head thrown back to meet his eyes squarely.

"Honey Bowman, you're a peril to all mankind! Your philosophy could destroy the entire world given enough time. It's certainly wreaked upheaval with my peaceful existence since our meeting."

"Ready for lunch?" She decided it best to ignore his tirade.

"Yes, as soon as I wash off the cat hairs." He headed toward the bathroom, shouting over his shoulder, "Can you believe that fur-shedding catastrophe had the gall to purr during the elevator ride and trip through the lobby?"

"Apparently anything female finds it hard to resist your manly charms." Honey giggled, rushing into the kitchen to rescue their lunch and get Brett a cold can of beer from the refrigerator. His fury was met with a contented smile, knowing how enjoyable it was to cajole him into a loving mood.

She entered the front room as he sat down on the couch. Placing the heavily laden tray on the coffee table, she noticed with satisfaction how his eyes scanned the plates with visible pleasure.

Refusing the glass she set alongside the tall can of beer, he raised it to his lips, taking a long satisfying swallow before picking up his plate. Thin-sliced corned beef was piled in a heaping mound between soft rye bread spread with mayonnaise and dark horseradish-mustard. A serving of homemade potato salad, mammoth black olives, and kosher pickle slices put any deli lunch to shame. A shallow wooden bowl holding salty pretzel sticks completed his meal.

Brett reached up, drawing Honey down beside him. Any pretense at anger was gone as he placed a kiss of appreciation on her cheek. "All's temporarily forgiven with this delicious lunch."

"Hmmpf!" she responded, wiping with the back of her hand to dry the sticky dampness. "How typically male you sound."

Her eyes filled with tenderness, locking with his in a silent moment of deep communication—a mute sharing of intense harmony.

"Better turn the TV back on, Brett. I think we missed the sound of the last few innings." Honey picked up her own plate, just picking at the food. Having him beside her was the only sustenance she needed.

With the plates setting on their laps, they watched the ending of the game in playful discord. Honey rooted loudly for her home team when they scored and disagreed with the umpire when they didn't. Brett, less vocal, still managed to convey he was equally interested in seeing the L.A. team win.

Content in Brett's company, Honey scanned his appealing features through the heavy fringe of lashes shadowing her eyes. He looked breathtaking in brown slacks and beige knit pullover. Her eyes lingered, taken by the sinewy bronze muscles of his arms, visible below the casual short-sleeved shirt.

Turning suddenly, he caught her look and held it. His vivid eyes narrowed, hiding his erotic thoughts to carry her into the bedroom. The phone ringing interrupted the heightened tension. One dark brow lifted, raised in query.

"You'd better answer it," Brett burst out grimly. "If it's one of those young, idiotic statisticians you work with, tell him to butt out permanently!"

Smiling at his jealous command, Honey lifted the receiver, the phone cord stretched across Brett's lap as he hurriedly took their plates and placed them on the tray.

He settled back, handing the phone to Honey, curious

to see who was calling her now. If this kept up, she'd need an answering service.

Speaking with exaggerated cheerfulness, Honey responded. She put her hand over the mouthpiece, whispering to Brett, "It's Bernard calling to tell me about his visit to Happy Hearts. Relax. I'll only be a minute or two."

"Excuse me, Bernard. I have company. No, don't hang up. He's not important."

"What do you mean I'm not important?" Brett made no attempt to lower his voice, jealous of all the intrusions during his visit. He returned Honey's glare, leaning back with arms crossed behind his neck to listen. It was hard to keep from laughing at Honey's attempt to matchmake. She'd get her comeuppance this time. Old Bryson was happier now than he'd ever been during his forty nagging years of marriage.

"I'm anxious to hear about your visit with Aunt Gladys." Her voice was soft and sweet without the slightest hint of her spitfire temper.

Brett couldn't believe it. Was he the only one who received the edge of her sharp little tongue? The only one she battled with?

"Of course there won't be any problems if you take the night off," Honey assured him. "Everything here ran so smoothly, your boss will never dream you were away."

Slipping beneath the strained phone cord, Brett stood up. He prowled around the living room, listening to the pleasing tones of Honey's lilting voice telling his manager to forget his job. Waiting impatiently for her to complete the call, he paced restlessly. Relieved to hear the lengthy conversation come to an end, he turned to face her. Not giving her time to comment, he blurted out grimly, "What the hell's with you anyway? Everyone you meet seems compelled to devote their life to looking at you, visiting you in person, or talking with you on the telephone!" His eyes pinned her, not surprised when her chin began to rise with a beginning retort. "The worst part of it is," he continued, his voice level despite his annoyance, "they feel no remorse at all taking your ill-given advice."

"Quit complaining, Brett," Honey admonished him,

her voice filled with mounting excitement. "I want to tell you what Bernard said. Would you believe he thinks he's in love already?"

"He's what? That must have shocked Aunt Gladys right off her velvet chair!"

"I guess it must have. That's who he's in love with. He told me he took one look at her and that was it. He thinks she's a fine figure of a woman. Even told her not to bother showing him any of her single ladies, as it would only waste her time and at their ages each day was precious."

Smiling wistfully, Honey raised shiny eyes to look at Brett, delighted with the unexpectedness of Bernard's disclosure. She sighed softly, a dreamy expression changing her features to tender anticipation.

"Isn't that wonderful?"

"No!"

"Why not, for pity's sake?" she scolded, piqued by his behavior.

Brett loomed over her, hands raised to his masculine hips, his voice filled with smug confidence. "He won't have a chance with Aunt Gladys. She's never dated a single man in her entire life and will run him off before he knows what hit him."

"You're really in for a surprise, then, Brett," Honey taunted impishly. "You're also a poor judge of character." Her delighted expression radiated confidence as she explained quickly. "Aunt Gladys closed her office and is now dining with Bernard at a local club. Bernard excused himself to call me from the lobby instead of waiting until he got home, he was so excited. In fact, he said by the end of their evening he'll have her convinced that he's the only man she'll ever want."

"The apartment manager and Aunt Gladys?" he scoffed in disbelief.

"Yes! He also confessed he's going to see she buys some new younger-styled dresses and a different perfume. He told her lavender toilet water was for old people."

"My God! This was all your idea too. I can't believe the constant turmoil that surrounds you." His brows drew together in contemplation. "Besides, I like the smell of lavender," he added, stunned at the thought of his aunt going on a date.

He paced the floor, trying to imagine his aged aunt involved romantically after decades of arranging love matches for others. It was impossible. Honey had to be mistaken. A sudden thought crossed his mind.

"Doesn't he realize he's dating a seventy-five-year-old virgin?"

"Probably not, though I think it's wonderful she's having a fling at last," she pointed out. "They're perfectly capable of enjoying an active sexual love affair. Men and women are never too old for romance."

Brett's attitude surprised her. He seemed unusually bothered.

"As Bernard said when we discussed age last week, he'd rather be over the hill than under it. He also recounted it's better to use it than lose it." She chuckled, her eyes alight with amusement.

Brett slapped his forehead in chagrin. "My gosh, the old lecher's a comedian too! I just can't believe Aunt Gladys would go out with him, much less close her marriage bureau for the afternoon."

Shrugging his wide shoulders, he added contritely, "Well, at least he can't get her pregnant."

"Stop it, Brett. You're acting horribly," Honey scolded adamantly.

Unconcerned, he retorted with emphasis, "Who'd want a seventy-five-year-old virgin anyway?"

"You would, if you were seventy-three!" Honey shot back, a touch of laughter lingering in the room.

"You're right, sweetheart." Brett smiled, acknowledging that Honey could be right if she was the one seventy-five and he Bryson's age.

"Well, I for one think it's fantastic news and I'm going to phone her later and tell her so. I might even help her pick out a new wardrobe." She looked thoughtful, thinking how she could advise Aunt Gladys.

Unaware of Brett's intent gaze, he stood watching her with total skepticism. Her stunning announcement about his spinster aunt was a shock he would never forget.

Honey stood up, walking to Brett with a wide smile, heady with the dramatic success of her first matchmaking attempt.

Brett pulled her into his arms, raised her chin, and dropped a firm kiss on her parted lips. "You pack a lot of power in your little body. Unfortunately, you also create unlimited devastation with your overactive scheming brain."

Pulling her face to his chest, he cradled her close, stroking her hair with tender indulgence. "I don't want to hear another word about Aunt Gladys and Bryson." Trailing kisses across her forehead and down to one dainty ear, he whispered, "I have a present for you."

"For me?" she asked, uncaring of anything but his hands plying their magic up and down her sensitive spine.

"For you, if you promise me one thing." His breath was warm on her neck as he nuzzled beneath her lustrous waves.

"What...?" Her voice trailed off, unable to think held so close to his firm chest.

"That you won't question my motives and accept it graciously." He tipped her chin up, kissed her, then drew away. "It's important to me you have this. Do you promise?" He eased her away, sat on the edge of the couch, and beckoned her closer.

Intrigued, Honey nodded her head in agreement. She moved forward, stopping between Brett's knees. She took a small flat box he removed from his hip pocket, opening it to find a single gold chain. Perplexed, she looked at him, stating curiously, "I don't understand. You already gave me three necklaces."

"No questions, remember?" he reminded her in a husky voice, his eyes raising to pin hers with commanding solicitude. "Give me this chain and I'll show you how it differs from the others."

She handed it to him and her breath caught when he reached for the tail of her T-shirt and tugged it away from her body.

He looked upward, catching her startled gaze. He

grinned, amused by her wary look. "You're safe, darling. I have no intention of seducing you tonight." Eyes lowering, he lazily scanned her shirt's bold lettering.

Releasing her breath, Honey smiled back. "I didn't know what your intentions were." His actions were a continuous puzzle, it seemed.

"Hold your T-shirt up," he told her, his eyes lingering on the creamy expanse of rib cage exposed.

Honey bunched the material beneath the swell of her breasts, obeying without question.

"Now hold still while I unfasten your jeans."

"What . . . what for?"

"You'll see, love," he informed her in a slow, deeply sensual statement. He unsnapped the waistband of her tight cut-offs, his hands trembling at the contact with her soft abdomen.

Honey's stomach lurched, quivering at the touch of Brett's fingers as he took the gold chain and fastened it around her waist. Bringing the ends together, he clamped them shut as she arched her back in a vain attempt to lean away from the torment of his gentle caressing touch.

Lowering his head, his breath was warm on her skin, his tongue moist when he probed her navel before placing a lingering kiss across her soft belly. His hands left her waist to tug on the front zipper. He wanted no barriers between his mouth and her abdomen.

Honey clasped Brett's shoulders. She could feel his touch from her fingertips to the end of her bare toes. His gold waist chain was the most sensual gift she had ever received. She reveled in the symbolism of being bound to him and yearned to ask when he would divulge his reasons for giving it to her. For now, it was enough to know it was important to him she wear it.

She leaned into him, yielding to the tempting contact when his face moved lower, widespread fingers sliding down to cup her shapely bottom. He slipped beneath the wispy lace of her bikini panties, uncaring her denim shorts hung precariously. Trailing a series of wet kisses across her belly, he lingered to follow the path of his gold chain encircling her narrow waist.

Honey clung to his head, holding him close. She knew he could feel the involuntary clenching of her stomach muscles. Her hands slid to his broad shoulders, aware his muscles contracted as she kneaded the hardened flesh unconsciously.

When she thought she'd collapse, one bold hand moved forward, probing errantly. Slowly regaining her senses, she tried but couldn't force herself to pull away.

Brett stretched the elastic to lower the last barrier between his mouth and her untouched femininity. The overpowering need to worship her with his mouth vanquished his former decision to tamp the irresistible appeal of her seductiveness. Before he could expose her totally, her voice warned, the throaty murmur more like a purr than a threat.

"If you go any lower, you'd better be prepared to buy me a wedding ring too."

Brett raised his face, his eyes alight with tenderness. The last thing he had expected was an ultimatum. She would never cease to amaze him. He cradled her close, whispering with barely concealed humor, "Won't an engagement ring do?" His lips pressed intimately lower, seeking and finding their goal for a brief span of pleasure so arousing, a film of perspiration covered his heaving shoulders.

"Not a make-believe one," she moaned.

He nibbled her waist gently, licked the rounded curve of each hip, and placed lingering kisses into her navel. His hands returned, fingers widespread to curve around her shapely bottom. He wanted to explore her body thoroughly, to show her the multitude of ways possible to give her fulfillment.

"Okay, my love," he growled against her belly, his lips reluctantly trailing upward. "If I can't continue south, I'll detour north."

Honey squirmed, held between his knees while his insistent fingers kneaded the soft flesh below her hips. "You're...you're crazy," she husked, straining backward.

"Lean forward, sweetheart," Brett urged, his mouth

above her gold waist chain, working upward across the underside of her breasts. With lazy precision he erotically kissed the straining curves, letting his tongue lick the enticing fullness before pressing his opened mouth over the tip to draw the tautened nipples inward with deep sucking motions. He couldn't get enough of her. He wanted to devour every inch of her.

Before Honey's knees buckled, Brett pulled her down, his hips pressing hers deep into the soft cushions of the couch. She stared mutely, squirming in a vain attempt to ease out from under him.

With both elbows bracing his weight above her, he scowled, pretending anger. "Lie still." His growling order was lessened by the series of soft kisses on her cheeks and nose.

Oh, Lord, she cried inwardly. It was such unbelievable sexual torture when his muscled thigh moved against her. The erotic pressure when she clenched her limbs tight against his brought a cry of delight from her throat, enhanced further when she felt his mouth surround the erect tip of her exposed breast.

Honey shuddered, her entire body on fire for the man above her. Without needing to ask, Brett knew how to impart maximum pleasure. Every sensitive area of her upper body was now under siege from his roving mouth and gently kneading fingers. The moist warmth of his tongue licking the curve of her breast, the leisurely sucking motions that were followed by flicking vibrations, spread a flood of urgency downward.

Drawing forth with his mouth, the sensual assault continued. The cautious tugging bites with his teeth on her erect, tingling nipples elicited a frank gasp of unbearable pleasure from the depth of her throat.

"Stop! Oh, Brett. I—I—!" Honey couldn't speak. She was too aroused and inherently aware she couldn't handle any further lovemaking. She felt disoriented, as if her mind had fled her body, leaving nothing behind but nerve endings, each suffused with yearning for satisfaction. Would it always be like this when he touched her?

"So soon?" Brett whispered on her breast, overcome

with fragrance exclusively hers. Her own fastidiously
clean aroma was more heady than the finest perfume. He
could feel her shudder, watching remorsefully when her
dreamy eyes began to shimmer with unshed tears.

Pulling abruptly away, he brought her up with him, his
arms cradling her across his chest. His hands stroked her
back in an attempt to undo the havoc of his lovemaking.
He felt cruel. With his experience he should never have
instigated such lustful hunger.

"I'm sorry, darling." His voice was deep and sensual,
drawn out with the depth of his bitter remonstration.
"Not sorry for the pleasure you brought me but apologetic
for any uneasiness you experienced."

Honey's voice was muffled, her honest admission tearing him apart.

"You never need to apologize for making love to me,
Brett. You know I love you." Her slender hand stroked his
arm, delighting in the abrasiveness of the dark hair around
his heavy gold watchband.

Brett's breath was warm on her skin, the gentle kiss on
her forehead a silent apology for his actions. He pressed
her flushed cheeks onto his chest, his hands stroking her
dampened curls with soothing strokes. He waited calmly.
Her breathing slowed gradually, as delayed in subsiding as
his tautened body was to return to normal.

"I'm going to need a lifetime's convincing, you know?"
Even that wouldn't be enough, he reflected silently.

Honey raised her face, her mouth agonizingly close to
his lips. She scanned his features, a hand raising to let her
index finger run over the taut planes of his face. When it
came near his lips, she stopped, lingering to outline their
sensuous shape.

"One day at a time, hopefully," she suggested, still
breathless from his touch. "Right now, I think we'd better
turn on the TV. Maybe there's a double-header today."

"TV won't help now, Honey. The safest thing is for me
to go home."

Brett stood up, drawing her to her feet alongside him.
He smoothed his knit shirt around his hips. He doubted if
Honey was aware her hands had clenched his back, trailed

to his nape, and finally cradled his head to her body with surprising strength in their slender grip.

One arm embraced her while they walked to the door. Turned into his hold, he cupped her face, placing a teasing kiss on the end of her straight little nose. "Good night, Honey, and sweet dreams." Without thought, his hand reached out to fondle the gold band around her waist.

His hand dropped from her side, lifted to wipe a shimmering teardrop from each cheek, raised her chin to meet his lips, and bent to touch her mouth in a caress so reverent, it shook her to the depth of her soul. Without saying a word to break the spell of love radiating between them, he turned, shutting the door firmly behind him.

Honey staggered to the couch, sinking weakly onto the deep cushions still indented from the weight of Brett's body. His tantalizing clean smell clung to the material, as familiar now as if they had been lovers for years. She buried her face in the corner where his head had lain, unashamed that tears trickled down her cheeks. The trauma of his emotional visit hovered in the silence of the room.

Raising herself from the stupor of her thoughts, she went to the bedroom. A sharp tug pulled the T-shirt over her head. She shrugged off her jeans and underpants and headed for the full-length bathroom mirror.

She stared at her body critically. The gold chain hung freely around her slender waist, drawing attention to her curving hips and flat abdomen. Her stomach muscles clenched remembering his probing tongue.

Exacting eyes raised to the rounded swell of her breasts. With the memory of his mouth coaxing urgently, savoring as a gourmet might over and over, it brought each sensation to life, instantly hardening the rose-colored tips to pulsating erectness.

"Brett Weston, I love you!"

Overcome with emotion, she prepared for bed, her rapturous cry breaking the silence of the empty rooms.

Chapter Ten

Propped up against the headboard, Honey placed a small sliver of rye bread crust on the tray beside her. She sat cross-legged on the satin sheets, finishing the last of her leftover lunch. It tasted much better not having Brett's distracting presence beside her. With a firm tug she tried vainly to pull her short nightie over her legs, giving up in disgust when the soft material refused to stay below the top of her thighs.

Engrossed in an extensive, well-written survey of women's sexual fantasies, Honey chuckled out loud. It appeared that most women with any imagination at all envisioned an ardent male the image of Brett.

"My gosh!" she burst out. She didn't have any idea he was *that* much more amorous than the average man. It seemed unlikely he would ever be satisfied making love five or six times a month.

The phone rang, disrupting her concentration. She leaned over, picking up the receiver. A flush tinged her cheeks when she heard the deep sensual tone of Brett's voice.

"You're terrible, Brett," Honey scolded sharply.

"Now what have I done?" he shot back, wondering what had happened.

"According to the story I'm reading, everything," she teased, her voice filled with laughter. "And often!"

"What the hell are you talking about, woman?"

"The sex survey I'm reading. Did you know that some men only have sex once or twice a year?"

"I'd heard that. Did they happen to mention how many

times a year those men's partners indulged in the act? That would probably be even more enlightening," he chided with disgust, not the least interested in some female author's viewpoint of a male's libido.

"No, but I haven't finished the article," Honey told him seriously. She was enjoying the story despite his obvious derision.

"Well, don't bother. You're not ready yet to start keeping score. That comes *after* you've joined the realm of experience. At this point you're not qualified to explain the facts of life to the average fourteen-year-old."

"Hush! I'm not that naive." She pouted, remembering their interlude that afternoon. "Especially after today."

"Hell, I barely got to first base. The Dodgers scored more than I did and they lost the game!"

"Why did you phone me, Brett?" It was definitely time to change the subject. She was still shaken by his sensual onslaught earlier.

"To thank you for the delicious lunch and to tell you to go to your front door at nine o'clock sharp." He glanced at his watch. "That will be in exactly ten minutes time."

"Why?"

"You'll see. Just do as I say," he told her, relaxing in his office. The vast building had an intriguing silence with he and the security guards the only ones present. He knew it was the one time he could get through his backlog of work uninterrupted.

"By the way, in case your article fails to mention it, an ice-cold shower or a couple hours of racquetball helps."

A wide smile of deep satisfaction changed his expression to one of smug arrogance. He had finally managed to have the last word, hanging up on her stunned gasp at his blatant remark. He could picture her reading the study, comparing his insatiability with other men and not realizing she had to share the blame with her challenging personality and intensifying uninhibited response.

Honey slammed the receiver on the hook, annoyed Brett had been faster. She had intended to hang up on him for the third time. She wasn't so unsophisticated she didn't know what his suggestion was about.

Shrugging into her worn robe on the foot of the bed, she walked barefoot into the living room. She was five minutes early but too inquisitive to wait until nine. She opened the door, peering around the edge.

A large man was walking toward her, his long arms literally filled with a conglomeration of articles. Following at his heels, tail straight up, was Beauty. When the man neared the partially opened door, the elusive cat streaked through, hiding behind the couch.

Honey eased the door shut, knowing she hadn't been observed. When she was certain he had left, she opened the door, noticing Beauty sneak out, ready to retire for the night on her favorite pillow.

"You terrible cat." Honey laughed, enjoying its soft body rubbing her bare ankles. "Someday you're going to sneak into an elevator stopping at the wrong floor. Then what will you do, Beauty?" She reached a hand down to stroke its arched back affectionately while curiously scanning the things set before her door.

A cumbersome scratching post with an egg-shaped bed on the top, covered in plush burgundy carpeting, stood on its wide base. Four pints of fresh cream. Where had Brett found this stuff at night? she wondered. A case of the most expensive cat food. Litter box, Kitty Litter, flea collar, hairbrushes in assorted size and types. Apparently he didn't want cat hairs on his elegant clothes again. She laughed. Even a stuffed toy rat with a long tail.

"Look here, Beauty. All this is for you. Can you imagine?" she told the cat who was busily investigating the bottles of cream. "After the horrible names he called you, he spoils you like a pedigreed Persian."

Honey dragged everything in, setting the scratching post in the corner of the living room. It looked horrible, but she didn't care to carry it around the vast apartment, looking for an out-of-the-way corner.

Everything but the cream was placed in the service porch. She poured some rich fluid into a cat dish, laughing as Beauty lapped it up with greedy licks, getting it all over her whiskers. She looked over the canned food, deciding to open tuna and egg combination.

Beauty sniffed as her mistress emptied the can in her new dish. She walked away, her head raised in disdain, while Honey scolded her haughty behavior.

Returning to the living room, Honey watched the cat climb into the egg-shaped bed through the side opening and then scoot quickly out to jump onto the couch. Leaving her favorite cushion, she padded to the other end, lying down where Brett had sat watching the ball game. Curled into a fat ball, she tucked her head on her paws and went to sleep.

Honey laughed at the cat's antics, thinking how annoyed Brett would be to know his cat bed was not to Beauty's liking. She returned to the bedroom, finished reading several stories, and spent a restless night thinking of Brett's intriguing personality and continued generosity.

Preparing for work the next evening, Honey thought over the long Sunday with Brett. Each visit gave her further insight into his complex character. Today's had been the most revealing of all.

He had wakened her before dawn, told her to dress in old clothes, as if she had any others, sturdy shoes, and to grab a Windbreaker. Before she could ask him where they were going and finish dressing, he was knocking on the door.

Dressed in faded jeans, worn deck shoes, and a short-sleeved sweat shirt, he looked casual and endearing. She had never seen him dressed in anything that didn't look like it was straight out of a display window. Sweeping her out the door, he had rushed her to the car and sped north to Flat Rock Point. Informed that today was a low tide, he had assisted her down the breathlessly steep bluff to explore the tide pools.

He drove her through the Palos Verdes Hills, slowing when she remarked on a hilltop home sprawling behind a rail fence on its grassy, tree-shaded acreage. Parking in a lay-by with a panoramic ocean view, they had eaten a gourmet picnic lunch, complete with a bottle of chilled champagne.

He touched her all the time, not sexually as much as affectionately. She'd never realized before how important human contact was. She was starved for it and responded openly, unashamed to let him know how wonderful it was.

Ready for bed, she lay awake thinking about his actions. When he had helped her over a slippery seaweed-covered rock, he had held her hand longer than necessary to assure her safety. While watching waves break, he would nuzzle her brow or just let his palms linger on her hair. At her door, a brief kiss and abrupt good-bye left her even more puzzled. The man was a complete enigma at times.

Six days passed, nearly a week of misery for Honey as she waited for Brett to contact her. Walking to work early each morning, she paused long enough to talk with Bernard. Pleased with the knowledge he was breaking through the flimsy romantic barriers imposed by Aunt Gladys, it made her turbulent affair with Brett seem much worse.

Disgusted with her abominable mood, she asked Aunt Gladys to meet her at Buffum's department store as soon as it opened. She dressed carefully, piqued it would be another week before she was paid. It seemed impossible she had spent all her money so soon. For some reason the ninety-dollar purse and a forty-dollar shoes were so much more to her liking than anything cheaper. She had known she shouldn't have gone into that exclusive store first last Monday night.

It never occurred to Honey when she was clasped to Aunt Gladys's ample bosom in a warm greeting that the old lady was Brett's aunt and aware of her nephew's continued subterfuge.

They spent the entire day searching through the finer dress shops in the downtown area. Honey suggested bright-colored pantsuits in vivid blue, delighted at how much more attractive and younger she looked.

Aunt Gladys's eyes shone, admiring her changed appearance in front of the full-length mirrors. Filled with energy and determination to impress Bernard, she added suits and dresses to the growing pile of boxes. Material and prints were styled to conceal her short, stumpy figure. Strappy sandals and neat court shoes replaced her thick-heeled leather shoes. Modern costume jewelry caught her eye, replacing the old-fashioned pearls.

Flushing at Honey's prompting, she let the saleslady fit her with lace undergarments in soft stretch materials, admitting with laughter she felt naked after so many years of being bound in tight corsets. Naked, but unbelievably more comfortable, she added truthfully.

Honey went to the perfume counter to browse around. She bought a decorative glass vial of Chloë, surreptitiously opening a charge account to pay for the gift. Bernard would love it too.

Not finished with her protégée, Honey encouraged Aunt Gladys to have her hair styled. A conditioner did wonders, smoothing the frizzy locks into soft, feathery curls. The beautician was given a haughty setdown when she advised toning down the vivid orange tint. Aunt Gladys informed her that was her trademark and there wasn't a living soul in the world who could talk her into changing the color.

Eating an early dinner together while the stores delivered the numerous packages to her home, Honey thanked Aunt Gladys for a new dress. A lovely gratuity in appreciation for moral support. A lifetime of dressing a certain way could not be changed in one morning's shopping without some twinge of doubt. Honey's bright smile and constant encouragement, plus assurances Bernard would think her beautiful, eased the old woman's moments of uncertainty.

Aunt Gladys hailed a cab, anxious to show her secretary the new wardrobe before she left work. Tears filled her sharp blue eyes, watching the lovely young girl wave goodbye. In one day she had grown to love her as a daughter. It was time to have a serious talk with Bretterson Robert Weston, she told herself with a decided frown.

Honey walked home, enjoying the cool evening breeze as she scanned the busy tourist-filled sidewalks. Stopping to chat with Bernard, she warned him about the transformation he would see when he picked up Aunt Gladys for their date that evening.

Carefully hanging her chic new dress in the long wardrobe, Honey looked at Beauty.

"You did it again, cat. I just don't understand how you

manage to sneak past Bernard and into the elevator sight unseen." She cradled the obese cat in her arms, amused how much heavier it had become since indulging daily in a bowl of rich cream and choice tidbits from Honey's plate. Beauty batted at the gold charms with her flared paw. Scolded softly, she was placed on the carpet.

Honey wanted to look at her dress. Pulling the protective wrapper up, she caressed the delicate folds lovingly. It was a romantic dress as glamorous as anything on the current fashion scene. The tucked bodice draped softly across her rounded breasts in a perfect fit.

Aunt Gladys had told her the pale ivory silk enhanced her vivid, lustrous hair and the short skirt hit her knees at a perfect spot to emphasize her shapely legs. She could hardly wait to model it for Brett.

Monday morning Honey stalked off to work with the beginning of a fine temper. In her arms she carefully balanced a carrot cake. It had taken hours to fix, yet Brett hadn't called or come by. With her chin raised defiantly, she placed it on her desk, inviting her co-workers to help themselves.

Within forty-five minutes there wasn't a crumb left. Unfortunately, the praise did nothing for her low spirits. She found little pleasure in being defiant if the man she wished to aggravate wasn't even aware of her belligerence.

Expending most of her restless energies on her job, Honey managed to get through further days without hearing from Brett. Her nights were the hardest. Self-doubts about the wisdom of declaring her love haunted her. He had demanded her commitment but never volunteered his.

Walking into Honey's office a few minutes before quitting time, Corkie placed the pay envelope down. Hiking her hip on the corner of Honey's desk, she relaxed, enjoying a few minutes of gossip at the end of another productive week.

"You look tired, Honey," she remarked sympathetically. "Any problems with the job, or is it too much night life with your boyfriend?"

"Actually, the difficulty is the lack of any night life at all," she answered truthfully. "He's been busy working and I haven't seen him lately." She straightened her desk in preparation to leave, casting a look of chagrin at her supervisor.

"Your mystery man sounds like our illustrious boss," Corkie told her offhandedly. "According to the latest scandal sheet, the Panther's been missing from his usual haunts for the past month."

Corkie rooted through her capacious shoulder bag, found her lipstick, and applied a heavy layer of glossy color. "Everything has really been dull for the staff since he appears to have dropped out of circulation. No one's as exciting to gossip about as our boss."

"Maybe he's collapsed from fatigue," Honey quipped shortly, disliking the sound of her employer more all the time. Her only concern was hearing about Brett anyway.

"No way! He's reputed to have the stamina of a sexual Adonis." She smoothed a wayward strand of hair over her brow. "One of the security men told my friend on the fifth floor that he's been burning the midnight oil upstairs." Satisfied she looked presentable, Corkie stood up, waiting for Honey to get her purse.

"Undoubtedly he's intent on making more money in order to buy expensive trinkets for his partners in passion," Honey scorned. Deciding to follow Corkie's example, she outlined her mouth in moisturized lipstick. A quick check in the compact mirror reflected her hair didn't need combing.

Her eyes widened, filled with mischief as she commented in a teasing voice, "If he's as active as you say he is, and changes women like a taxi driver changes customers, it's no wonder he has to take some time off from his love life to work overtime. He must need a breather as well as the cash."

Corkie ignored Honey's humorous sarcasm, her expression serious. "My personal opinion is he has some cutie holed up in an apartment. Another gorgeous blonde, no doubt."

"If so, I hope she takes him for every penny she can get

her hands on. He sounds like he'd make her earn every cent and give her hell too!"

"That kind of hell I'd put up with any day or night of the week." Corkie lowered her voice, threw her head back, and closed her eyes as if swooning. "Wait until you meet him. You'll flip out too, and I'll bet your fiancé will look as second-rate as my lover did after I first met him. Honestly, I don't think there's a woman who works here, married or not, who isn't in awe of our employer's arrogant good looks."

For the first time Honey became intrigued with the man. She had been deluged with gossip each workday. "What does he look like anyway? I've never seen his picture."

Corkie taunted, getting back at Honey for not describing her fiancé. "Now, that I'll not tell. Next Monday I'll show you a company photo. In the meantime it would spoil the shock if I detailed him inch by inch. Your first sight will be a jolt, I assure you."

Honey scoffed. No man could look that good. Not even Brett was perfect, though she hadn't found any flaws in his looks she could remember. Just his occupation and volatile personality.

They left the building, talking over weekend plans, then parted outside the main doors.

Cashing her second check, Honey spent hours walking in and out of boutiques in another self-indulgent spending spree. She returned to the apartment lobby loaded with packages and carrying an empty billfold in her new purse. All she had left was some loose change.

"It was payday again, Bernard." She laughed, a tantalizing smile expressing her pleasure. He looked totally stunned at the number of boxes and sacks balanced in her arms.

"This time I splurged my entire check on myself. You've bragged so much on how pretty Aunt Gladys looked in her new outfits that I thought I'd add to my wardrobe."

Bernard took the largest packages from her arms, talking on the way to the elevator. "Honey, I'll never be able to express how much happier I've been since meeting Gladys. The fact she's never been in love before makes her all the more precious to me. Our concern for each other has driven the loneliness completely from our lives.''

Entering the apartment, Honey caught a sidelong glance of Beauty darting behind the couch. It was uncanny how that cat managed. This time she hadn't seen it enter the elevator. She thanked Bernard, closing the door behind him.

Picking up the cat, she cradled it close to her breast, reflecting that loneliness was no exclusive trait of the aged as she stroked its fur. She was desperate for Brett's company and furious with herself for missing him. The momentary lift of buying new apparel had ended. Clothes didn't bring happiness when she yearned for the company of the man she loved.

She took the packages into her room and unwrapped them slowly. They were the nicest clothes she had owned in years.

Fearing she might miss Brett if he came by or phoned, Honey never left the apartment on Saturday. By evening the massive rooms became claustrophobic. Beauty had long before retreated to a back bedroom to escape the continuous verbal blastings while her mistress paced.

Determined to stay away all Sunday, Honey rose early, her angered vocabulary muffled by putting on a whimsical T-shirt imprinted with a cuddly teddy bear holding three balloons. A firm tug pulled deep-brown form-fitting Vanderbilt jeans over her hips. She strode off purposefully, her Jordache tennis shoes the same cocoa color.

Her entire paycheck was wasted, she speculated. She might as well be wearing old cut-offs and her college shirt instead of expensive designer fashions, for all anyone noticed.

"Brett Weston, you're an odious beast!" she hissed out loud.

Cutting down the sharp sloping street to the wide beachfront walk, she spent a long day exploring the noisy arcade. She watched couples playing games at the many booths each side of the pike. Laughing teenagers knocked head-on into each other in electric bumper cars or threw baseballs attempting to knock down weighted bottles in hopes of winning a cheap plaster doll.

Just before dark Honey entered the apartment. Dusty and tired, she kicked off her shoes, wiggling her toes in relief. She felt like she had walked for miles. She slumped into the corner of the couch. It had never felt softer.

She reached for the telephone. Brett had been on her mind all day and she was determined to find out what his intentions were once and for all. She dialed carefully, a sigh of relief escaping her lips when she heard Aunt Gladys answer in her high reedy voice.

"Aunt Gladys, this is Honey."

"Hello, dear. I've been meaning to call you and apologize for not coming to dinner last week. Bernard left a short time ago and I told him I had to have one free day for you."

"That isn't why I'm calling," Honey said, exhaling sharply.

Aunt Gladys excused herself to shut off the whistling tea kettle, returning to ask, "Is everything all right?"

"No, it isn't, actually. I want to get in touch with Brett," she explained firmly, making no attempt to hide her chagrin. "I haven't heard a word from him in over two weeks."

"Yes, I know, dear," the older woman soothed. Her loyalties were divided. Only last night she had talked with her nephew after a week's try to find him. Annoyed by his gallivanting all over the country, the unusual continued put-off by his enigmatic secretary, and avoidance of her oft-repeated calls, she had finally tracked him to his plush hotel in New York City. It had been foolish to let Brett's eloquence persuade her to keep silent about his identity until he returned to Long Beach. A moment of guilt touched her conscience, knowing she had been so involved with Bernard, she had been unconcerned about Honey's problems.

"How can I help?" Her ready voice softened, filled with sympathy.

"You'll think I'm foolish, Aunt Gladys, but I fell in love with Brett." Honey's eyes turned stormy, matching her mood perfectly. "Frankly if he has been so busy escorting other women that he can't even bother to phone me, I want you to tell me. I refuse to tolerate his occupation any further and won't hesitate to inform him of my decision."

"Settle down, love," Aunt Gladys pacified. Her eyes were bright with excitement. Brett was going to get the shock of his life at Honey's daring ultimatum. "You've no need to be upset, dear. Brett has been out of town. He has other job interests too, and doesn't spend all his time with women."

"I can't imagine what I did that he hasn't even phoned me," Honey spoke with dejection. She had never been more miserable since her father died.

"I would think nothing, child. Hasn't it ever occurred to you that Brett is an experienced man with strong passions? He's not used to leading a celibate existence. It's possible he feels threatened by your innocence. Even doubtful of his own self-control in your presence," she told her frankly.

"I don't think so," Honey disagreed quickly. "It was my constraint that was lacking. Apparently I'm not sophisticated enough for him."

"You underestimate him, Honey. He's an honorable man, despite what you think, and wouldn't commit himself to starting a relationship without complete understanding from his partner regarding the eventual termination."

"But," she cried out, "Brett never said he wanted to terminate our relationship. Only that he was busy working!"

"Don't you think it's highly likely that by devoting all his time to his work he is avoiding an encounter he feels you are both wise to shun for the time being?"

Loud, repeated knocking on the front door checked their conversation. Honey excused herself, exclaiming in a high, excited voice, "Hold on, Aunt Gladys. Someone's here and I think it's Brett."

Dropping the receiver on the corner cushion, Honey

ran to the door. Her heart beat wildly, animosity over Brett's behavior left in the eager impatience for his company.

She pulled open the door, her soft passionate-shaped mouth welcoming with a dimpled smile. Her expression changed to one of immediate distaste, widened eyes scanning Wendell Foster standing in the hall. She clutched the edge of the door, apprehensive over his surprising emergence. How could he have found her? She had adamantly warned her mother not to give out her new address.

Wendell's handsome face with its smooth, well-cared-for looks and soft pampered features repelled her. Heavy lids shielded his thoughts.

"I've a message from your mother," he lied smoothly. "Aren't you going to invite me in?"

Honey shook her head no, too wary to speak. She moved forward, intent on closing the door to her unwelcome visitor. She remembered each detail of their last encounter alone. His brutal sexual advances would remain a bitter memory forever.

"No! I don't ever want to see you again," she told him firmly, pushing the door forward. "Tell my mother to write. She has my address here."

With overpowering strength, Wendell pushed into the door as Honey slammed it in his face. His force knocked it open, narrowly avoiding hitting her. Angry eyes never left her startled features as he kicked it shut with his heel.

"Get out, Wendell!" Honey screamed. She trembled, furious at the sudden fear that ran up her spine.

Ignoring her frantic demand to leave, he sauntered into the room, deliberately staying between her and the door.

"I see you're still wearing Weston's ring." His eyes glittered with sudden lust as they roamed the swell of her full breasts and rounded hips.

Honey stood braced, her hands clenched, uncertain what to do. Her mind reeled. He was strong and fast and blocking the only unlocked exit from the apartment.

"I've planned for years on being your lover," he ground out harshly. "For years I've fantasized about you; you've haunted me from the first time I saw you."

Honey's face paled, perspiration beading her brow. Wendell was crazy. His obsession made him dangerous. She prayed for Brett to come to her. Her legs were trembling so badly, she doubted if she could even run if she had the opportunity. She swallowed, her throat suddenly too dry to protest. She'd let him talk. Isn't that the advice the experts gave when confronted by a madman? Or was it to fight? God in heaven, she couldn't remember.

"If your frantic fighting hadn't drawn the attention of those curious do-gooders months ago, you would be mine today. From the first moment your greedy mother introduced us, I've wanted you. I've thought of nothing else."

His chest rose and fell, the glimmer in his eyes more wild, his mouth thinning with the force of spewing forth the bitterness and lust that had haunted him for years. "You're no different than the other one. In the end your cries to stop would change to a plea for me to stay."

Honey's temper over his sheer gall that she would ever tolerate his attentions overcame her horror. Never easily intimidated, her voice rose, defying him unwisely. "I hate you, Wendell! I detest the very sight of you and always will. Brett will be returning shortly and he loathes you as much as I do." How dare he state she would ever want him!

He didn't raise an eyebrow at her threat, taking a step forward, watching as she cautiously backed away, her frosty eyes flashing a warning.

"Weston's in New York. Foolish of him to stay at the same hotel all the time. It was easy to check his whereabouts prior to coming to visit his mistress."

"I'm not his mistress!" Honey blurted out, trying to keep Wendell talking long enough to ease toward the front door and make her escape.

His bitter laughter filled the room. "No man sets a woman up in his high-rise oceanfront apartment without getting all the sex he wants in return."

"This isn't Brett's apartment! I'm watching it for his friend."

"Save that lie for some gullible fool like your mother," he threatened sarcastically.

"It's not Brett's apartment, I tell you," she retorted belligerently, wishing the bedroom had a lock. He was still too close to the front door to rush past. Where had he heard such erroneous gossip?

"Are you really that naive?" Wendell questioned smugly. Convinced of her innocence by the dogmatic mien on her face, he added with malice, "Your lover not only owns this apartment, the entire building is his as well. Why the hell do you think it's called Weston Towers?"

Delighted with the obvious shock of his words, he continued to taunt her. "Just like Weston Towers is named after your philandering lover, P.P.C. is his too. Lock, stock, and barrel!"

Honey slumped to the couch, too stunned by Wendell's disclosure to be alarmed by his threat to do her bodily harm a few moments earlier. She felt like she'd been kicked in the stomach, the unbearable pain spreading throughout her body. Her eyes were dark pools of misery in her chalk-white face.

"Is...is all this true, Wendell?" she questioned hesitantly. "Does Brett really own the apartment and P.P.C. as well?"

"Don't tell me your fiancé didn't tell you he's not only your landlord but your employer too?"

Honey buried her face in her quivering palms, uncaring of anything but Brett's perfidy. Feeling she was the butt of a horrible joke, she looked at Wendell. She hadn't even noticed when he moved to her side. Alarm crossed her face instantly, appalled by the unchecked hunger in his eyes. They lingered with sickening intensity on her body.

She scrambled to her feet, making a sudden attempt to race to the door. A cry of pain was torn from her throat when she was grabbed from behind. She was spun around, her plea for help smothered below the force of his mouth.

Honey fought like a wild creature, hitting at his heavy shoulders repeatedly with both hands. Her continuous pummeling aroused him further. Thrown to the couch, his taut body forced the imprint of his desire on her. She twisted sharply, her limbs pinned beneath the weight of his thighs as he pulled at her clothing. Avoiding his repulsive kiss, she gagged at the pressure of his mouth buried at the base of her throat. Her nostrils flared, inhaling his costly hairdressing.

A scream was broken off by the harsh pressure of his palm. Frenzied with the knowledge Wendell was intent on revenging his battered pride, that he had prearranged his encounter by checking that Brett was out of town, she knew he was beyond reasoning with. She heard his heavy breathing and saw the beads of sweat on his brow above eyes glazed with lust. His desire seemed based as much on wanting to revenge some past harm from Brett as it did on possessing her.

"Stop fighting me!" His mouth raised from its plundering, his voice a low animal growl. "Nothing will stop me this time. Nothing, you hear?" His palm groped for her heaving breast. "No one to help you now. No one!"

Honey managed to free a leg, kicking at his shin before making a valiant attempt to raise her knee into his groin. Angered by her continued struggles, he smothered her verbal protest with his mouth in a violation so vile, it caused her stomach muscles to clench. Sinking her teeth into his lower lip, she bit with all her strength, hearing his startled yelp at the same time she felt a spurt of blood from his cut mouth.

Raising his arm to grab her, Wendell was unaware of the three men who burst into the room. They pulled him from Honey and twisted his arm behind him in a painful arm lock, subduing him with a choke hold until he slumped forward in speechless obedience.

Looking at Bernard's concerned face, Honey clambered off the couch and stumbled forward to cling to his wiry body as he commanded the men to take Wendell to the office.

Between sobs, Honey explained what had happened. Fearing the far-reaching consequences of prosecuting him, she beseeched Bernard to have the security guards release Wendell.

Feeling a semblance of composure return, she pulled from the old man's hold to sit on the couch. "I'm fine now, Bernard," she told him, trying vainly to stop her hands from shaking. "He won't bother me anymore. I'm absolutely convinced he hates me now."

She forced the information about Brett to the back of her mind, intent on convincing Bernard to release Wendell.

"I don't agree at all with your decision, Honey. The man should be arrested; he tried to hurt you." He paced the floor, uncertain what to do. He wished the boss were there to advise him, knowing he should call the police. He listened to Honey's stricken pleas and grudgingly agreed.

"If he's a good friend of your mother's, we'll give him a severe warning and see he leaves town immediately. My security guards are real tough and know how to persuade his kind with firm conviction. They'll follow him all the way out of the county too."

"Thank you, Bernard," Honey said fervently, her eyes brimming with tears of gratitude. "How did you know I needed help?" He had never come to the top floor that late at night before.

"My Glady girl phoned me. You left your phone off the hook to answer the door. By the time she was aware something was wrong and walked downstairs to the office phone to call me, it was almost too late."

He retrieved the receiver from the couch and replaced it, shuddering at the thought of what would have happened if Honey had hung up before answering the door.

Bernard wiped his brow. It's a wonder he hadn't had a heart attack. "Too bad Mr. Weston wasn't here. He'd have known what to do, for sure."

"He would have probably ended up in jail. He hates Wendell Foster as much as I do. This would have ended in a major brawl between the two."

"Was that Wendell Foster?" Bernard asked in a stunned voice.

"Yes. Do you know him?" Honey was recovering quickly, aware she was safe from further attack. Poor Bernard, he looked stricken.

"No, although I know about him," his voice interrupted her thoughts. "One night me and Mr. Weston was sitting around the office, having a few drinks together. We started talking all chummy like when he confided he had nearly broke a man's neck in college. Said it was the only time he'd lost his temper to the point of wanting to commit mayhem.''

"What happened?" Honey asked. She had known from the first there was something between the two men that had made them bitter enemies. Their verbal exchange at Marcie's wedding had been violent.

"Well, Mr. Weston confessed that Wendell Foster had brutally attacked a local girl he had picked up while they were in college. A young, virtuous girl who had fallen for Foster and dreamed of marriage. He said she was naive and impressed by his good looks and obvious wealth. Instead of her calling the police, Foster talked her into continuing to see him until she found she was pregnant."

"How awful," Honey whispered, imagining the poor girl's agony.

"It gets worse," Bernard complained. "When she told Foster, he gave her money to have an abortion. The inhuman quack almost killed her. Brett accidentally found her hemorrhaging, alone near her apartment late at night. She was nearly dead. He took her to the hospital, remained with her until she was okay, got the full story from her, then sought Foster for his own revenge."

Honey could envision a youthful Brett filled with anger. He would be a formidable enemy to any man.

"The girl was hospitalized for three months at Brett's expense. He visited her, saw she wanted for nothing, and arranged for her to move to a small midwestern town where she could live with her distant aunt. He supported her until she found a decent job. The night he was talking to me, he'd just received word she had married and was very happy...except for the fact the butcher who performed the abortion had botched the job and she'll never be able to have children."

Honey listened to each word. Bernard seemed to want to talk and it gave her additional time to calm down.

"Mr. Weston has never told another person about his involvement. No one even knows he knew the girl, much less spent thousands of dollars on her medical care and months of personal, brotherly attention. He showed me the letter. She thanked him profusely for saving her life."

He looked at her bright auburn hair and slender fingers clasped in Honey's lap, admiring the young girl's amazing composure. She was the bravest little thing he'd ever met.

"You've quite a man there, Honey. When I tell him about Foster daring to lay a hand on you, he'll break my neck to know I released him."

Troubled by the tale of Brett's concern for an innocent stranger, Honey looked at Bernard. "That's all the more reason to release him. I don't want Brett involved with Wendell. I'll—I'll tell my mother what happened and ask her to explain to Wendell's parents. They can deal with his antisocial behavior. Apparently there haven't been any further problems since that time and with me. He's a very reputable businessman in San Diego now."

"I don't like it, child. He should be locked up," Bernard insisted.

"No, please," Honey pleaded. "If you don't mind, I'd like to be alone now." She couldn't handle any further discussion at the moment. "Thank Aunt Gladys for me. I owe her and you more than I can ever repay."

Honey stood up, walking on trembling legs to the door, her voice weary as she thanked Bernard again. She bolted the door behind him and rushed into the bathroom. Stripping off her clothes, she dropped them carelessly on the carpeting in her eagerness to feel clean. She stood under the needle-sharp spray, taking a shower for the first time in the tiled stall. She was desperate for the touch of heated liquid streaming over her body. The water healed as it poured over her upheld face, rinsing the profuse suds from her vigorously scrubbed flesh.

Wrapped in a velvety bath sheet, Honey curled up in the middle of Brett's bed. Her eyes scanned the room with new awareness. Knowing the apartment was Brett's, that he owned the entire building and was her employer, made their entire relationship a farce.

Discarding the towel in favor of the warmth of the feathery soft quilt, she curled it around her. She had to think. Had to decide what to do. Her mind became hazy, reeling with the turmoil of confronting Brett. The trauma of Wendell's abrupt appearance and his physical attack seemed less important than his devastating disclosure relating to Brett's identity. Sleep gently brought oblivion, temporarily easing all stress.

Awakening slowly, Honey stretched her cramped limbs before rolling onto her back. Momentarily confused about her reason for falling asleep on top of the bed, she sat up, stifling a weary yawn with her palm. Luxuriant strands of hair tumbled about her shoulders, vivid against her pale skin. Dark shadows beneath her eyes attested to her panic-stricken evening.

She remembered with explicit clarity each detail. Her mind was sharp, her plans clear as she impetuously prepared her day's actions. She temporarily erased the traumatic encounter with Wendell from her thoughts. Her coming meeting with Brett would take all her concentration.

She scooted out from under the quilt and swept into her morning ritual of bathing and dressing. Only today she took extra care, wearing one of her new outfits and applying her makeup meticulously. Slipping into leather pumps with high thin heels, she grabbed her purse and headed toward the front door.

"Come on, Beauty," she hissed, calling to her cat. "This is Brett's pet-prohibited apartment and you and I have just spent our last night sleeping in it!"

Determined to give the arrogant, double-dealing monster a verbal farewell he would never forget, she pictured leaving his cowering figure begging her forgiveness as she victoriously departed, her chin held regally high.

Taking a brief detour, she made her purchases, determinedly ignoring the owner's questioning glimpse when he did as she asked. Stuffing two of the items in her capacious purse, she reached for the other.

"It'll be heavy, miss," he warned. "I used to sell a lot of these in the early fifties. Too tacky for most folk now."

"Not for me," she told him sweetly. "It's the perfect gift for my, er... my friend. He doesn't have any class at all."

She stormed out of the souvenir shop, heading toward the towering marble building on the corner. "Preferred Pension Counselors!" she spoke out loud, wondering how she could have been so involved with her own problems not to pick up on some of the comments he and her co-workers had made. She felt like a dolt not figuring out his identity by herself.

"The Panther!" she fumed, unaware of the numerous glances following her determined strides. She adjusted her arms, rapidly becoming strained from the weight of her burden. The shop owner was right. The ugly thing was heavy and over two feet long and a foot tall.

Honey entered the lobby, walked to the waiting elevator, and sighed with relief that it was empty. She pushed the top-floor button for the first time. Watching each floor number light up, she was whisked soundlessly to the executive suites.

With a deep breath and a keen temper, she had the impetus to face what difficulties lay behind the paneled door ahead. Taking in the serene smile of the impeccably proper secretary seated behind a wide desk, Honey was awed. One quick glance found the luxury of the top floor suite unbelievably stunning. Doors led off in different directions, their gold lettering stating the use from board room to the one she was seeking, the private office of Brett Weston, President P.P.C. It wouldn't surprise her one bit if he actually was related to Rockefeller, Getty, and all the other monied names dropped so casually.

Honey returned the secretary's curious gaze, speaking firmly.

"I'm here to see Mr. Weston." She swept past her desk, not cognizant Lillian rose in a futile attempt to stop her.

"Mr. Weston's busy. You can't go in there, Miss—" Lillian called out, her voice faltering as Honey stalked to her employer's closed door. He had just arrived from New York City and would be very irate that someone dared invade the privacy of his inner office.

Honey turned the knob with one outstretched hand and

stalked into the room unannounced. Slamming the door shut, she stood just inside, staring belligerently at the un-ruffled expression on Brett's face, one dark eyebrow raised in question as he calmly scanned her from head to toe.

Outwardly matching his composure, her glance swept around the room. Seated before his desk were several men and women. With a faint flush she recognized Claude Jordan, the closest one to her, and Corkie Anderson, sipping coffee in one corner, her eyes wide pools of shock. Honey hadn't anticipated he'd be having a staff meeting, but it didn't matter. Nothing would interrupt her intended behavior.

She stormed up to Brett's desk, wishing his plush carpeting hadn't muffled the sound of her assured stride. Annoyed further by his casual attitude, her gray eyes turned a dark charcoal black, glimmering with soon-to-be-released temper. She faced Brett for the first time since finding out about his true identity. Chin tilted, her face expressed indignation at his persistent nonchalance.

Unconcerned by Honey's unexpected appearance, Brett leaned back in his high-backed executive chair. The gray suit stretched across his broad shoulders and pristine white shirt added to his look of confidence.

The deep burnished tan of his handsome face caused her stomach to quiver with fascination. She forced back the sudden longing and the reason for her wildly beating heart. Staring rebelliously, her glance lingered for a moment on his raven-black hair shining in the morning light, taking care to avoid his compelling eyes.

His mouth twitching with amusement, Brett watched with admiration the fiery beauty of Honey's stormy face.

"Good morning, sweetheart. Did you miss me?" he asked casually, as if it were a common occurrence for her to intervene in a meeting with his key personnel. Damn, she was really something special!

His voice acted like a catalyst. Her eyes flashed as they locked with his, her breasts heaving sensuously with the force of holding back her wrath.

"Sweetheart! Miss you! Why, you...you perfidious, black-hearted rake. How could you? How could you, Mr. Brett—*the Panther*—Weston?"

"Did you bring me a present?" he asked in an infuriating, innocent tone, staring at the hideous object in her arms.

"Yes, I did!" she shot back, placing a snarling ceramic panther, glazed shiny black with glittering vivid green glass eyes, on the edge of his massive desk.

"A most appropriate one, don't you think, you arrogant lying beast? You actually had the gall to claim to be everything from a gigolo to a thirty-four-year-old virgin too shy to attempt premarital sex! My God!"

Laughing uproariously at Honey's daring, Brett turned to his stunned staff. "Meeting adjourned, ladies and gentlemen."

His blasé attitude at her finding out about his deception added fuel to her provocation. She turned to the men and women rapidly rising from their chairs.

"Stay put! I'm not through chastising this depraved debaucher! As department heads, you can hand a memo of his deeds to the employees on your particular floor."

"Shove off," Brett warned, his voice changing to whip across the room in a serious command. "I think my fiancée has something to tell me."

He turned to Claude. "Jordan, you might as well see about hiring a new actuarial assistant. I have a distinct gut feeling my company will be minus one female staff member shortly."

"I'm not finished," Honey interrupted loudly. "First—"

"Get the hell out now," Brett growled, angered that his employees dithered, not wanting to miss a word of the young woman giving him a scathing blast with her sharp tongue.

"You'll hear all the despicable deeds I'm accused of later. I don't want any witnesses in case I have to subdue her with my own brand of dominance."

He leaned forward, fingers widespread on his desk blotter, his deep-timbred voice filled with mischievous laughter. "The last time she gave me this much trouble I kissed her into submission and it looks like I'll have to do it again before the day's over."

They filed out of the office reluctantly, careful to close the door behind the last person. Corkie gave Honey a departing, envious smile, reeling with the evidence that Brett was her mysterious lover. Grouped around Lillian's desk, they all listened on the intercom to the events taking place in their employer's office.

Honey raged angrily, her sparkling eyes not leaving Brett's face.

"How could you do this to me? How could you have the nerve to let me think you were nothing but a gigolo for hire and all the time you were my boss? The Panther! *You* deliberately prevaricated."

"*I'm* untruthful? After all your lies?"

Honey ignored Brett's contradiction. She had waited all night to let him know how she felt and wasn't going to be cheated out of one angry word.

"You deliberately coerced me into falling in love with a gigolo. Seduced me into forgiving your horrible occupation. Let me belittle your way of earning a living. Encouraged me to brag about my excellent job and mathematical ability. You even let me worry that you couldn't afford to buy me a present. From the office grapevine I hear you could buy any damned thing you want. That your girlfriend's good-bye gifts alone support half the jewelers in Long Beach!"

"I missed you, sweetheart," Brett interrupted nonchalantly, remaining seated behind his desk. He drummed his gold pen without concern on the protective blotter as she faced him.

"Don't call me any more false endearments. You pretended to be a *rentable Romeo* just to make fun of me." Both hands were clenched so tight along her hips, the knuckles were white as she continued furiously.

"Well, Mr. Weston, I hope you enjoyed your laughs, because I'm through being the butt of your jokes. I quit!"

She took his heavy ring from her finger and held it out to him, her dainty chin tilted defiantly.

"I'm leaving your office, leaving your apartment, your

life, and since it wouldn't surprise me to find out you own the whole damn city, I'm leaving it as well!"

Brett's hand raised, deftly catching his ring flying over the desk when Honey threw it across the distance that separated them. His dark eyes narrowed, a look of aggravation crossing his face when she flung her engagement ring aside as carelessly as if it were a cheap dime store toy.

He had heard enough. It was time to give her a quick setdown. Imagine having the audacity to order *his* employees to stay put, he reflected grimly. He started to stand up, pinning her with the force of his intimidating glance.

Honey decided she had said enough. Glancing warily at his darkening eyes, she spun about, running from the office. It was time to beat a hasty retreat.

His taunting laughter added to her anger as she stormed by his staff without a single glance.

Their last glimpse was of a shapely female figure with flashing legs rushing furiously from the room into the waiting elevator. Her molten hair shimmered, flying away from her shoulders in silken waves.

Brett loomed in the doorway, staring at the guilty faces of his department heads. His eyes were alight with mirth.

"Gorgeous, isn't she?" He turned to his secretary. "Lillian, phone Aunt Gladys and have her and Bernard Bryson meet me at the Long Beach airport in one hour, wearing their best clothes. Phone the airport, charter a jet for a flight to Las Vegas, ready to leave at a moment's notice. Call Las Vegas and reserve their best chapel, then let my aunt know which one it is."

"What's up, Brett?" Claude questioned. He had known his boss longer than anyone in the room. Nothing had ever happened like that before and they were all consumed with curiosity.

"None of your business," Brett retorted truthfully. "But, I'll explain anyway. I'm going to be married this afternoon to the most exquisite, tempestuous little minx in the whole world. As of now, I'm delegating my authority to each of you, so don't expect me back for one full month." He stared in turn at each shocked face, warning explicitly, "The first—and I'm totally serious—person from this office who interrupts my honeymoon with a phone call can expect to be fired!"

He returned to his office, heading toward the closet. Removing a dark formal suit wrapped in a plastic carrier bag, he draped it over his arm. Smiling at his stunned employees, he nodded good-bye, passing them without a word on the way to his private elevator. He drove to a local florist shop, waiting impatiently while the clerk fixed him a bridal corsage of white orchids surrounding a single burgundy rose bud for Honey and gardenias for his aunt.

Adding two carnations for the men, the clerk smiled. He was the most restless man she had ever seen and the most generous. It was the first time she'd ever been told to keep the change from a hundred-dollar bill.

Stepping from the cab hailed at the front entrance of P.P.C., Honey paid the bill by check, cajoling the driver to accept it with promise of a lavish tip. She would have to quit blowing all her money on paydays. She didn't even have a dollar's worth of change in her wallet.

"My gosh!" she cried out, suddenly realizing she had no place to stay, no job, and no transportation. Just a plush new wardrobe and a disreputable calico cat. Racing into Weston Towers, she was too enraged to care.

Warned by Aunt Gladys what to expect, Bernard was waiting for Honey to appear. Dressed in his only dark suit, he was ready to leave as soon as his boss gave the okay.

Honey spotted Bernard, asking foolishly, "Call me a taxi and have it here in fifteen minutes."

"But you just left a cab." She sure didn't look like a woman preparing for her wedding. Her eyes were filled with sparks of fire.

"I know it, Bernard. I want a different one!"

She sniffled, trying hard to hold back tears. Adrenaline still pumped through her heart following the fiery encounter, making it difficult to plan her next course of action in a calm and reasonable manner.

Confused by Brett's impassive attitude and backfiring of her plan to disconcert him, she knew she had blundered again. With reluctance she was forced to admit he bested her during each encounter. How could she have ever been so dense to presume anything she could do or say would leave him cowering and her the victor? He had outmaneuvered her continuously from the first moment they had met.

Taking her anger out on the apartment manager, Honey scolded, "Why didn't you tell me, Bernard? He said I was helping protect his friend's apartment while he was away. I had no idea Brett Weston owned this entire building and was my employer as well."

Not giving Bernard time to explain why he had kept silent regarding his boss, Honey rushed to the elevator. Dashing down the hall when the doors opened at the top floor, she swept into Brett's lavish suite.

Suddenly breathless after her wild rush from his office, she swiped at indignant tears streaming down her cheeks. Blinded to everything but the task in front of her, she pulled the package from her purse. A grimace crossed her face as she held the articles before her. They would be her final coup de grace.

Finished, she walked to the bedroom... *his bedroom*... nervous fingers fumbling as she removed her dress and shoes. She threw the new apparel indifferently on the rug, too upset to care about being neat. Intending to change into jeans and a T-shirt when she had finished packing, she pulled on her old flannel robe, unconcerned that the frayed cord hung limply from the belt loops.

Oblivious to everything but her need for haste, she failed to hear Brett enter the apartment.

Carefully locking the door behind him, he walked into his master bedroom, fully aware he would find Honey frantically gathering her personal items together in a foolhardy attempt to escape him.

Unabashed by her rampage and long tirade of verbal abuse in front of his staff, he smiled indulgently. His eyes blazed with adoration as they lingered with delight on her shapely outline.

Despite her statements to the contrary, he was confident of her love. Her soft poignant whimpers tore at his heart as she continued to pile her clothes carelessly into an overflowing orange carton.

About twelve hours of married life ought to resolve everything, he speculated with the boldness of a man certain that his skillful, attentive lovemaking would give his wife enough pleasure all hint of rebellion would desist.

Chapter Eleven

"Going someplace, sweetheart?" Brett asked calmly, standing in the doorway, arms crossed with deceptive nonchalance over his chest.

A shocked gasp escaped from Honey's throat at the sound of his husky query behind her. She whirled, facing him fearlessly.

"Of course!" she lashed out, marks of tears still lingering in her eyes. "I'm leaving as soon as I cram my things in this darn carton."

"You're not."

"I am!"

"The hell you are! Not now or ever," he stormed back. His braced stance brooked no argument. Blocking her only exit from the room, he was fully aware of his forbidding power.

Honey stood motionless, defiantly facing Brett with her trembling chin held high. Despite unvarying vulnerability to his dominant personality, her eyes locked boldly with his, the faded robe draped across her heaving breasts unnoticed while she revised her plans.

Deliberately giving him a haughty, quelling look, she turned her back and tugged the front of her robe open. Grumbling furiously, she pulled without success at the chain encircling her waist. Her hands shook, desperate to break the bondage she felt from its gold links.

"What in God's name are you doing now?" Brett demanded brusquely.

Looking over her shoulder, Honey stared at him with acute distaste.

"I'm removing your abominable waist chain!"

"You can't. The lock's unbreakable." He stared at her, a harsh frown drawing his brows together, his narrowed eyes dark slits of green.

She turned to face him, clasping the robe together, eyes flashing. Giving him a contemptuous look, her spine stiffened.

"Why on earth would you give me anything I couldn't remove?"

"Originally," he told her without apology, "it was meant to satisfy my male ego. A gold circle of love you couldn't remove when we were apart."

"That's ridiculous," she snapped derisively. "I hate it and I want it off now."

"For that remark I'll see it stays on until you're pregnant."

"Then the stupid thing will stay on me forever, as I don't intend to have children." Adding as a final thrust, she informed him icily, "And especially not by the likes of you!"

"*They* damn well will be mine." He shot her a hard look as dangerous as the deepened timbre of his husky admonition. He pointed to the carton, his patience running out fast. "Put that stuff back, leave it there, or throw it out, but get moving. I'm in a hurry!"

"Tough," she sassed impertinently, uncowed by his threat to speed up.

Brett stared at her in amazement. Despite her impudent chin tilted at a fighting angle, she had an illusory mien of fragility. She always made him feel protective, though he doubted if there was any female who needed it less. Not as long as her tongue went uncurbed, anyway.

"Quit arguing. We're leaving to get married in ten minutes."

"We're leaving to *what*?" Her face paled, stunned by the physical impact of his words. His emphatic, blasé declaration wrought instant change to her features. Her eyes lost their fiery spark, becoming a dreamy slate-gray. Her lips softened, the dimple appearing as she whispered sweetly, "You mean to...marry...me?"

"Only if you're ready to leave on time." He watched each changing expression flicker across her face, marveling as her fierce defiance was replaced by a look of wondrous yearning.

Honey reached for the hanger, removed her new dress, threw it on the bed, then bent to root through the carton for a new pair of evening sandals. She had no intention of letting him change his mind. Auburn waves fell forward, pushed back with anxious fingers attempting to rush.

"I can't believe it. Ah, here they are." She straightened, holding up a fragile pair of sandals. "Cute, aren't they? Er, when did you ... ?"

"Decide?" he answered with amused clarity. "The first moment I saw you at my aunt's office on her new videocassette recorder."

"Aunt Gladys is actually your real aunt? What other surprises do you have in store?" He was more complex than Rubik's cube.

"A lot more if you don't get this engagement ring back on your finger."

Honey's head tilted, eyes brimming with humor. Graceful strides took her forward. She stood with left hand outstretched. "Can I have a kiss too?" she begged saucily. It seemed like years since the last.

"Definitely not!" He gave a short laugh. "Not with a jet waiting to fly us to Las Vegas and my urge to possess you becoming embarrassingly more evident the closer you get." He replaced his ring on her finger, again prompting her to make haste. "In three hours you'll be my wife and in six satisfied with the memory of my kisses exploring every sensual inch of your enticing body."

"Not even the Panther is that fast," she retorted mischievously. Enjoying her devilish ploy and secretly hoping it would precipitate a hard kiss, she quipped, "Who knows, I might even end up writing my own survey."

"As frustrated as I am now, no one would believe you because I'd probably raise the entire male population's median average by several—"

Honey flushed, pushing against his back to ease him from the room. Taunting his sexual prowess had been unwise. Maybe he really was physically gifted too. She'd heard he was a genius and a member of MENSA.

With Brett out of the room, she threw the faded robe on the floor, slipped into the pale ivory dress Aunt Gladys had given her, fastened the gold chains around her neck, applied fresh makeup, and walked from the bedroom. She was immaculately groomed, though breathless. Whether it was the rushing or the vision of later that night, she wasn't sure.

"You don't waste time when you make a decision, do you?" Honey asked, leaning her head on the seat back to admire his dark suit. She was overwhelmed by the speed with which he had ushered her from the apartment into his Ferrari. It seemed impossible they were already at the airport.

"Not if the end result is you being my wife." He was getting damned tired of sleepless nights and cold showers.

Honey stared at his straight profile as he pulled into the parking place. His raven-black hair tumbled in unruly waves close to his well-shaped head. Her hands trembled from the effort it took to keep from touching him. His fingers clutched the wheel, knuckles strained white. He exuded passion held in tight control. She could feel the magnetic force of his virility close in on them in the confining space. She couldn't tear her eyes away, staring at him with disturbing awareness.

"If you don't shield your romantic fantasies, I'll anticipate our marriage vows in broad daylight, despite being much too big and way too old to make it in a damned sports car."

He leaned over, unfastening her seat belt with shaking fingers. A brief kiss brushed her irresistible lips. "I want you, Honey. This very instant." He was burning with unspoken words of love.

His breath fanned her face, the harsh revelation as erotic as the sweet promise of his mouth. Their glances locked, mysterious forest-green and polished silver-gray.

"I love you so damn much, it's eaten my guts out suppressing my true identity."

"Why did you, darling?" she crooned in a sensuous throaty entreaty.

"My entire deception was for desire. Desire to curb your impertinence, alternating with desire to make you mine." His hand raised to cup her chin, one finger tracing the edge of her molded cheekbone before lingering on her soft mouth. "From the first a mania too potent to quell."

Honey parted her lips, moving to probe his palm with her sensuous tongue. He jerked his hand away, his hoarse moan quickening her pulse.

Brett climbed out abruptly. Despite his size he moved gracefully, as lithe as his predatory nickname, the Panther. When he assisted her from the car, Honey hesitated, seeking his guidance. "What about Mother?"

"For now, nothing. I'm filled with animosity when I think of her trying to force you to marry that pervert Foster. I'll phone her in a couple of weeks, after we've been married long enough for her to realize she can't interfere in our lives."

The vehemence in Brett's voice talking about Wendell assured Honey of the wisdom of her decision to have Bernard release him. She knew Brett would commit lasting physical damage if he ever found out about the attack.

Honey's high heels clicked loudly, attempting to match Brett's long strides across the walkway toward the charter offices.

Brett paused momentarily when he spotted Bernard. Whispering out of the corner of his mouth, he questioned Honey, "What's that with, Bryson?"

"Aunt Gladys," Honey told him proudly, pleased with her part in the transformation of the happy old lady.

"My God! I thought it was a tent with glasses. The only thing the same is the bright orange hair."

"Shush, Brett," Honey scolded. "She looks lovely."

"I guess," he grumbled, not entirely convinced Honey was right. "I suppose you're responsible for that change too. I loved her like she was. Lavender perfume, dowdy clothes, and all."

Aunt Gladys rushed up to them, her chubby arms outstretched and short stumpy figure covered in a bright blue float dress. Numerous pleats blew, billowing out to expose both tiny feet clad in strappy sandals. Crystal costume jewelry glittered on her ample bosom as she clung to first Honey, then Brett. Her fashionable dark glasses failed to hide the bright sparkle of her tear-filled eyes.

Bernard held her arm proudly, reprimanding with a soft voice, "Come now, Glady girl. The kids don't want you gushing all over them yet. Wait until they're married."

He shook Brett's hand, congratulating him on his choice of a bride. "There's no doubt we two men are escorting the most beautiful women in town, huh, Brett?" he solicited, sincere in his compliments. He couldn't believe the difference in Honey. She was glowing with happiness without a trace of anger or tears visible.

"Agreed," Brett said, laughing, reaching to pin on Honey's orchid corsage while Bernard did the same for Aunt Gladys.

Interrupted by their pilot's arrival, they followed him to the waiting plane. Awed by the luxury of the gleaming white jet, Honey remained quiet as she was seated in one of the sumptuous upholstered chairs placed for the maximum efficiency in flight.

The shrill whine of the jet engine throbbed through the aircraft as their pilot prepared for takeoff. Honey's momentary alarm left as Brett drew her hand to his mouth, searing the palm with a poignant kiss.

Aunt Gladys chattered continually during the short hop over the barren rust-colored peaks of the jagged Providence mountains and during the smooth landing in the sprawling neon-neighborhood desert town.

Honey's mind reeled at the speed of events happening since early morning. Brett's expression of worship when the minister pronounced them man and wife brushed a pale rose flush across her cheeks. It was hard to believe her self-confident husband trembled, fumbling when he slipped the wide gold band on her finger.

Unbidden tears slipped down her face when he handed her the matching groom's ring to slip on his finger. A surge of yearning for the powerful man standing at her side made her oblivious to anyone else.

The touch of his mouth as he bent his head to place the final seal on their union with a betrothal kiss was so perfect, she raised on tiptoes to increase the pressure. Her slender arms wrapped around his shoulders, holding him close as her lips clung, offering a promise of eternal love.

Aunt Gladys intruded, breaking the shattering intensity of their silent exchange. She kissed Honey, crying with happiness, her hand surreptitiously taking Bernard's handkerchief. Knowing her adored nephew had found love through the subliminal manipulation of her matchmaking at Happy Hearts Marriage Bureau made all her past pairings insignificant.

Hovering attentively near Aunt Gladys, Bernard congratulated his employer heartily before placing a shy kiss on Honey's cheek.

Brett took command, paid for the services, and ushered them with arrogant impatience to the waiting limousine for the short drive to the airport and the return flight home. He could see his aunt and apartment manager anytime. Honey was his and he wanted her alone. And soon!

Arriving at their destination, Brett bid Aunt Gladys and Bernard a hurried good-bye, uncaring they exchanged a knowing smile. His grip was firm on Honey's elbow, seating her in the Ferrari quickly, then walking to the driver's side without comment.

Wide tires squealed when he pulled forward with a roar. Intent on he and Honey spending their first night as man and wife in his home, he drove silently, his attention held as he maneuvered off the freeway onto the winding mountain road leading to his hilltop estate in the prestigious Palos Verdes Hills.

"Oh, dear," Honey cried out, breaking the silence. "You'll have to pay off my college loans now that I won't be working." A frown creased her brow. There were so many questions still to be answered. "What about my education?"

Brett slanted Honey a quick glance, a wide smile lifting the corners of his mouth, his keen eyes filled with amusement. "I'll be glad to pay off your loans, if..." Another quick scrutiny of her curves.

"If?" she prompted impudently, having an idea what was coming next.

"If you pay me back with, er..." He broke off, his meaning clear.

"I may not be good." She knew darn well what he had in mind.

"I hope the hell you're not." He shot her a leering glance. "In our bed I prefer a wild and wicked auburn-haired witch."

"Intent on making a good girl go bad?" She chuckled, thinking of the song by that title.

"You bet!" he taunted. "As to your second question, your education continues tonight. By tomorrow you'll have earned a master's degree and be well on your way to a doctorate in advanced physical sciences."

"Sounds interesting." She slanted him a teasing smile. "Especially the homework." She reached for his thigh, letting her fingers trail slowly up and down, deliberately raking her nails across the fine cloth.

He placed her fingers back on her lap. "The best part will be the tests as you appear to be an apt student."

Brett's banter stopped, his voice serious. "You can't imagine how delighted I'll be to know I can discuss my work with you intelligently. Sharing my problems will be a new experience that I'm looking forward to. If you want to help my with my public relation work, you'll be un-equalled." His eyes swept quickly to her firm little chin. "With your daring personality, you will have no problem talking my most voracious competitors into hiring the ser-vices of P.P.C."

"I'll give it my best shot." She chuckled, shooting him a stricken glance. "Oh, dear! Your staff must think me terrible." She really did have a wayward tongue, thinking of her shameful outburst in his office.

"Hell, they loved it," Brett assured her. "They've been waiting for ten years for me to get hooked. Today's inter-lude will be their pièce de résistance."

Honey raised her hand to caress his strong shoulder, her next words suddenly reflecting something she had hidden for years. "I'm not really a career-oriented female, darling. It was more fun decorating your plush apartment than your office." Frankly, she had worked enough jobs to last her a lifetime.

"My office? I don't understand." He'd do anything to make her happy.

"Your male stats said I was the most decorative woman on the staff."

A deep frown furrowed his brow as he floorboarded the pedal to pull around a lumbering motor home. "It's a damn good thing I'm taking you home, Mrs. Weston. You're a menace to my peace of mind. Probably to Danny's, Enrico's, and what's his name's as well."

Pleased by his rush of unnecessary jealousy, she watched the coastline abstractedly. She never dreamed he would remember their names.

"I'm afraid to ask about your home. Thinking you were a gigolo until last night, I didn't expect you to have one. Now that I know you own Weston Towers, P.P.C., and undoubtedly this Ferrari, I can reasonably presume I'll feel totally overcome."

"You'll love it at first glance. It's my family home. My father purchased twenty acres several decades ago when the homes were sparse and land inexpensive. He built my mother a large, rambling ranch house and, until the day they were killed, it was filled with love and laughter. She was a minx just like you and my father adored her. I had a wonderful, extremely happy childhood."

"I wish they were alive now." She was envious. Her home had always been filled with uncomfortable tension. Her parents should never have wed.

He recognized her sudden dejection. "When I fell in love with you, I realized why I'd held on to the estate during the years when I had no need for it." He wanted to assure her their life would always be filled with love. "In the future, our sons will play on its vast green lawns and climb the huge trees my father planted, as I did."

"Sons! What if we have daughters?" Honey taunted, upholding her sex.

"They can stay inside and learn to sew." That should rate a censure.

"Sew! You've a lot to learn, husband. I distinctly remember being able to outclimb any boy in the neighborhood when I was younger."

"That's not the least surprising. There's probably nothing in the world you couldn't accomplish if you wanted to. You captured me!"

"Serves you right for letting me rent you. Stop!" Honey cried out, gripping his forearm. "We have to turn around, Brett. We forgot to get Beauty."

"Don't worry about that abominable thing. I had it taken home with your clothes." Here he was rushing to start his honeymoon and she was worried about an ugly old stray cat.

"But how did you catch it? It's terribly independent."

"The damn thing ran out of the bushes at me when I went to the apartment." He slowed to make a steep turn, grimacing. "Intent on shedding more hair on my clothes, no doubt. I caught it and put it in a cage for transport to its new home."

"Won't she run away?" Honey had never had a pet and was worried.

"Hopefully," Brett retorted with a decided scowl. He slowed the car to turn into a wide paved entrance. A white rail fence, barely visible beneath a profusion of blooming multicolored roses, joined an impressive arched brick gateway. "We've arrived, wife."

"You're a very secretive man, my darling husband. You drove me by here after our outing at Flat Rock Point. You listened to my comments on your—"

"*Our,*" he pointed out. For the first time he felt like he was really coming home.

"*Our* home," she continued, "and never said a single word about it being yours. What if I hadn't liked it?"

"I'd have changed it to please you," he told her matter-of-factly. "Something I'll be doing throughout our marriage, no doubt."

Honey took in the gigantic maple trees shading broad velvety lawns as Brett slowed the Ferrari to a slow crawl. Well-tended flower beds bordered the drive leading to an elegant sprawling ranch home painted a soft yellow. Glis-

tening diamond-paned windows edged with white shut-
ters were sheltered beneath a wide porch. The hand-split
shake shingle roof was dark with age, visible above the
heavy beamed wide eaves.

"Just as I suspected," Brett remarked with disgust.
"Look in front of the door." He eased to a stop next to
broad used-brick steps.

Honey's eyes shone with happiness. Beauty was staring
at them, seated on the door mat as if she had lived there
all her life. Too excited to wait for Brett, Honey opened
the passenger door and rushed up the stairs to her cat.
Hugging it to her breast, she smiled at Brett.

"I'm so happy now." Brett's residence looked perfect
for them both.

"Glad one of us is," he grumbled, removing the purring cat and placing it back on the porch. "If you want to
clasp anything to your breast from now on, you'd better
make sure it's me. I don't have fleas and don't shed!"

He unlocked the glistening white door held by black
wrought iron hinges, pushed it open, then swooped
Honey up into his arms. He made deep growling noises in
his throat as she arched her neck for his caress.

Trailing kisses upward, he covered her face while deliberately avoiding her mouth. She tried vainly to hold his
head still and touch his lips. She was as eager to make love
as he was. Laughing together, they started in.

Brett cursed beneath his breath, his first step narrowly
missing Beauty, who darted inside, stopped a moment,
then sauntered ahead with lopped-off tail and comical face
held straight up.

"Undoubtedly the greedy beast will head straight for
the kitchen service porch and find the cream and canned
tuna my housekeeper set out."

Honey scoffed at Brett's sneer about her cat, asking to
stand. She just had to look through the house. Hand in
hand, Brett led her from one room to the next, not giving her time to do anything other than give it a cursory
glance. It was huge. Much bigger than his apartment.
Leaving the absolute dream of a mammoth country kitch-
en, he stopped her.

"Your first wedding present awaits you." Swept into his arms for the second time, he pushed the door open. A smile lit his face when her eyes widened to scan the unique decor. "Renovation started the day after we met, keeping me in continuous turmoil that they wouldn't finish before you caught on to my deception."

Honey pulled from his arms. She stood a moment. It was shocking after the modern, masculine decor of his apartment.

The vast room was dominated by a grand four-poster brass bed, draped with rich burgundy velvet, drawn back at each corner from the arched canopy to expose a gleaming headboard. Two cupids with arrows pointing to the center were suspended in hearts made entirely of solid brass. They were an exact replica of those on Aunt Gladys's front window.

Honey's expression was rapt. It appealed to her whimsical sense of humor and was symbolic of their unique introduction.

"I love it, darling," she murmured, turning to lay her head on his wide chest. "It's a very passionate-looking room, husband."

"A fitting one for my wife." He kissed her brow, both hands rubbing her spine. His body trembled involuntarily when she moved against his hips.

Honey quivered, pulling away from his intoxicating hold. She walked to the bed, her sandals silent in the deep velvety dove-gray carpet. She touched the spread, running her fingers across the sensuous material. Soft pink satin sheets with a delicate print of wine-colored rose blossoms and soft green leaves were laid back invitingly over the corners of the spread. Propped in the middle of fat goose down pillows was a heart-shaped needlepoint cushion. She smiled, amused by her husband's dazzling sense of romantic capriciousness. It would take no time at all getting used to such indulgence.

Across from the bed, matching velvet was pulled to the side, tied back in a loop behind an artistically draped and tucked swag. Shimmering white nylon made into pouf drapes covered the window with fragile shirring. The furnishings were exquisitely Victorian and she adored everything. A pleasing mixture of gleaming brass, antique marble-topped carved chests and end tables, brocade chairs, and authentic Tiffany lamps blended to create luxurious warmth.

"Oh, darling, you're a big bluff," she cooed, spotting an identical miniature brass bed, complete with canopy, for Beauty. "No man would indulge an animal as you have my cat unless he cared for animals." The only thing out of place was the orange carton stuffed with her old clothes, apparently set there by his housekeeper by mistake.

Brett ignored her consensus of his feelings about the cat. He shrugged out of his suit jacket, throwing it over a lounge chair near the fireplace. Loosening the top button of his shirt, he dragged his tie off in one jerk.

"Present number two is by the bed."

On the bureau was a jewelry case opened to expose its priceless contents. Curious, Honey touched the gleaming necklace with her finger. Her voice broke, barely above a whisper. "It matches my ring."

"Yes, wife. It's the Weston family necklace and following a centuries-old custom given after consummation of the marriage to a virgin bride in gratitude for giving her innocence to the eldest son." He shrugged his broad shoulders in acceptance. "Quite chauvinistic, but nevertheless appreciated."

Touching the pendant's magnificent diamond, sparkling in a circle of rubies, Honey was speechless. She'd never even seen heirloom jewelry.

"There are earrings and a bracelet to match, which are traditionally given after the birth of the first child," Brett told her with lowering voice. His smoldering eyes transmitted he was ready to claim his bride.

"I intend to see you'll be wearing the entire set in nine months!"

"Don't be in such a hurry." Honey spun around, her filmy ivory dress clinging along her thighs, outlining their beauty and accenting the erotic tilt of her full breasts.

"In a hurry! I've waited thirty-one days, seventeen

hours, and"—checking his watch—"thirty-seven minutes for you. That's enough to try the patience of any man illogically forced to live a celibate existence. In one third of that time I've become bored and bid good-bye to a female... yet, you claim I'm rushing you!"

Honey turned away, resentful of the women he'd known before.

Sensing her discomfort, Brett took her in his arms, asking her to look at him. "Do you want an explanation of my past?"

Honey's eyes absorbed him, sudden maturity resolving her twinge of jealousy. She told him truthfully, "No, Brett. I have no right to question what you did before we met." She reached up, placing a lingering caress on his taut chin. "The future, now, is another matter."

"I suppose you have a plan already formed to keep me in line?"

"Certainly," she sassed, nipping his neck when he moved her back and forth against his hardened body without embarrassment. "I intend to give you so much loving at home, you won't have any energy left for anyone else."

"You're really asking for it now, little Miss Innocence." Damned if she didn't mean it, he reflected with pleasure.

"I know." She raised up to kiss his chin, then drew away to reach for his shirt buttons. Her fingers tugged them open deftly, one by one.

"Let's get started, husband. You're much too excitable still for me to feel safe." She glanced down at his tensed body, then raised her twinkling eyes. "Especially with you near a well-stacked blonde, which, I have on good authority, is your decided preference."

"Past preference." He grabbed her hand, squeezing.

"Good enough for a start, since I don't intend to dye my hair and I hate wearing wigs." She looked around, then swept him a coy glance beneath her heavy fringe of lashes.

"Aren't you supposed to go smoke a cigarette or pace the rug while I change?"

"I don't smoke." He turned her around, telling her

where the bathroom was. "I'm not in the mood to pace and if I leave this room, that furry monster will probably want to shed on my dress slacks."

"What *will* you do?" she asked, giving him a gamine sideways grin.

"Wait and see," he warned her, reaching for his belt.

Honey scooted into the closest door, quickly removing her clothes with fingers that had suddenly grown clumsy. Her eyes surveyed the most sumptuous bathroom she had ever seen. It appeared her husband's generosity was unlimited.

She leaned over a raised octagonal tub of marble surrounded on three sides by a glassed-in greenhouse literally filled with exotic plants. It would be like bathing in a tropical island pool. With one twist, water cascaded from the open arms of a fat cupid-shaped spout.

Avoiding her reflection in the full-length mirrors, she poured bath salts in the water. Ascending the two carpeted steps, she eased into the lukewarm water, sighing at the pleasure of it.

Brett burst in unannounced. Braced in the doorway, he held her startled glance. His pupils dilated, lazily drinking in the intoxicating sight of her exposed nudity.

Honey stared back. She raised a hand, trying ineffectively to stifle her laughter. She had forgotten all about *those*!

"Apparently you found my final coup de grace?" He really did look funny, though she had to admit his legs were quite gorgeous for a man, despite being awfully hairy.

He wore a gray T-shirt, form-fitting across his wide chest and down below his waist. Imprinted on the front, at Honey's request, above the stalking form of a black panther, were neat black letters in two rows:

"PANTHERS DO IT AT NIGHT—TO THEIR PARTNERS' DELIGHT."

Below the T-shirt he wore skin-tight bikini underpants in gray with the snarling faced, fangs-bared, tongue-showing, head of a black panther.

"Oh, dear," she added gravely. Apparently her mischief-making hadn't cooled his ardor any.

"You damned little devil," Brett scolded, pulling the

T-shirt over his chest and throwing it beside her underwear. "I couldn't believe my eyes. After tearing my hide off in a blistering tirade in front of my staff, I come rushing to drag you off to the altar and find this crap on the front door of my apartment!" Strong hands tugged the last offensive garment over his legs.

Honey's eyes roamed over his naked body for the first time in a slow inspection. His shoulders rippled as he moved closer. His broad muscular chest was covered in dark hair forming a vee past his flat navel.

Placing both hands on his hips, he made no attempt to conceal his chagrin. "Now, woman, it's time you heard the Panther growl and felt the force of his desire when he stalks down from his lair to pounce on his chosen prey." Having spoken, he moved forward with obvious purpose. Within an hour he'd damn well be hearing his wife purr.

Honey could feel her pulse increase alarmingly. He was stunning. Totally uncowed by his ill temper, her eyes followed his hips, taut thighs, and well-defined calves to his feet, then back up a more intimate route.

"My God, don't tell me you've never seen a naked man before?"

"Not this close." A faint flush touched her cheeks, caused by excitement, not embarrassment. She'd never believed the male body was so beautiful.

He shook his head in disbelief. She was unbelievably chaste for her age. Stepping into the deep tub, he eased into the water as if they had bathed together often. He reached beside him, taking the new bar of soap in his palm. His eyes linked with hers, the soap dropping unnoticed into the water.

Reaching for her smooth shoulders, he held her, his deeply tanned hands a startling contrast next to her creamy skin.

"It's time I kissed you, Mrs. Weston."

"Thank heavens, Mr. Weston. I thought you'd never ask." She flung herself into his waiting arms, her mouth raised to accept the pleasure of his.

Insatiable for the taste of his wife, Brett cupped her sleek body the length of his. His lips claimed hers in the way he'd visioned for the first time in weeks. The playful banter between them ended the moment they embraced. Their agony was over.

Honey was trembling with frustration. She had loved him so long, she feared it was a dream. The insistent pressure of his tongue parting her lips to explore the sweet warmth inside made her head spin. It was no dream. Just pure sensual pleasure racing across each nerve beneath her sensitive skin. While his mouth coaxed hers into total reciprocation, one hand slid to her breast, cupping the heavenly weight in his palm, his thumb leisurely stroking the taut crest.

His mouth tempted, lingering on her lips sensuously, lifting then briefly pressing down to tease again. His tongue darted in and out until she cried out with disappointment. She wanted it to remain inside, to plunder with hunger. In response, she enticed with extended access, then teased with fleeting vigor before capturing to hold with the slow sucking motions she knew had the power to drive him wild.

A harsh moan was torn from his throat after moments of pure heaven buried in the heady moist interior of her mouth. She kissed like no woman he'd ever known.

"Easy, Honey," he choked. "One more kiss like that and you'll be sorry." He leaned sideways, his weight resting on the curved edge, one sinewy leg drawing and holding her intimately close in the water.

Arching her throat, Honey lay back, letting Brett stroke each pulse point with his searing mouth. Ecstasy was hers, handed out in endless portions by the man she loved, from the base of her throat to her jaw, along the side of her neck and behind her ear, ending with the erotic intimacy of his tongue circling inside its dainty cavity. Deep emotion burned inside her, flaring like the flame lighting his eyes.

"I adore you," she murmured when he drew away.

"Feel good?" he asked, his breath teasing the sensitive area behind her ear.

"Wonderful," she gasped, feeling his tongue lick her neck. She ached for him. Unhappy when he paused, she pleaded, "I'd like some more."

"You're going to get more, wife," he murmured back. "A lifetime's more!"

Leaving her delicate ear to pursue the exciting softness of her full breasts, he reached his goal. Moving his thumb aside, he let his strong fingers cradle and lift. He took the erect nipple and surrounding sweetness into his mouth. With his tongue beneath the hard bud, he closed his lips, sucking to give pleasure but receiving it tenfold. He pulled his tongue back, stroking, circling, then flicking the peak until she cried out. His head raised, satisfied with her response, lowered, then worshiped the other breast with equal intensity.

Honey's hand stroking his side brought him back to sanity. He'd been so lost, he had forgotten they were making love in water. All he had intended was a brief bath together to ease any nervousness about the intimacies of seeing him unclothed.

He sat up, drawing her with him, then easing her in front. His breath caught at the beauty of her high breasts, the nipples erect from his recent manipulation. Her eyes questioned, waiting for his directive. He found the bar of soap, placed it in her palm, and dictated.

"Wash me, darling." He held out his hand, fingers spread while she laved it. "When you're finished, I'll do the same to you."

Bemused by the force of his virile personality and her own desire to touch him, she rubbed the bar of soap over his wet, hair-roughened chest, working up a thick foamy lather. Her fingers explored his rock-hard shoulders, kneading each muscle of his back, his long arms and sides. She kneeled beside him, wanting to reach all of his back easily. Soaping his chest, she rubbed his flat nipples, circling until they stiffened, centered in his solidly sculpted pectoral muscles.

He lay indolently, letting her learn the pleasure of touching one's partner. Teaching her, there was as much enjoyment in giving as receiving. She never hesitated, her slender fingers sliding the bar of soap over his navel to disappear beneath the water.

"I've always wanted to touch you, Brett."

Her honesty tore him apart. He couldn't believe her passionate declaration, nor the exquisite exploration going on. Her fingers were driving him crazy. She unerringly knew how he had fantasized she would act. He reached down, holding her hands still, covering them with his own.

"My turn now, wife." His voice was ragged with the force of holding back. He had wanted her for so long. "It's quite impossible for me to hide the hunger I feel for you."

The cooling water surged turbulently around their heated bodies in soft, fragrant ripples when he pulled her upward, allowing her sleek form to lay full length over his. His fingers threaded through her hair, cupping her face still while he covered her mouth in a series of fierce kisses.

Honey stirred languorously, returning each caress with increasing passion. She squirmed, pressing her abdomen down, her legs entwining his.

Abruptly sitting up, Brett placed her gently over the contoured edge of the tub. "You're playing with fire, woman," he scolded in a pretence of anger when she reached to draw him to her.

"Hardly," she teased, her voice a throaty murmur. "Not in the water."

Finding the soap dropped during their ardent embrace, he lathered his hands. Starting with her shoulders, he rubbed deftly, stopping to knead her breasts tenderly. His fingers were gentle, caressing with the slippery suds, bringing her to a fever pitch of excitement.

Soft moans of unfulfilled longing escaped her parted lips as she lay beneath his skillful touch. Her eyes closed. She wanted nothing to interfere with the sensations aroused by her husband's hands lowering across her abdomen. She lay back, clenching his shoulders while he searched her body as intimately as she had his.

Brett was aware her nerves were pulsating beneath his questing hands. He ran a finger around her navel, stroking lower until she voluntarily raised her hips. He cradled her in the crook of his arm, drawing her head onto his shoulder. His fingers descended to continue their amorous siege. He wanted to extend the glory of knowing he could touch her without protest, could know her as intimately as he knew himself.

Honey parted her limbs, beseeching him to continue. Shifting sensually, her breath caught when he parted the most protected area of her body to probe with gentle loving strokes inch by inch until she could accept the tantalizing motions with total rapture.

She turned fully into his arms, her mouth resting at the base of his throat. With deep, whimpering murmurs, she pleaded, "Love me now, Brett. Please?"

Releasing the water, Brett stood up, drawing her supple form with him. With trembling hands he wrapped her in a velvety bath sheet. Cradled close to his damp chest, he carried her into the bedroom. He set her down near the edge of the bed, drying her thoroughly. The thick nap of the towel soaked up the moisture of her body instantly before he ran it quickly over his own limbs, then let it fall to the floor.

He kneeled before her, clasping her naked form in his strong arms. His hands clutched her bottom, holding her still while he buried his face into the smooth flesh of her abdomen.

Honey shook, her knees threatening to buckle. Clasping his solid shoulders, she looked down at his glistening ebony hair. A low moan escaped her lips when he probed her navel with his tongue before descending to press fevered kisses where his fingers had wrought such erotic delight. The thought touching her could bring him to his knees was overpowering. She knew instinctively no other woman had been the recipient of such worship.

Brett shuddered, raising his face. His hands still clasped her close while he bowed down before her.

"I worship you, Honey. Every gorgeous inch of your innocent body and with every breath that I take."

Tears of love shone in Honey's eyes when he rose, holding her in a tender embrace. No words were exchanged. It was enough that they be together. Both arms circled his lean waist, her flushed face turned to rest on his chest, until he lifted her reverently to his bed.

He lowered his body, covering hers while he took her mouth in a tender kiss, surprising her with its gentleness. She could feel the erratic pounding of his heart pressing the throbbing warmth of her breast. She was awed he would hold himself back, waiting until he was satisfied with his own knowledge that she would receive equal release.

She teased his tongue, kissing him the way he preferred, until his sudden gentleness deviated and he was devouring her mouth with fierce urgency. Each kiss blended, increasing her mounting sexual awareness. It seemed impossible to think of life without him.

His hand cupped her breast, holding it delicately as he prepared to take the hardened nipple into his mouth. Bold eyes scanned her body, languorously stretched in the middle of his bed. He kissed her breast.

"Please, darling. Please..." Honey pleaded, moaning softly. She could feel the warmth of her body waiting to receive him. Frantic fingers that had been kneading his shoulders unconsciously slid down his body, encouraging him, touching him. She let her body arch, limbs raised to place their silken length along his sides.

"Don't stop," she whispered, pleading for the pulsating ecstasy to continue. Her body stretched, molding to his, accepting him inside her with gratitude. Her wildest fantasies had never been so perfect.

When he was certain she had reached the peak, was ready to climax in heights never before reached, he relaxed, letting his own desires supercede. The sexual urgency escalated until his body shuddered over and over again with release, his arms and limbs assuring her tremoring form remained in his total possession.

They lay quiet, too moved by the bliss of their first passion to speak. He caressed her, running his hand lovingly up and down her supple spine, insisting without protest her face lay cradled on his shoulder.

Her eyes were as soft and gray as a dove's feathers, filled with the wonder of her husband's lovemaking. A smile of infinite wisdom touched her mouth, still moist from his final kiss. Her nostrils flared delicately, glorying in the heady smell of his heated body. She stretched languorously, her silken limbs parting with regret from their entanglement with his. She felt lethargic, quietly relishing the emotional contentment of sensual satisfaction. It was as perfect as she had known it would be, transforming the physical to ascend to spiritual heights as well.

Hours later bright sunshine penetrated the wispy nylon pouf, its golden rays invading the cozy seclusion of their bedroom.

Honey woke slowly. In the hazy moments before full awareness she scanned the velvet canopy over their king-size bed, knowing how much her husband loved her to go to the expense of recreating the Victorian atmosphere of his aunt's marriage bureau.

Nothing could have been more romantic than the consummation of her love for Brett in the sensual privacy of their draped bed. It was like a velvet lair, one prepared by her Panther for her alone. She had never been happier and would always remember the wonder of the past hours.

Lazily turning her face, a shy smile exposed the enticing dimple when her dreamy eyes locked with those of her husband's, watching her with indulgent adoration. She wore only his jewelry, accepted only hours ago.

Rolling to his side, he cradled her resilient form close, his mouth tracking the gold chain of the family necklace surrounding her neck.

Honey arched him a seductive smile, squirming closer. Her hands trailed down to his hardened body. It pleased her to touch him.

"It's a good thing your kitchen's well stocked, Mr. Weston. I've never heard of anyone raiding their refrigerator four times in one night."

"I had to do something between—" Brett broke off to lean over her naked body. His glance left her flawless skin, absently looking toward the opened bedroom door. He couldn't believe his eyes.

"Good God, wife. Look at what that horrible pet of yours has done!"

Honey turned over, drawn the length of Brett's body. His hand cupped her soft breasts tenderly, knowing they were still highly sensitive from hours of unaccustomed lovemaking.

Her eyes shone, her heart filling with the wonder of life as Beauty carried in a newborn kitten.

Tail erect, head held high, the cat padded to the custom-made velvet canopied brass replica of their bed. She circled it twice, jumped out, and walked to the unpacked orange carton containing Honey's faded robe. With haughty disdain, she leaped into the box and deposited the steel-gray limp body of her mewing kitten on the soft flannel.

Brett and Honey watched in amazement as Beauty followed the same pattern five more times. A long-haired calico, a sleek ebony-black who looked like a tiny panther, two varied alley-striped, and an orange as bright as Aunt Gladys's dyed hair.

Brett nuzzled his wife's neck, his breath warm on her skin. His fingers slid to her stomach, stroking the quivering flesh with definite intent. He couldn't keep his hands off her, or her him. He had been astonished at her willingness to do anything he asked and overcome with reverence at the pleasurable suggestions requested so freely while he rested.

"This is really a miracle," Honey whispered. "My cat actually having kittens the first day of our marriage."

She shifted to get closer, feeling warm and protected within his hold. Her head tilted, eyes devouring his deeply tanned masculine face.

"Can you believe it, Brett?"

"Easily!" He hugged her tightly, deep laughter following his low teasing. "That obnoxious fur ball is as wanton as you are."

"Not hardly," Honey scoffed, turning around to plant an impetuous kiss on his warm upraised mouth. "Each of Beauty's kittens looks like it had a different father, and I'm quite satisfied with only you."

Harlequin Stationery Offer

Personalized Rainbow Memo Pads for you or a friend

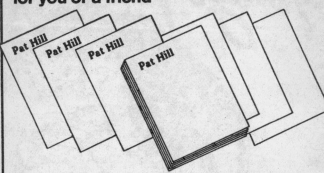

Picture your name in bold type at the top of these attractive rainbow memo pads. Each 4¼″ x 5½″ pad contains 150 rainbow sheets—yellow, pink, gold, blue, buff and white—enough to last you through months of memos. Handy to have at home or office.

Just clip out three proofs of purchase (coupon below) from an August or September release of Harlequin Romance, Harlequin Presents, Harlequin Superromance, Harlequin American Romance, Harlequin Temptation or Harlequin Intrigue and add $4.95 (includes shipping and handling), and we'll send you *two* of these attractive memo pads imprinted with your name.

- -

Harlequin Stationery Offer

(PROOF OF PURCHASE)

NAME_____

(Please Print)

ADDRESS_____

CITY_____STATE_____ZIP_____

NAME ON STATIONERY_____

Mail 3 proofs of purchase, plus check or money order for $4.95 payable to:	Harlequin Books P.O. Box 52020 Phoenix, AZ 85072	4-3

Offer expires December 31, 1984. (Not available in Canada) STAT-1

RIDE A PAINTED PONY

by **BEVERLY SOMMERS**
The third
HARLEQUIN AMERICAN ROMANCE
PREMIER EDITION

A prestigious New York City publishing company decides to launch a new historical romance line, led by a woman who must first define what love means.